I0524942

THE PILOT'S MATE

A novel by

MARTY DUNCAN, ED.D.

Historical Fiction by Marty Duncan, Ed.D.

The Harant Family Series:

Gold …then Iron

Iron Lake Burning

Black Powder, Gray Hope Book I: Vengeance

Black Powder, Gray Hope Book II: A Civil War Romance

Black Powder, Gray Hope Book III: New Americans

Ancient (Anunnaki) History:

The Pilot's Mate

Shin'ar, My Love

THE PILOT'S MATE

The Anunnaki War of 2024 BCE

A novel by

MARTY DUNCAN, ED.D.

**In Earth's forgotten history an Anunnaki princess
leads her people from a dying Mars to rebuild
an old village in the years before nuclear war
destroyed Sodom and Mohenjo Daro**

The contents of this work including, but not limited to, the accuracy of events, people, and places depicted; opinions expressed; permission to use previously published materials included; and any advice given or actions advocated are solely the responsibility of the author, who assumes all liability for said work and indemnifies the publisher against any claims stemming from publication of the work.

This book is a work of fiction. Places, events and situations in this story are purely fictional. The history (in the background) is a shortened, condensed retelling of early Earth history. Any resemblance to actual persons, living or dead is coincidental.

The reader is invited to visit the author's website at *www.martyduncan.us*

Cover Art: *'Dara landing on Mars'* (Author's Title) Artwork by Andrea Dante, licensed by Adobe. Cover Design by Creative Ad Solutions, North Mankato, MN. Illustration by Colby Marble.

Library of Congress Number: 2015960862
All Rights Reserved
Copyright © 2016 by Marty Duncan, Ed.D.; 2nd Revision-Nov 2016

No part of this book may be reproduced or transmitted, downloaded, distributed, reverse engineered, or stored in or introduced into any information storage and retrieval system, in any form or by any means, including photocopying and recording, whether electronic or mechanical, now known or hereinafter invented without permission in writing from the publisher.

Publisher: O'magadh Media
Publisher Address: 1210 Pine Point Curve, St. Peter, MN 56082
Visit our website at www.martyduncan.us

ISBN-13: 9780692606025
ISBN-10: 0692606025
Pilot's Mate, The, Saint Peter, MN

FORWARD

The novel '*The Pilot's Mate*' presents an alternative paradigm of history founded in the work of Zacharia Sitchen, Graham Hancock and Robert Schoch. The landing station on Mars actually existed. The underwater large constructions actually exist in our oceans. The Anunnaki Rebellion that resulted in the creation of *Homo sapiens* actually happened.

With Appreciation of the hundreds of archeologists, historians and translators of Sumerian, Akkadian, Chaldean, Hebrew, and Hittite cuneiform tablets, *please remember* this novel is fiction. The novel is a salute to all those translators.

The old myths frequently referred to an ancient, highly technological global civilization that was destroyed twice by a worldwide cataclysm sometime in the prehistory of today's world. This novel takes place during the Age of Egypt and the Age of Akkadia and Sumer (also called Shin'ar) (circa. 2050 BCE to 2000 BCE).

The symbol ⋇ represents the 'Star' symbol used in Sumerian cuneiform to indicate names of Anunnaki lords, thus ⋇Anu, ⋇En.Lil, and ⋇En.ki etc.

Arya, Aryan

"An Arya is one who hails from a noble family, of gentle behavior and demeanor, good-natured and of righteous conduct. "*Amarakosa (a Sanskrit Lexicon)*

Anunnaki, Anunnaki Lords

The Anunnaki Lords came to Earth from Nibiru, with the intent of mining gold in South Africa. When their sons rebelled, they used their sciences to create a new race of slaves, the ancestors of *homo sapiens*.

Anunnaki Rank (the Council of 12)

60 Anu (King on Nibiru)	55 Antu (His spouse)
50 Enlil (Lord on Earth)	45 Ninlil
40 Enki (also Ea)	35 Ninki
30 Nanna / Sin (Nan.Nar)	25 Ningal
20 Uta / Shamash	15 Inanna / Ishtar
10 Ishkur / Adad	05 Ninḫarsag

Anu Naki: 'Ant Friends' (Hopi Mythology)

The 'Anu Naki' saved the Hopi people *First* from Fire, then *Second* from Water disasters.

Timeline in Pre-History (Approximate Dates)

40,000 to 20,000 BC est. – Anunnaki Lords create *Homo Sapiens*

12,800 BC est. – Vela Supernova, 45 light years distant

11,000 BC – Balbek, in Bekaa Valley, Lebanon (Landing Platform)

11,000 BC – The Era of Enoch, builder of the Sphinx and Great
Pyramid

**10,800 BC – Vela Supernova debris 'firebombs' Laurentian
Ice Shield**
'Great Cataclysm' floods the Earth

10,800 BC (alt conjecture) **multiple airbursts & comet strikes
Ice Shield**
Great Flood and Younger-Dryas Small Ice Age
begins

10,800 BC – Acapana Pyramid/Tiwanaku buried in mud

9,600 BC – Second comet wave hits North America & Northern
Europe

9,600 BC –(+/-150 yrs) Younger-Dryas Small Ice Age ends

9,600 BC – 1st Temple at Göbekli Tepe (SE Turkey) under
construction

8,400 BC – Aşikli Höyük, hunter-gatherers with wild grains, wild
goats

8,200 BC – Jericho becomes a small village, begins its long history

7,640 BC – Seven cometary fragments strike Earth

7,500 BC – Çatal Höyök men domesticate wheat, barley, sheep &
goats
--use of copper, barley, and cattle development

6,500 BC – Early Neolithic Period: Mehrgarh in Indus Valley

3,200 BC – Mohenjo Daro & Harappa (Indus Valley)
   --contemporary with Dynastic Egypt
3,113 BC – Date: 4 Ahau 8 Cumku (Maya Date 13.0.0.0.0)
   --new World Age begins
3,102 BC – World Age begins in India *(kali-yuga)*
2,807BC – Mesopotamian Flood:Three-mile wide asteroid
   hits Indian
   Ocean 935 miles SE of Madagascar
2300-2100 BC – Scriptural *Rig Veda* composed in Indus Valley
2,024 BC – Nuclear War destroys Mohenjo Daro, Harappa,
   Sodom, Gomorrah, Zoar
   and Sinai Spaceport; *An unintended consequence*: The
   Black Cloud killed all living things in southern
   Sumeria: Ur, Eridu, Larsa, Erech, Nippur (the command center) Lagash, and Babylon. (Src: Sitchen, *The
   Wars of Gods and Men)*.
1,900 BC – Great Cataclysm: Urban collapse in Indus/Sarasvati
   culture
1,628 BC – Explosion of Thera; Moses parts the Sea of Reeds
220 BC – Qin Shi Huangdi; united China; first Emperor
830 AD – (10th Baktun) Maya people 'went home' to Pleiades
1960-2040 AD – Maya Date 14.0.0.0.0>>new World Age begins

Chapter 1

"Your people …*you* will lead. Much sorrow …*you* will see. Much joy …in a new child's first cry. *Your face* …I see …looking at a great black cloud filled with anger, red with vengeance."

The little girl watched as the old haggard woman pulled her hand away. A tear formed in the girl's eye. There was a muffled sound from inside the girl. The old woman turned her head to listen. Her eyes were sightless, cloudy with gray matter. Her gray hair straggled to her shoulder. She wore an old coat of faded leather that reached to her feet. She sat with her feet on the bottom step. Behind her an enormous pier stretched along the shore. It was the meeting place; once the place of fishing boats.

The little girl watched the old woman's hands come to her shoulders and move down. The woman's gnarly hands felt the puffy sleeves of the girl's dress.

"I know you will lead. What color is your dress?" she asked.

"Yellow."

"You are not afraid?"

The girl looked down at the woman's bare feet. "A little."

"Remember my words. You will lead. You will see a great black cloud."

"Yes, Málóid, I will remember."

"What is your name, child?"

"Say-leest-ay" my mother says. She spells it *C-e-l-i-s-t-e.*"

Celiste turned away from the wooden pier and the old woman. She walked up the sandy slope toward their village, a collection of stepped pyramids built on the edge of the Great Lake that stretched to the north. She was expected to return quickly. A soft breeze scattered her unruly hair. She looked up and saw her father Essa on the third level of their pyramid.

Celiste would remember the words of the village seer. She would also remember this day. She could not know that her world was about to lose its atmosphere and her people would embark on another long journey, a return from exile.

Celiste joined her father on the balcony of their quarters. She saw light clouds above their colony Ibri. To the south she saw the highlands above the lake and heavy clouds with the promise of rain. Sadly, a strong wind blew down the lake and pushed the rain clouds away, where the rain would do little to benefit her people.

Essa pointed at the clouds. "This is how I want to remember the day I joined with Dea: a day of promise but no rain." He smiled a soft demure smile that melted many hearts among the ladies of his village.

Essa's best coat of pale leather had been cleaned and stretched by a friend. He wore a light yellow shirt, imported from Kien; in a material they called cotton. His face was newly scraped and his hair slicked back with an oil of desert palm. His role this day was to walk the path from the Gathering Plaza up the small slope to a copse of trees. There he was to wait for…

Celiste's mother, Dea. She remained in isolation while her friends fussed over her hair and her gown. In the early morning she put river mud all over her face; now she fairly beamed with expectation. Her clear blue eyes put the lie to her heritage. She did not have the black eyes and black hair of the Aryan lords who ruled *Kien*, also known as Earth. She had the aristocratic nose of the lords, but her mouth was wider when she smiled.

Essa and Celiste left their pyramid and walked together across the plaza and up the small slope. The few trees were ancient, imported from *Kien*, planted by the original exiles to their planet, called *Lehmu*.

The trees were dark green, with wispy fronds on slender branches. Essa stopped and waited. Celiste went ahead to meet her mother.

A piper strolled in front of a small group; they approached from beyond the trees. The piper led Dea's parents and their guests. Two of their guests were Counselors; witnesses when a person of Dea's rank mates to another of less rank. She received the rank of 25 when she agreed to mate with Essa. Her grandmother (on Earth) held the same rank.

The small group came up the slope and stopped. By tradition the parents stepped apart and Essa saw Dea in yellow, with green ferns in her hair. Later he was told that his face turned pale; some thought he tried to smile.

Essa stepped to her side and stood beside her. "You look," Essa began, "you look ...oh ...charming."

"Essa ...you dear man ...flattering you are not," said Dea. His face began to grow warm. They stood together and waited for the musicians to arrive. The music would bring Captain, their village leader by acclamation. Dea and Essa stood inside the trees, with branches intertwined over their heads and yellow banners flying in a mild breeze. The arbor stood at the edge of the village Ibri. A path lined with stone blocks led from the small hill and its ancient trees down to the old pier.

"I am patient," Essa added while he tried to smile at her. *Mother,* he thought, *this is for you.*

Dea must have sensed his nervousness. Her lips curled, slightly. A small stone turned in Essa's stomach. Dea held his hand, briefly. She wore a flowing yellow gown that reached her ankles, cinched at the waist by a tan belt. Her hair was topped by a fashionable garland of woven ferns with white berries. Dea's face was handsome; her eyes inquisitive, her lips carried a smile. Those present heard the lilting sound of pipes and small drums and their friends coming; color appeared in Dea's cheeks. At her side her daughter held her mother's hand and smiled at her.

"Your mother is blest; you honor her," said Dea.

"The blame is mine," he said. Among the Aryas, when a death occurs, the son or the husband or the father takes responsibility for the death. He knew his mother was working in a field near a cliff when a large rock fell and crushed her. "There were reports; she should have been warned."

"She made me promise to join with you," Essa added.

"Is that the only reason we are …here?" Her lips formed a soft smile. Essa felt heat in his cheeks. He knew when he was nervous or defensive or worried the color came in his cheeks. There was little time to worry about her question. The musicians and Captain approached and stopped a short way back from the gaily decorated trees. Their guests knew Dea and Essa were expected to go first to the wooden pier by the lake, and prepare the way.

Chapter 2

S ilence. A crisp breeze ebbed across the ancient platform, built originally for the Gathering. It was a large wooden pier; it extended
along the edge of the lake. Carved posts supported a platform of flat-
edged planks, eight strides deep and one hundred strides long. Benches
were built into the railings; steps at each end descended to the water.
In the middle of the platform a white cloth covered a small raised platform. The cloth carried the symbol for water: two smaller circles were
laid over the rim of a larger circle. The cloth fluttered gently with the
breeze; the platform waited.

The musicians waited; they caught their breath. *Lehmu's* atmosphere was thinning. The pipers wore light green tunics over black
leggings. They began to play a soft melody on their hollow pipes. The
tune drifted down the stone-lined walkway from the village until it
spun across the platform and sailed out into the lake. Dea and Essa
waited; they stood under the trees next to their large cask, half-full
of water.

The music drifted into silence. Dea and Essa raised a wooden yoke;
held it to their shoulders. Suspended from the yoke was the cask; the

symbol for water painted on its side. They held the yoke with one hand; with their other hand they held the top of the container. Together they walked slowly down the walkway; their friends and musicians waited behind by the trees. Celiste followed her mother.

Essa glanced at Dea. Her face was flushed with excitement. After they crossed the sand of the beach they stepped onto the ancient platform. Together they placed the water container on the raised stage. Essa unhooked the yoke and placed it on a nearby bench. They moved to opposite ends of the small stage. They stood silently and looked at the lake. The small moon *Phoebe* moved toward the eastern horizon, the moon *Dorn* was not visible. There were few clouds; the lake shimmered with sparkling yellow diamonds. In the direction of the setting sun a few clouds hinted at rain.

Celiste, who was but four years old, moved to her mother's side and stood silent.

When the sun touched the horizon the Captain, dressed in a green robe with his black hat with the curled brims, stepped away from the leafy bower. He was tall, as befit his role in their village. He carried his ancient frame with dignity; he was one-half head taller than Essa. He led the crowd down to the walkway, across the sand, onto the platform. When he reached the small raised stage he turned back and nodded at the musicians. They began to play the same lilting melody; the crowd unfolded seating devices or sat on the floor of the pier.

"I remove my hat," said Captain slowly.

"No, you did not," came a shout from the back of the crowd. There was scattered laughter. Captain raised a hand and seemed to discover his hat upon his head. He smiled.

"In order to grant a favor," he added, "I remove my hat."

"The People," came the response, "ask you to remove your hat."

"Well said," answered Captain. It was a traditional ritual, from the earliest days of the colony. Captain smiled and said, "The Captain removes his hat."

"Thank you," said the crowd.

"What is the favor you ask?"

There was a noisy rumble of voices. A slim, tall man with the scars of age upon his face stepped forward and said in a clear voice, "We ask you to grant the Joining of Essa and Dea."

Captain turned to face the lake. After a moment of silence, he asked, "Do you have an oath to swear so that I may record your Joining?"

Essa turned to Dea and said, "I am Essa." She looked up into his eyes and said, "I am Dea." Together they repeated, "We pledge to be faithful to each other, to share equally in trials and tribulations that happen during our lives and to share our water for all time."

When Essa was a boy his grandfather remarked, after a Joining, that the original pledge contained the words, 'to obey the commands of our Lord.' Those who were exiled did not feel compelled to obey the words of a lord who was on Kien, the third planet.

"As it was done in the beginning," intoned the Captain, "it shall be done today. Our people cherish the water; we store the water, we share the water in difficult times. Let your sharing be your contract," he started then paused, "…Essa and Dea, your contract with your village."

From inside his long cloak Captain produced two small shiny goblets made of metal. He gave one to Dea, one to Essa. They turned away and walked to opposite ends of the platform and down the steps to the lake. They filled their goblets from the lake and returned to stand on both sides of the water cask. Essa offered his goblet to Dea. She sipped from the water and offered her goblet to Essa. He sipped and poured her goblet into the water cask. Dea did likewise.

His eyes were drawn into her eyes. In her shimmering blue pools, he saw reflected her trust for him. His hand, of its own volition, reached up and touched the soft skin of her cheek. His eyes began to produce water. Dea smiled; Essa felt a sense of exhilaration.

Captain turned to the crowd and intoned slowly, "In accordance with the rules set down by the first colonists, whereas Essa and Dea have pledged to be faithful and have shared their water, I declare they are joined. Come and drink; share their water." The crowd broke out in laughter and the musicians jumped into a raucous song that celebrated the joys of living and having a mate and children. From somewhere in the crowd a voice shouted, "Bout time, darn it!"

"After five years of sly meetings, 'twas 'bout time," shouted another voice. There was laughter. The crowd formed a line to share the water and to congratulate the newly joined couple. Essa admitted later to being embarrassed; among his friends he was last to be 'Joined.'

The musicians resumed playing an exciting, uplifting version of an old song from the years when the People, the proud Aryas, were exiled from *Kien*. Dea and Essa continued to pour water from the large cask into small mugs or clay bowls held by relatives and friends. Essa's friends, bless them, were busy moving two casks of fermented grain that produces mental confusion, onto the platform. Some of the men gravitated toward Essa's 'rowdy' friends.

They were right to celebrate. Essa must produce an heir or there could be a battle over his seat as Comhairleoir, the Advisor to the Council, second only to Captain. The people of Ibri, his village, knew Celiste was his daughter; she carried his smile and his lighter brown hair.

Dea smiled at Essa. He saw her watching him; it was difficult to pour and not waste the water. It is the traditional role for the man. His task requires concentration. When he finally looked directly at Dea, she was smiling. His face cracked into an enormous grin.

"Later," she said.

"Yes, my love."

Chapter 3

S ilence. The forest of tall, straight spires was quiet. The little furry ferrets were still, unmoving, watching four humans as they passed through their forest. A woman led three men. They wore leather coats inside thick padded vests. Brown leaves crunched under the woman's feet. They moved quietly and looked for danger. The forest floor was a carpet of brown and yellow leaves. The woman Dea smiled, she was proud to lead; she could not know her efforts would lead to her death.

A sonata in wind tones whispered among the trees; more leaves began to fall. *'Too early,'* thought Dea. She looked up. The trees were partially bare. *'Far too early,'* she added. The trees were tall, straight trunks covered with white bark. The year had been dry; the trees suffered for lack of moisture. In the distant past Dea's father used the trunks to make chairs and beds. Her mother used the thin willowy branches to weave containers for vegetables. Their small colony was in its third and fourth generation since landing on the planet. In these dry years there were few calls for new furniture.

It's the moisture, Dea knew. She knew the ice caps were growing and atmospheric moisture was on decline. Dea knew her people and their enemies the Beag faced a decision: would they leave their planet?

"The trees struggle," she said aloud. Behind her, one of the three men in her team mumbled a 'Huhn!' while the other two looked both ways into the forest of tall white shafts with leafy crowns, searching for threats.

Dea stopped on the path and turned to the three men behind her. They were armed as she was …long attack poles with knives attached. She was their Major, chosen by the Council. Dea knew her team could defend themselves; they were proud, tall men with straight noses and flat foreheads. Rath's face carried an old scar from a knife fight; Marder was known for closely held, unspoken, opinions. Aaron was a youngster, of perhaps sixteen years.

My team, she thought proudly. Aaron, Marder and Rath looked at Dea, each with a question on his face. She picked up a few leaves and waved at the trees. Her team nodded. They understood. It was the lack of water that affected all their people.

Her lips curled softly under her straight, royal nose. Her blue eyes flashed; her light brown hair fluttered in the breeze. Her team loved the manner in which she commanded their attention. It was hard not to love her smile, her soft voice and her manner when in the field. Dea had now served the Aryas, her people, for ten Earth years, or five cycles of their planet around the yellow sun.

"Our planet struggles," said one of the men. A small breath of air rustled leaves in the tree tops. A tiny four-legged animal scurried up to Dea's boot, sniffed once and ran back into a low bush. Dea smiled at the image, momentarily. Then her mouth turned down. She knew that somewhere in the future the grandchildren of the little ferret would probably die when her planet died.

She turned to the path and looked ahead. A shallow stream of brownish water meandered across their path. Dea remembered her grandfather the day he planted these trees. He was remarkably patient with her. She wanted to play in the stream; he kept her from the swift current. She remembered the clear, cool water. But that was before the ice pack on the poles began to grow, before the stream turned brown with burned residue from an upstream fire.

Dea stepped into the stream; the water barely covered her ankle. She waded across. On the far bank she urged her team to cross. Her boots were soaked. *Time to oil the leather?* she pondered. She brushed little pieces of forest dirt off her tunic. When she looked down she glanced at her leather trousers and thought, *Time to oil these leggings.*

The far side of the stream seemed to be lower; the ground held more moisture. There were a few scattered white shafts but most of the trees were thicker with large, floppy leaves. The heavy trees with their gnarled branches threw shade on the path. Dea and her team walked quietly, as if to speak would break the solemn silence among the garishly ominous trees. Ahead she saw light and knew they approached a wide space of grass and sunlight. She slowed their progress; caution was a watchword.

Her team stopped. Aaron adjusted his backpack. He was her 'rookie' and carried their supplies of water and vegetables. Marder surveyed the darkness inside the trees, searching for a threat. Rath, the unmated team member glanced at Dea's hip and saw a flash of his last visit to Rachel, his intended mate, and smiled to himself.

The team wore similar uniforms, leggings of thin leather covered by a leather tunic that reached their knees. The collars of their tunics held a silver emblem of a pyramid inside a circle, the symbol of the Aryas colony. Their tunics held hoods to keep out the rain. Looking at the hoods, Rath smiled. There had been no rain for a very long time.

Chapter 4

They stopped in the shade. Ahead was the open field of knee-high grass. Three crows arose from the distant trees, as if scattered by a loud noise.

Dea saw the crows and said, "We wait."

Out of the silence Marder asked, "They accused us…?"

"Yes?" asked Dea.

"Of stealing their water?"

"They actually used the term borrowing," she added.

Marder, the oldest of the three men turned to look to his right, as if he heard something. Behind him Rath said, "It was a screecher."

Aaron suddenly lifted his lance into a defensive position. He pulled it back as if to throw it. They heard the 'whuff, whuff' of a large bird while the owl climbed above the tree tops. A shadow moved over the leaves above their head.

Marder laughed. "Easy there, Aaron."

"Only a rookie," said Rath laughing. "Did you think the owl was about to attack our noble leader?"

"No," said Aaron, confused. "I thought…"

"That is all," said Dea directly at Rath. She raised a hand that signified 'quiet' and listened to the wind in the leaves. There was the music of drying leaves. She watched a few yellow leaves fall.

"But I thought…" said Aaron.

"We know," said Dea quietly. "These two brave stalwart men before you love to admonish and chastise those who are younger."

"We do out of concern," said Marder.

"For our younger brother, here," added Rath laughing.

"Enough," said Dea. She saw the color rising in Aaron's face when he turned away from them, as if to look into the forest. "The Beag accused us of stealing their water," said Dea to Marder. "You are correct."

"Those short minded thieves," snorted Rath, using an old expression. The Beag from the other side of the Great Lake were two hands shorter than the taller, thinner Aryas. "Shorter, thicker, stronger, maybe…" he added.

"Good for farming," said Marder. "Strong backs, thick arms. Even their women are strong workers."

"As they should be," snarled Rath. He looked at Dea to see her reaction. There was none.

"Their grandparents, and ours," said Marder. "You know the story. How they asked for better conditions in the mines. More water. Large bellows to move the air. No children in the mines until age of eight."

"My grandmother is a royal in the house of ꭓLord Enki," said Dea. Her lips turned down, slightly. She knew not to ask about the exile. It was her mate Essa who found the old records of the rebellion.

"Now the Beag accuse us," noted Marder.

"Those short dwarfs…" snarled Rath. "…with stumpy brow ridges."

"Their brow ridge betrays their evil nature," said Aaron quietly.

"You cannot know that," remarked Dea. Aaron looked away. Rath had a frown between his slim eyebrows. Marder's face was a blank. "Enough!" she commanded. She turned up the path and took three steps toward the sunlight.

Dea smiled to herself. *Unfair how we describe the Beag.* She knew the south waterfalls emptied directly into the Great Lake. Their two tribes lived on opposite sides; both tribes depended on the lake for enormous fish that provided meat and oil.

Rath stepped up to her side. Dea turned toward him. She saw his hand coming up to her hip and grabbed his wrist.

"You make me uncomfortable," she said. Her face betrayed her confusion.

"Do you ever wonder about having a younger man in your...?" he began before her fist came up and smacked him hard in his chest.

"Back off," she said with solid determination. She pulled her hand back as if she were about the hit him again. Marder stepped around her and grabbed her hand.

Dea looked at Marder and briefly thought, *Thank you.* Then she saw him tilt his head in the direction of the clearing ahead.

In the full sunlight across the field of grass she saw six Beag armed with lances walking single-file in her direction. With their heavy legs and muscular arms and blunt faces they looked nothing like Dea's team members. The leader was the most handsome; his nose was prominent below the heavy brow ridge that marked him as a Beag. All six Beag were one hand shorter than Dea, perhaps one and a half hands shorter than Rath, Marder and Aaron. She knew they were Sons of Earth, bred to be slave labor in the gold mines. These six Beag were grandsons of the original agitators who protested working conditions and were sentenced to be exiled.

Dea pointed at Marder and waved him into the trees to her right. She poked Rath in the chest and pointed to her left; Rath and Aaron moved quietly into the dense copse of heavy wood. When her three men stopped moving she stepped up the path to where the Beag could see her. The leader had his head down, watching the path through the knee-high grass. *Afraid of snakes,* she thought, and smiled. When the leader looked up, he stopped. He saw a tall female with a lance. She blocked his path, with a smile on her face.

"The sun is warm," said the man. "Come into the sunlight. Let us see you."

"I think not," she responded. "The cool shade sharpens my wit; the sun dulls my mind."

From behind the man a voice said, "Sharpens her wit?"

The man ignored the question. He looked anxiously into the dark shade beneath the trees. "Are you alone?"

"No," replied Dea.

"I think not," said the Beag, the obvious leader. He knew the silver ankh she wore on her chest indicated her rank of Majority, a position of trust. "There must be others," he said quietly. He took two steps closer.

"You are too close," declared Dea firmly and stepped back. Dea knew the man's lance was a dangerous tool. The blade had a double barb; it had been used as a harpoon on the big lake. A twig snapped inside the trees.

"Order him to come out," the man said quietly.

"No," Dea responded with grim lips. "I take no orders from Beag."

The man raised his hand to shield his eyes. He looked at her and remembered Dea's people had a ceremony. "I am Ragar, team leader," he recited and waved his arm to indicate his five men. They were dressed in battle gear with thick vests over chain mail on their arms.

Ragar wore a long blade used for gutting the large fish they sometimes caught on the lake.

Dea made a small bow towards Ragar; it was a slim exercise, a thin meaningless bow toward this younger 'team leader.' She stood straight and taller, if that was possible. "I am Deacair. I hold a Majority, a *thromlach* or verdict by a decision of my people. We are here to stop you."

"Stop us?"

"You are on our land. We will send you back."

"We are hunters," Ragar added.

"O'magadh?" she stammered slowly. Her demand 'Oh, really?' was a direct challenge. Her lance tipped down and pointed at his armored vest. "I think not …fisherman Ragar."

He tried to smile. The men behind him began to spread left and right behind Ragar. Behind Dea she heard twigs snap; her men stepped to where Ragar could see them. Their lances were pointed forward, held on their shoulders, in throwing position.

"Did I tell you to move?" she growled at her team. She lowered her lance until it pointed at Ragar's feet. He wore fisherman's sandals with double straps across his feet.

"Our Counselor would wish for you to come with us. We are your escort," she said quietly, and added "to a Gathering."

"So your people can make fun of us?"

"No. We listen. You explain how you are injured. We vote."

"You steal water for your fields."

"No. All water from the tall falls goes into the lake."

"You steal water," Ragar repeated.

"We do not steal water," she said with a fierce scowl. She looked at each of Ragar's men in turn. "There is a stream. We use what it brings. The excess goes into the lake."

"We come, we destroy," said Ragar. He saw that his men were in a ragged line facing Marder, Rath and Aaron.

"You turn and leave. We will report your complaint." Dea's teeth were clenched; her face did not smile. She saw Ragar was silent.

"You are armed. You seek death." Dea's face betrayed anger.

Ragar looked at his men.

Dea added, "Your leaders can send three men. We talk. We listen."

Ragar seemed to pause, considering her words.

"We do not seek death," added Ragar. He lowered his lance until it pointed at the ground. He nodded and his men lowered their lances.

"You lie, you Beag," shouted Aaron.

There was a long moment of silence. The men on both sides glared at each other. Two of Ragar's men began to raise their lances. They suddenly charged into the trees. Both of their lances struck trees when they tried to follow the sudden movement of Aaron and Rath. A lance came out of the shadows; it struck a Beag warrior in the shoulder just outside his chain mail; he fell. Rath avoided a lance; he side-stepped his opponent. Then he hit him using his elbow full-force into the man's head. The man crumpled and began to moan before he collapsed onto the forest floor.

Ragar's men began to advance on the trees. He looked at Dea and began to raise his lance. She used her lance to deflect his lance. His sharpened harpoon head ran up her arm and nicked her shoulder. She flinched. Ragar's movement caused Dea's lance head to slide under the strap of his sandal. Her sharp blade cut tendons across the outside of his foot. He stumbled forward while he was pulling his long knife from its scabbard.

The biting pain in his foot caused him to instinctively raise his long knife. The point found the side of Dea's leather tunic. The knife would have glanced off harmlessly had it not run into a flap under her arm. The knife sliced through the leather and entered her side. Dea tried to turn away from the blade but her motion caused the blade to slice through her lung and its tip nicked her heart.

Her face went blank. She knew she was hurt. She had a vision of Essa, with his strong arms holding Celiste. She saw the curls in her little girl's hair, the curve of her lips and her slightly pudgy nose. She looked into the eyes of her beloved Essa and saw his love and his sorrow for her. 'My love,' she thought, 'it was not to end this way.'

"Stop!" She heard a man's voice, loud and commanding. It was Ragar; Dea was suddenly at the edge of the clearing. "Your Major is hurt," shouted Ragar. His men were trying to thrust their lances; the trees interfered. Aaron went down with a lance embedded in his leg. He was trying to stop his opponent from pulling out his lance. The man suddenly shouted, "He is hurt …the one who called us liars."

Ragar shouted again, "Stop!" His men began to step back. The man with the shoulder injury was helped out of the trees. Ragar looked down at Dea; her face looked pale. Ragar saw two men with savage intent coming at him; he ran back a few steps.

"We were to harass and confuse, to harm no one," said Ragar.

Dea was down on her knees, her eyes open. Marder put a hand on her shoulder and pulled out the long knife. She winced in pain. Her body fell sideways away from Marder. He looked at the knife and threw it toward Ragar's men. Rath pointed his lance at the Beag and made to throw it. The Beag, especially Ragar, stood still.

"I have failed," said Ragar. He pointed his lance at the ground; he bent over to retrieve Dea's lance. "I am your prisoner."

"That is enough," said Dea weakly. She reached out to grab Rath's legging and held on. "Enough," she repeated.

Rath nodded at Ragar and the older man, the fisherman, turned the two lances upward, toward the sky. Marder walked to him and reclaimed the lance, the old family weapon of his Major, Dea.

"The Council will deal with Ragar," said Dea. Her voice turned whispery and slight.

"My Council will exile me for my failure," added Ragar. He began to back away, still facing Rath and Rath's lance. With each step he left drops of blood on the pale yellow grass. One of his men came to him and put Ragar's arm over his shoulder. They turned to walk away. They were five. One of Ragar's men was in the trees, unconscious.

Marder knelt by Dea and put his hand on her side. He felt warm blood. With his other hand he took her hand and lifted her arm. It felt limp. Rath bent over and said, "Is this how you want it? They are walking away."

"Tell my Essa. The man stumbled with my lance stuck in his foot. I tried to turn and his knife went into my side."

She smiled, momentarily. Marder turned her head and saw a blank face. She rallied for a moment and squeezed his hand, but weakly. "You will tell my love, my Essa?" She looked up at thin, scattered clouds in the sky. In a quiet voice she said "No rain" and her eyes closed.

Chapter 5

There were five enormous pyramids surrounding the central plaza. These stone and cement buildings housed the residents of Ibri, the village of the Aryas rebels. The step pyramids had balconies on the five levels above the first. Each balcony was covered with food plants; many hung down from the railing. Celiste was watering the plants on their balcony when she looked down and saw Essa walking toward a group of men. The three men walked slowly, heads were down. They came from the direction of the southern falls that fed the Great Lake. The men were carrying an object wrapped in a ground cloth, such as they used to sleep on when they were in the field.

She continued to water their plants. Most were the long green plants they cut into parts before boiling. There were strong vines that held a red bulb they used for seasoning; many hung down the outside of the balcony. Celiste had to pluck the red bulbs before they were out of reach. A frown formed on her face.

Dea led those men. Where is she?

She put her watering can down and looked down at Essa. He was listening to the three men. One of the men held a lance that he gave to Essa.

Her father looked up at Celiste. He raised a hand in a 'halt' motion. He turned to walk toward their building. Celiste waited.

———— ᨇᨇᨇ ————

Minutes passed. Celiste moved to the entry hall of their quarters. She heard the sound of steps on the inner stairway. She had the impression that Essa was walking slowly.

He rapped on the door. This was unusual. She turned her head in wonder at his behavior. She unlatched the door and watched as he walked down the hall to their central room where they ate and talked and prepared food and played games and worked on her sense with numbers. He stopped in the opening to the balcony.

She stood and looked up at her father. He stood silent, a hand in front of his face. His shoulders shook. He stood and stood and stood. Celiste looked around and the unthinkable began to form in her mind. She said "No!" and went to her father. She put her arms around his waist. They stood together for long minutes until she backed away and said, "What about her team? Are they all dead?"

Essa raised his hands and put them, one on each side of her face. "She told them to stop. The Beag leader was injured."

"They did nothing?"

"She told them …to stop."

"They lose their leader and…"

"The Council told the team, No killing."

"But…"

"No, Celiste. No one wanted to start a war over water."

"They are bad, my father. Bad like dead fish on beach. Everyone says so. This will end with war." She added, "Where is she?"

"They are bringing her." Essa walked to the balcony of their quarters and looked down. He saw a solemn procession of women bringing Dea home, wrapped in a long sheet. "Your mentor, old Sleam has told us for years that the Beag are evil. He points at the heavy ridge of bone above their eyes."

"He is right!" she said from behind him.

"You are thinking with emotion, Celiste.

"And you are not?"

"I want vengeance, also. The man Ragar killed your mother. He will be tried. By their Council, I am told."

———— ❦ ————

The long wrapped package was moved into her mother's bedroom. Two women of the village went quickly to work, demanding water and towels.

Other women arrived at Celiste's third level residence. They seemed to be concerned about her mother. A time later, as Celiste remembered it, one of the women brought her into the bedroom and she saw her mother lying on the bed. She seemed peaceful. Celiste reached out and touched her mother's hand. It was cold.

While the older women watched, Celiste bent over and kissed her mother's hand. When she straightened up there was a tear below her eye. The tear made its way down her face, drawing a track across the slight dust on her face.

Her father came into the room and wrapped his arms around her and said "It is you and I now, Celiste. We will be strong for our mother Dea."

Celiste did not whimper. Nor did she cry. As far as her village was concerned, Celiste never shed a tear for her mother.

Chapter 6

At the age of eight Celiste began her formal learning. There were six plus Celiste in her group. They studied the principles of numbers, the history of their people, and the qualities of leadership. Their learning tools were ancient tablets that were exposed to the distant sun for part of each day. The tablets recharged themselves and provided problems for Celiste and her peer group to solve. The tablets told the story of the two generations of Aryas who came through the Deep Black in a small planet, now called Phoebe. Their ancestors, many generations back, left Phoebe in a west to east orbit and settled on *Mars,* called *Lehmu* by the Aryas. Their young men and women mined ores and smelted the ore into useable beams and sheets of impenetrable metal. One entire generation was devoted to building six transit vehicles for travel to the third planet, *Earth,* called *Kien.*

Celiste had an inquisitive mind. She explored the history of their people and found notes about a rebellion among the Aryas. When her history tablet was silent she asked her father, Essa. He sat down with a large mug of steaming beans and slowly told her the young Aryas worked in the mines on Earth. They asked for better working conditions. They were exiled to *Lehmu*. They were his grandparents, condemned to work as fishermen and builders to survive.

Essa, always the patient father, looked at her puzzled frown and asked, "Do you understand?"

She was a smart and precocious student with the curiosity of a budding scientist. She looked at her father and said, "But tell me. Will we go back to the land ruled by Anu and his sons, this planet with its one moon?"

Essa was silent. He could not force himself to tell Celiste about her heritage, for her true father lived on Earth, the third planet.

Celiste and Essa, daughter and father, could not see down the path of the future. The old, blind seer had said Celiste would lead her people ...and she would see vast devastation by a great angry black cloud. She could not see herself on Earth. She could not see her friends conscripted to serve in the Army of ✖Enlil. Nor could she see her father's decision to remain with the older generation on *Lehmu*.

Celiste was content. She wanted only to live her life and to have children. If she found a male to which she could bond, that would be a bonus. She knew her father rarely told the story of the rebels and how they came to be exiled on Lehmu. She listened to Essa when he told the story of her people to children around an evening gathering...

"I shorten the story," he began, "of how we came to be here..."

"In the far distant past an enormous chunk of a smashed planet grabbed smaller rocks and sent them crashing into our planet. They formed pock marks and valleys. These depressions were filled with blowing rock dust and decayed organic matter. Tiny streams blended with others to form rivers that cut channels and filled large lakes. The smashed planet became our moon. We call it *Dorn*, or dark.

"Our planet cooled. Moisture condensed and fed streams. The nitrogen-based atmosphere was slowly replaced by a mix of nitrogen and oxygen. Plant-eating animals prospered. Ice packs formed at the poles. The atmosphere shrunk; a desert began to swallow up a nearby forest. The planet could be colonized.

"And then my grandparents and their grandparents came. They came in a round oblong of rock. Hollowed out. Their rock came past our planet, swung around the yellow star and found an orbit around Lehmu.

"What do we call that rock, the other moon in our sky?"

"Phoebe?" said a small girl, shy with eager excitement.

"Yes," said Essa. He smiled at her. Celiste handed out small emblems of their planet, the six-pointed star.

"How many of you know why there are six points?"

"I do, I do!" shouted a young boy near the rear of the group. He stood up and re-arranged his leggings before he scratched his bottom. Two girls nearby giggled.

When he had the attention of the children and adults he added, "Our planet is the sixth planet from the edge of our star's collection of planets."

"Excellent," said Essa. He did not tell the children the deep space habitat called 'Phoebe' was empty; that technicians once each year went up to check on 'her' operating systems and power sources.

Chapter 7

The year Celiste passed her twelfth Naming Day was also the year the Counselors met to discuss her uncle Sleam's provocative new ideas. The fishermen of Ibri for years had complained the Great Lake was shrinking. Could no one see the shore as it walked away from their pier? Did no one realize less water fell across the Great Falls that fed the lake?

They met on the plaza between the five pyramid structures that housed the population of Ibri. At the plaza center stood an ancient stone altar, a solid base with a five-sided slab. The five Counselors sat in ceremonial chairs at the five points of the altar. They included Captain, their leader; Essa, their advisor; the female Gastina with Sheb.Sin and Sleam.

Four of the counselors wore their long black coats. Captain wore his black hat with silver bangles, his symbol of office. Essa wore the skull-cap of the Advisor. Each of them, by accident, was the oldest member of their family. Their graying hair and craggy faces portrayed their wisdom, if such was to be found in this 'Gathering' of the leaders.

The plaza was surrounded by the men of Ibri, with a few of the young women to the outside of the circle. The majority of the women chose to listen from the second and third story balconies in the housing pyramids.

Sleam jumped right into his proposal. He suggested that 300 reflectors be built and situated on the polar ice cap in such a way as to send melted ice water down to the planet's rivers. When Essa asked why? The old man said, "The moisture is disappearing. It does not rain."

A voice among the observers said loudly, "Bruscar!"

"No, you must listen!" shouted Sleam. His arm swung wide and clipped a slender, black cup carved from crystal obsidian. The black goblet wobbled, then fell, spilling its water. The stone plaza absorbed the water and cracked the cup.

Sleam was respected for his dedication to saving water; he looked down and said, "Wasted!" He stood there, confusion showing on his face. He was a tall male, typical of the Aryas; he was thin of face with a long nose and long, bony fingers. His undistinguished tunic was old and gray; he wore trousers with ragged cuffs. His boots were not polished. His face was thin, almost gaunt.

The word 'Wasted' is a horrific word of condemnation. Sleam was embarrassed. He was always serious about the need to conserve water. The Ibri colony was dedicated to saving and preserving a life-giving resource. A shallow river had been diverted to irrigation. A thin stream from the highlands filled the Ibri reservoir. The colony prospered in the years before the rain stopped.

"That is a bad omen," said Essa when he bent to retrieve the black goblet. His finger snagged a deep crack before he added, "You say the atmosphere is becoming drier."

"Essa, you and the Counselors ...must listen," Sleam stammered.

"You believe. My fellow advisors disagree," said Essa.

"For almost one hundred fifty cycles around our yellow sun, the crops have flourished, the tarb have grown fat and provided meat, and the Mother Lake has given us enormous finned creatures," said Sleam before he added slowly, "The atmosphere has been calm; the rains arrived as predicted."

"It will rain again," said Essa. "Your idea is radical."

Sleam is older and given to emotional outbursts. Essa's friends said Sleam became unreliable after his mate Alonna died. In his youth Sleam was a noted technician; he gathered data and reported on crops, soils, and fertilizer. His team dried fertilizer; it was made from excrement collected from the people. His 'role' became the origin of the nickname 'Sludge,' although no one dared to say that to his face.

Captain, the oldest advisor, added, "The goblet is also wasted." Captain wears the ancient black leather hat with silver bangles that symbolizes his role of Captain. When our people made the long Traverse, a trip across the Deep Black that required two generations, Captain's ancestor was the navigator and arbiter of disputes. On the Council of five the Captain is the final arbiter. He sits in a chair padded with cushions of leather, symbols of his rank. His face shows the years of his life amid the scars and furrows of his sun-darkened skin.

Sleam raised the black goblet so all could see. There were fifty or sixty of the Ibri clan scattered around the edges of the raised platform. Sleam then threw the goblet hard against the stone at our feet. Shards spread in all directions. Essa's leg caught two shards; the pain was sharp.

"That is our atmosphere," growled Sleam. "Broken."

No one said a word. Essa bent over and removed two thin daggers of obsidian from his leg. They hurt briefly. Two drops of blood formed.

When Essa straightened up, Sleam was looking at him. He made a gesture; he opened his hands. He turned one hand toward Essa. His friend Essa nodded and accepted his apology. The tiny wounds did not bleed.

"You claim the atmosphere is drier?" said the old Captain.

"Yes."

"Where is your evidence?"

"The highland rivers to the east of the Beag have dried."

"Proves nothing," said the Captain.

"The Beag live on the east shore of our Mother Lake. They need water also. They are becoming desperate."

"We know all this," said Essa. It was known, from two cycles past. The Beag, the people with short stubby legs and strong arms tried to divert water in the highlands behind their colony. Their failure persuaded Essa's friends that the Beag were incapable of solving their own problems. The bony ridge above their eyes demonstrated, to some, that the Beag are an inferior race, not to be trusted with technology. Essa added, "I question your conclusion."

"What evidence do you have?" asked Captain with patience.

"The old records," said Sleam.

"Your uncles have examined the records," Captain reminded him. "They voted three to one against your recommendation."

"The Beag have records, as well."

"Yes?" said Captain. He raised an eyebrow.

"Do you trust their records?" said Essa. The woman counselor Gasta nodded. "We do not trust the Beag," she said. "Their records stink."

"Essa," said Sleam. He turned toward Essa. "My family has kept the rainfall, water levels and moisture content records for nearly 300 years, what we call 150 cycles around our yellow star. My uncles are obstinate."

"Stubborn, yes …can you blame them?" laughed Essa.

"The family Donneann," said an old man among the fifty observers outside the circle. His weathered face told a story: he built and sailed long, shallow boats for fishing on the Mother Lake.

"My uncles …Yes," Sleam said quietly.

"Family Surly-ann, don't you mean?" said the same old man, a retired boat captain. It was an ancient joke by an old sailor who knew about 'surly' weather.

"We have heard his ideas," said the retired boat master.

"And the Advisors have listened," added Captain.

Chapter 8

Essa and the Counselors looked around the circle. The observers were silent. Beyond the silent men Essa saw three of the oldest grandmothers on the lower terraces of the nearby pyramid, watering their plants but listening to the Counsel deliberations. In his mind he said, *what say you? …honored mothers?*

Someone unseen outside the circle shouted, "Bruscar."

Sleam shouted back at him, "It is not rubbish."

Captain formed a fist; he raised it skyward and held it. Gradually the babble of voices diminished. A tense quiet fell across the platform.

"It is not theory," said Sleam into the silence "It is fact…"

"…that your uncles dispute," said the boat master in a louder voice.

"You say the planet's moisture is falling at a steady rate. You say we must rehabilitate *Phoebe* and our *Cead* to take our people *and the Beag,*" Captain paused, "…to where?"

There was silence. Someone outside the circle sniggered.

"You know where," began Sleam.

Captain raised his arm with a fist, to command attention. "No, we will decide at the next Gathering." He glanced around the circle of

Advisors, at the nearby pyramids, then out to the lake where *Phoebe* had risen above the horizon in the west.

"When *Phoebe* and our ship *Cead* cross the path of Dorn, when all three are aligned at the end of this year, you and your uncles will present data and arguments at a Gathering of our people."

"Who else?" asked Sleam, "do you invite?"

"They are part of the problem," said Captain.

"Does that mean we must ignore them?" asked Essa. He turned away from Captain and looked out at the fishermen and young 'farmers' who surrounded the plaza.

After several moments of quiet the old fisherman said, "Yes."

Another added, "This year they steal water."

And another added, "And our fish when they can get away with it."

"They must know," said Sleam.

"Know what?" asked Captain. He raised his hand for silence.

"Their planet is slowly dying," said Sleam.

"Sleam is correct," added Essa slowly. "We must ask."

Captain looked across at the pyramids and then at the people surrounding the plaza. His fist remained immovable; it demanded attention. When he spoke it was clear that he would accept no disagreement.

"We will invite the Beag. We will ask our technicians to propose a plan. We will ask the people to decide."

He paused to look up and saw *Phoebe* climbing into the sky and behind her *Cead* flashed in the sun. He could not know the power plant of the ancient habitat *Phoebe* was defunct, nor could he know those of us who were exiled from our neighboring planet Kien would vote to go home.

Chapter 9

Celiste walked with her head down. Her bare feet made soft, light impressions in the damp, nearly dry mud of the lake. Two containers of water were suspended from a carry strap that ran across her shoulders. Her long slender fingers steadied the containers and kept them from swinging wildly. She raised her head when she approached the old dock. It stood, silent and morose testimony to what had been a gathering place of her people. She mounted the steps to the dock; her feet slapped on wood smoothed by two hundred years of traffic.

They were married for two years, here on this dock. She walked with my father Essa here, on this dock. It was just after my sixth Naming Day that Dea led her squad against those Beag animals...

How long? She wondered then heard the words of her father: "...*your great-great grandmother Deacair was among the first born after we landed. One hundred circuits of this weak, yellow sun. A long time ago.*"

On the dock she set the water containers down and carefully placed the strap across the lids of the containers. Then she walked to a stool, took a cloth off a rack and dried her feet.

It was her sixteenth Naming Day when Celiste informed her father she was now on a water team. Essa responded with "Too slim." Her father said, "...too thin to carry water." But Celiste persisted and gained a measure of respect from her friends.

She was tired but proud of her second walk to the lake. Celiste brushed her hair away from her face and looked out across the lake. The far horizon was empty. To the north, just above distant rolling hills she saw sparse clouds. She shook her head. The clouds did not bring rain. There was not enough moisture to feed rain. The edge of the lake had slowly walked away from the dock. As a little girl she could barely remember when the water of the lake lapped the pilings of the pier her people built at water's edge.

Celiste glanced at the far end of the 'People's Pier' and saw a solitary figure sitting on a stool, hunched over a board game. She knew Aonar missed his daily game with his lifelong friend Sleam, the old codger who was known for his stubborn opinions. The two men played the same game with the little figures of people and animals at the same time each sunrise, sipping on 'Bitter Black' and disputing each other's theories about why the lake water was now a long walk. When they played a small group of men always gathered.

Aonar and Sleam played the board with black and white figures for ten long cycles. Many times they laughed, sometimes they cursed with a smile aimed at the other. Then five years ago the winds became stingy; they turned drier and colder. The Advisors met on the Plaza and argued and cajoled and then decided. They decided that Sleam should test out his idea that the polar cap was getting larger. The Captain sent Sleam and three assistants. They took markers that could talk to *Cead,* their monitoring station in the sky.

After half a cycle Sleam reported the ice cap was growing. He proposed the people should build five hundred reflectors to shield the ice cap from the sun and melt the ice, returning the water to the land.

And then a cycle later, thought Celiste. The work crews had 125 of the reflectors installed when word came that Sleam was lost, fallen into a deep blue crevasse. His men tried to reach him; there was no sign and no sound bounced back but the echoing of their shouts.

The girl saw Aonar sitting, hunched over his board. A few of the villagers had tried to challenge Aonar but he made quick work of their feeble attempts. She saw him move a piece. Celiste heard him laugh, as if Sleam sat across from him. She felt a stone of regret in her stomach.

Chapter 10

Celiste heard boards creak in the long causeway from the village and turned to her boots. She dried her feet a second time; she wanted to appear studious. The colony relied on the water. She began to pull on her boots just as her father's voice rang out,

"Celiste, my daughter!" She loved the way he emphasized the pronunciation of her name, *'Say-leest-aye.'* She was proud of her father, Essamehir, for he held the title of *Comhairleoir,* which meant Advisor to the Colony. The people called him Comhair, a short version of his title, or Essa, out of respect for his name. Essa was fully grown; he was a half-head taller than his lissome, slim daughter Celiste. He was equally proud of Celiste for volunteering to join the cadre of water haulers, thirty strong. It was no easy task, hauling water twice a day for five days, then resting for five days. The Colony depended on the haulers to supplement the water produced by the collectors.

When Sleam died on the ice cap the Counselors were quick to ask Celiste to join the atmospheric specialists, but she declined. She may have been Sleam's top student but she had not gone through the ceremony to be given the title of *Thromlach,* or *Throm,* for short. With the title she could direct research into atmospheric events. *"I should have been on the ice,"* she told Essa. He wisely told her not to blame herself for Sleam's death.

"Years ago," said Essa, when he glanced in the direction of old Aonar, "we had 300 persons in our colony. Our water supply was sufficient."

"Yes, Comhair," she remarked using his title.

"Now we have 70 persons, and thirty aboard *Cead* and *Phoebe* preparing the ships and eight aboard the shuttle *Dara*. The young techs in Water Resources say our reservoir is slowly gaining. Up an inch during the last 30 turns."

"So we heard," added Celiste. She did not remind him that a huge amount was about to be sent up to the *Cead*. She knew that each member of their colony was aware of the water issue. In public meetings they all swore to conserve, to bathe only once every three turns. "Did you speak to that snippy Gastina who always smells just so …so?" she paused before adding "…nice? …I guess."

"The Director spoke to her. Gastina has missed meetings. She does not come if she cannot smell just …so …so?"

"Appropriate?"

"Yes, well said, my daughter," said Essa laughing.

Celiste finished lacing her boots and stood up. She smoothed the folds of her long dress. A red and black band controlled her light brown hair. She tucked a few loose strands back into place. She reached for her carry strap. Essa leaned toward her and took the strap from her hand. He said nothing. She placed the strap over his shoulders; when he bent down she attached the two water containers. Essa straightened up with a grunt.

"Are you able?" asked Celiste.

"My knees …they do not like the strain," he snorted.

She watched him take a step, then another step while his back straightened up. He turned and smiled, as if to say, *See? …I be not as old as you think?*

Celiste patted his shoulder as he began to walk to the causeway. She knew it was 600 steps to the water reservoir. In a musical voice she chimed, "Mi Essa, so croga."

"No, my Celiste …I am not brave as you say." He stepped onto the old causeway and they heard its squawk of protest.

She said nothing. She watched as he walked ahead of her. It was an old tradition, old from the distant past. The father walked ahead of his family. In the distant past, she was told, there were predators that attacked the people. The father always carried the Lightning Bolt called *Shar Ur*. But in her memory there were no predators.

Essa stopped; he set down the containers. He readjusted the strap across his shoulders. Then he straightened up without a grunt. *So brave, and determined,* she thought. His face was weathered by many cycles, but broadly admired by the females in their colony. His nose was tapered, narrow near the eyes, broader above his mouth. His eyes echoed hers, blue with a hint of green. To Celiste his cheeks seemed gaunt; as did the cheeks of her people. His lips were turned in as were the lips of her people. They knew to squeeze their lips inward to protect the soft tissue from the arid air, dry and blowing dust.

They passed the squeaky wind gauge at the mid-point of the causeway. Her father jerked his head at it, as if to say *There was a time we had people to service our machines; even the smallest and most mundane.* The wind gauge ignored him and continued to turn in sedate squeaks.

"I know," said Celiste. "The techs are up in *Cead* and *Phoebe*."

They walked quietly up the slope toward the reservoir. Above them five enormous collectors of water stood silent in the afternoon sun. They were five-sided inverted devices that acted to channel condensed water in the early morning to the reservoir.

Chapter 11

At the end of the causeway Celiste and Essa tramped across an expanse of dry, dusty sand. Celiste remembered a turn long ago, her first trip to the sandy breakwater. She saw her people in bathing costumes, enjoying the slight breeze and slim waves of the lake. She saw lithe young girls dancing in the sand and boys playing a ritual game with long poles. She remembered also one of the boys crumbling after a hit to his head. When two boys were sent to the Medical Team with broken arms, the Captain banned the use of the wooden 'thumps' as they were called.

This day she watched her father. He slowly walked up the causeway from the beach. He straightened his back against the heavy load he carried. *This is the hard stretch,* she thought. She looked up with pride at the group's new collector; five bright yellow panels tagged LC#8. There were light-weight wooden poles at the corners, supporting the wide panels that diminished to a point at the bottom. The panels were joined by a channel that collected the moisture before it ran to an ancient pipe that took the moisture into the reservoir at the center of the village.

Her father walked up to the basin at the base of the collector and set his load upon an old stone platform.

"We will survive," he said slowly.

She looked up at Essa. He saw the sadness in her eyes.

"Yes, I suspect you will," she responded politely.

"But you will..." he started to say. He admired Celiste's thin nose, a nose like her mother's. Her slim cheekbones seemed to offset her sparkling eyes that some called blue, others called green. When Celiste smiled Essa saw the face of his mate, Dea, in his daughter's smile.

He paused. In his mind he saw Dea, his love. "You will make the Traverse," he finished.

"Yes, the Traverse ...we know that our destiny is to cross over," she said. Celiste bent over, unfastened the carry straps and raised the first container to the basin. While it drained she looked at her father. She was proud of him, the Advisor to the Village, the man of wisdom. His hair turned gray many years ago when Dea died. His face was crossed with ravines of age. She guessed, without knowing, that twelve maybe fifteen of her people would never leave their village. Essa, who they all called 'Comhair' would lead those who stayed to face the wrath of their enemies beyond the Mother Lake.

"The young men," she laughed, "have started a lottery. The winner, I hear, will hold the honor of courting me before the Traverse."

"Is that all bad?" said Essa.

"No, I am pleased. They are thinking ahead." She did not mention her 'once and only' friend Deem, the brave Captain on the *Dara*. His mission to the blue planet Kien had been approved by the Lord ✗Enlil, ruler of Kien. They would return shortly.

She watched the last drops of water drain from the container. Then she tipped it up and placed it on a rack that held perhaps forty similar containers. She raised the second container and tipped it into the basin.

"We will make a new home with our memories of our people and our story. We will choose three of our most lyric singers to create a long ballad of our time in the 'Deep Black' and our time on this planet. It will be told to our children and their children through the long cycles of the Traverse. It will tell of our journey, of our banishment from Kien and of our 'Face of Enlil' that we leave behind.

She glanced toward the dark moon they called 'Dorn.' It stood above the 'Face of Enlil' after rising on the bridge of Enlil's nose. *What a waste,* she thought, *to carve a face that can only be seen from space.* The 'Face' was an enormous project, begun in the days of her grandparents, a reaction to the Lord Enlil's banishment of her people, a deliberate attempt to say *'We were here.'*

Essa watched her take the empty container and place it on the rack. When she turned around she saw the sadness in his eyes.

"I know," she said.

"I miss her," he said. He looked down to avoid seeing the water that suddenly welled up in the corners of Celiste's eyes. She missed her mother Dea and knew that Essa mourned Dea, his second mate and Leannair, his first mate. They had both been brave members of the colony's defense force.

Chapter 12

A member of the current water team walked up behind them and placed his two containers on the stone step near the collector. He was about one-half head shorter than Celiste, with blackish hair and dark eyes. He unhooked both of his containers and emptied them into the basin.

"Greetings, Gastan," said Essa. He was always polite, even to the members of the colony with questionable lineage. The young man looked at Essa, said nothing and turned with a smile to Celiste. She saw his dark eyes and the brow ridge above his eyes; the brow ridge that her friends said proved he was the son of a Beag. Celiste felt sorry for the young man. His people were laborers; on the blue planet they worked in the gold mines.

He smiled at her.

"What?" she said with impatience.

He smiled. Then he turned to Essa and made a short bow toward the older man whose eyebrows were clinched in a frown.

"Your daughter," he began. Then he bowed even deeper toward Essa. "If it pleases you, Comhair, I am proud to announce that I have the honor of escorting your daughter at the next Gathering."

"Which will be when?" said Celiste quickly.

"When *Phoebe* hits its peak, in one turn. Perhaps you have not heard," he added and glanced at Essa. An eyebrow went up on Essa's face. Essa held up a hand to block any further comments from his daughter.

"Our mission has returned. The *Dara* is in orbit. A Gathering will be held to hear their report. First, they act to confirm my winning the lottery for your daughter."

———— ∞ ————

Father and daughter began to walk toward the plaza. The plaza was empty except for the five-sided altar and the five chairs of the counselors. Essa glanced to the west and saw *Phoebe* rising above the horizon.

"Strange, is it not?"

"Strange?" replied Celiste quietly.

"That we place so much of our hopes on an old chunk of rock."

"We talk of the 'Deep Black,' the long Traverse. As if we are proud of our grandparents," she paused, "but fear what the Traverse means."

"You should fear it."

"We do fear it," she said quietly.

They were walking past the chair traditionally reserved for 'Captain' when a voice said, "You must fear nothing,"

Essa and Celiste turned. The old woman they called Málóid sat in 'Captain's' chair with her feet perched on a box. She wore a new cloth coat of bright yellow. On her head sat a black hat with droopy brim. Underneath her hat there were wisps of gray hair moving in the breeze. Her sightless eyes were turned toward Celiste.

Celiste took three steps away from the old woman and stopped. The woman's face was lined with the crags of age. Her cheeks sagged.

Her nose was bent to the left. Her eyebrows were missing. She made a half-smile and revealed a gap in her teeth.

"Too many years since I have seen thee," began Essa. "Too many years. The Council thought thy spirit was in the land of our ancestors."

"Ha!" laughed the old woman. She began to hack and cough.

"Too many years," she said. "And I know thee, my friend."

"Málóid, this is my daughter Celiste."

The woman looked toward Celiste and said, "Give me your hand."

Celiste was reluctant but stepped forward and placed her hand in the outstretched bony hand of Málóid. The old woman closed her eyes; she had the appearance of one who looks into the past …and the future.

"Yes, you are the one. Many years ago. Do you remember?"

"Yes," said Celiste.

"You do not have to fear that Beag, the one they call Gastan. I see him in your life."

"Yes, but…"

"No, he will leave your life. You will send him on a mission."

Celiste nodded. *I understand, I think.*

"Your daughter will face the anger of an enormous black cloud … no, I see two clouds …black with anger near a white sea."

Essa reached out and removed his daughter's hand from the hand of the old woman. Málóid grabbed his wrist and turned her head toward Essa.

"She is right to fear the Black cloud," she paused then added, "As for you, I see a blinding blast of white light, what I saw once when young."

"A blast of white?"

"Yes, you are here in this plaza. You are talking to a Beag. He holds a device in his hand. There is a long black wire running to a large tube. The flash of white blinds me. And you …I see no longer."

"Thank you, Málóid."

Essa bowed toward the old woman. Celiste also bowed. "We bow to your wisdom," said Essa. They turned and walked away.

Chapter 13

When they looked down from space the exiles saw the mighty canyon that circled their new planet. They saw a great lake with small streams that fed into the lake. A bare desert was painted in a slight red twinge. Areas of old forest and plains of waving grass extended south from the northern pole. The enormous canyon ran around the middle of the planet, and thin rivers ran from the ice at the poles.

In the high lands above the great lake they saw a colony on the south side. The exiles were told the colony, called Ibri, belonged to their cousins from the highlands of Nibiru, their cousins who arrived in *Phoebe* and thrived in a thin atmosphere.

There was a waterfall that fell off the bluff east of Ibri. The water cascaded into a circular depression in a stone basin. The outflow wandered across an ancient plateau where it was used to irrigate crops. Eventually the stream fell off the plateau into the Mother Lake. This lake is wide, shallow on the side where the Aryas built their colony; deep on the north side where the exiled Beag would build their cabins and ceremonial center. The lake widens just west of the village of Ibri and disappears on the horizon. Somewhere beyond the horizon the lake falls between high bluffs and drops into the deep canyon that runs one-quarter of the way around the planet.

The exiles insisted on the right to make decisions. Too many years passed, they said, while the Lords and their *'high and powerful'* children lived like princes while the Beag (and a few Aryas) worked in the mines. The Lords ✗Enki and ✗Enlil decided it was in the nature of the Aryas to be rebellious and exiled their leaders. The exiles asked for a Council of five to resolve disputes. In the end they settled for a Captain, a Counselor and three Regents.

In the early years of the exile the 'Counsel Circle' met on the wooden pier they called the 'Gathering.' After the reservoir was blasted out and covered with limestone cement the people moved the 'Gathering' to the stone platform that sits over the reservoir. There were times in raucous dissent when a speaker stamped his foot a deep boom would be heard from below. A poet of the people called the 'boom' the *'Voice of Ibri'* which elicited laughter and the proverb *'Big Voice, no Echo.'*

Around the 'Gathering' plaza, at five points of a star, sit five pyramids. The first colonists built a wooden structure; it burned to the ground. Then they built a cement pyramid of eight levels, each level set back from the lower level in order to provide a balcony for growing plants and for enjoying the night sky. The balconies are festooned with green and yellow plants. The lower levels 'belonged' to the oldest of the people, those who could no longer walk the upward stairs. When the Council met it was traditional for the older women to tend their plants and listen to the voices below them.

Above the sixth level there were no setbacks; flat walls with small windows rose to a small platform at the peak. There were several metal devices for transmitting to and from the *Cead,* up in orbit.

The stone, they say, will last forever. Each apartment within the pyramid is responsible for the storage chambers inside the pyramid, where the occupants store food stuffs and fuel for their cooking stations.

It is of particular note that a boulevard extends west to east down the middle of the Ibri pyramids. It touches the 'Gathering' plaza before it stretches to the horizon where the people carved a mountain to represent the 'Face' as some say of Lord Enlil.

The first pyramid is called *Cead,* or 'First' in honor of the oldest of the grandparents who settled in the building. The second housing pyramid is called *Dorn* in honor of the old moon that lazily crosses the sky once a turn. The third pyramid was built when the second generation desired a place to raise families. Today it is called *Phoebe,* a reference to her hasty flight two times a day across the sky. The two smaller pyramidal buildings were built last. *Inanna*, also called *Ishtar* in the lands of Lord ✕Enki, houses any females who are not mated. *Croga* in memory of the brave men who led the colonists through the Deep Black houses the unmated males.

Mars, in ancient history, was hit by an enormous object (another planet or very large asteroid?) that created the Tharsis Bulge of the Mars crust. On the opposite side of the planet Valles Marineris, the largest 'grand canyon in the Solar System, reaches depths of up to 7 km (4 miles). There is evidence of water (river beds, canyons) that once flowed into this canyon. In the highlands, near a large lake that flows into the valley, is where the people of Ibri built their village of five pyramids.

The Beag exiles chose to build across the lake where an enormous forest of old growth trees provided them with ready building materials. They cut and shaped the wood and built square structures. The Beag are shorter with pleasant faces and long hair in defiance of Lord ✕Enlil's rule about short hair. The Aryas think the men of Beag wear their hair long to hide the bony ridge above their eyes. Some men bind their hair; many of the women cut their hair short.

Truth be told, the Beag tried to negotiate for land near Ibri but were refused. They settled, reluctantly, on the north side of Great Lake now called Mother Lake. Their village is below hard stone ridges that provide water and shelter from the occasional gale winds. When the strong winds blow down the lake there is an old proverb: 'Gone to the Cave' which implies the Beag have an inordinate fear of the winds.

Back in the early years the Aryas colonists declared the perfect time to hold a 'Gathering' of the Counsel was when *Phoebe*, their Deep Black vessel was climbing to the mid-point of the sky.

Chapter 14

There was a larger than normal crowd standing around the plaza. The fishermen were ashore; the herdsmen were present with clean boots. Captain Aonar led three short men to the edge of the plaza. They were dressed in black coats; their long hair was pulled back and gathered at the back. An old fisherman called out, 'Thief.' A man yelled 'Go home.'

A frown deepened Captain Aonar's face. With his hand he pushed his hair braid to the side. He wore his hair shaved on the right side, long and braided over his left ear. His old friends knew it was an insult to 'Lord Enlil' who wore his in the reverse style. He turned and said, "They are our guests, under a banner of peace."

From the back of the crowd someone shouted, "No peace."

"No treaty with Beag," shouted another. From the back was heard, a low chant, 'Sons of Kien.' It was picked up and repeated by several of the men.

Aonar held up a fist then turned and removed his dark green coat and hung it over the back of his chair. This was a symbol that the Gathering should come to order. An old man shambled up to the observers and rang the Chime. The people became quiet. Aonar turned and made a small bow toward the horizon and the 'Face of Enlil.' He saw the dark moon Dorn rising in the east while their habitat *Phoebe* reached the mid-point of the sky. "Two moons," he said. The oldest regent, Sheb. Sin added, "means good decisions."

Essa laughed and added, "An old wives' tale." A silence descended. The Regents moved to their chairs. Essa left Celiste where she stood near Deem, Captain of the *Dara,* and moved to his chair. The return of the '*Dara*' brought a sense of excitement and impending 'bad' news, according to the 'ancients.'

The Aryas were there to meet and decide their fate. The people stood in small groups across the plaza. A large cluster of younger persons stood around three of the newly returned crew from the *Dara.*

Captain Aonar indicated three stone blocks near the edge of the plaza and the three Beag sat. One turned and glared at the raucous men in the back of the crowd. The three Beag wore black coats and beards trimmed to a point below their chins. They were Beag, enemies of the people. They were short, stocky with hair falling below their ears and a pronounced ridge above their eyebrows. One of them chewed on a medicine stick.

Aonar was tall, regal, and solemn. He bent at the waist and intoned an ancient formula: "Listen and grant us your wisdom, all those who seek this day to decide."

There was a moment of quiet while Essa looked at the men who were present and the few women. Then he put a fist into the air. He hung his head and held his fist raised high. It was an old signal asking for silence. A slight breeze ruffled his thin brown hair. He lowered his hand to brush away a pesky insect near his strong, powerful jaw.

He waited. There was blunt silence; it was broken when the old man dropped the Chime onto the stone terrace. Several men laughed, nervously.

"The Beag suffer from the same conditions, as do we. They are working diligently to grow plants and produce food and teach their young …as are we. They are led by radicals who want vengeance on the Lords of Kien. They know our best are preparing *Phoebe* to return to Nibiru."

He looked up into the sky where their transport vehicle *Cead* was about to be passed by *Phoebe.* He marveled that *Phoebe's* orbit was exactly a half-day. "The Beag resist change and hold on to old beliefs, old sailor's tales of the long void and the black and cold when our ancestors first came here in Phoebe."

There were rumbles of agreement from several of the men. The oldest tales, handed down from grandfathers to their children were of the old land, the planet with long-tooth predators that appeared out of the grass and snatched young children. Many said those were stories meant to scare little children into staying close to their parents. Others said the stories told of a land the People fled 600 years in the past.

"The Beag must decide to join us on the Traverse," said Essa.

A murmur rumbled among the onlookers. Someone shouted 'No!' so loudly that heads were turned in his direction.

"There is no room," said the same man.

Chapter 15

"My daughter," Essa said slowly, "urges me to lead you on the Traverse back to Nibiru." He looked around the fifty people scattered around the plaza and recalled when 300 or more chose Aonar to be Captain. Among them he saw the face of worry, the face of sadness, the face of anger. "I know some of you want me to bring our young men back, to launch an attack on those who destroyed two of our collectors and three of our people."

The people were quiet. They looked at Essa in his long red tunic and black leggings and admired his badge of rank, the silver circle with the six pointed star that said, 'I am descended *Lehmu*, the Land of the Exiles'.

"I am angry," Essa said and turned toward the face of 'Lord Enlil.' The dark moon Dorn was well above the nose of the face. He bowed slightly and then lowered his arms. "Sad that our people leave."

Several of the old men grumbled. After dedicating their lives to their colony they were now told to leave on the Traverse to their home planet.

"Some of you wish to stay, you wish to honor loved ones who have passed before us and now lie in dream sleep with our 'old ones' from the past 300 years." Essa looked at their Captain, called Aonar by his polite friends. The old man waved a hand telling Essa to pause.

Aonar rose slowly to his feet. He looked around at old friends and younger men of his village. He was known for saying little at Gatherings. His hand came up and pushed his thinning hair out of the way. "I am the face of sad," he stammered. "I am sad."

"We are all sad," added Essa from the platform, looking across the People and the three Beag who sat listening. Essa enjoyed the respect of 'Advisor' and knew that same respect was due to Aonar for his earlier leadership.

"From the earlier time we have heard..." said Aonar, "...of the void and the cold and the hunger and the bad dreams of the little ones who were born during the Traverse. We have heard from our grandparents of the grassy plains of Kien and the blue waters in the hills. And of the terrible anger of Enlil when he executed 100 of our men and sent us to this barren rock."

"True," said Essa.

"For myself, I choose not to accept the Traverse," said Aonar loudly.

"That is your choice," remarked Essa.

Aonar and Essa stood silent for a long moment. Their friends and neighbors were caught in the dilemma of making a decision. They knew the question was coming. Essa looked down the broad avenue that led directly to the 'Face' his young men had carved for, what? Thirty years, now? His beloved Deacair, mother to Celiste, was buried with her parents and grandparents in the sacred ground near the boulevard. Essa saw several men turn and look in the same direction. *'They too think it is time to stop carving,'* he thought.

"It is your choice," said Essa a second time. "You know the reasons many will leave. How many of you will stay?"

Aonar raised his arm with a fist voting 'Aye.' A few of the older men did likewise. Essa counted the fists and counted the women on the balconies.

Celiste moved to the front, near the platform. She looked at her father with sadness. A tear rolled from her eye to her chin. Essa saw the sadness in her eye and said slowly to his neighbors while he looked at Celiste, "I will stay. That makes seventeen."

"Not enough for a full squad," said Aonar.

"We will organize our defenses and resist any attacks."

"They will come, you know," shouted a man.

One of the Beag turned; he wore a banner of white with the green and black stripes of his people across his chest. He stared at the man who shouted, *'They will come.'* The color was rising in his cheeks. He seemed to glare at the man. One of the Beag took ahold of his shoulder and turned him back to the platform. The second man raised his arm with a fist. Aonar motioned for him to speak.

"Forgive my friend, here. He is full of fire and revenge for attacks your men made in the time of his father and uncles."

"We remember," said Essa. Among his people the term 'remember' was an honorific term for those who died before their full lives of 300 years.

"We do not come," said the Beag, "to provoke you." He was a full head shorter than Essa and Aonar. His hair had recently been cut short; his beard trimmed. His face was lined with age; his hands gnarled with old scars; his arms dark from exposure.

"I am MarSin, of the house of Enosh. I am seventh generation from Enosh, third generation from Enoch, the builder. These two grew up without fathers. We do not come here to provoke more war."

He looked up at Essa, as if to say *'how much can I say?'*

"We remember," said Essa. Aonar turned and sat on his chair. Essa looked at his people and gestured that they could sit on the benches scattered around the plaza. Two young men near the three Beag come forward and grabbed the nearest bench in an effort to intimidate MarSin and his nephews. Essa raised a hand. Men nearest the two men stopped them. They put the bench down. One kicked the bench. The other made a gesture; he ran his hand across his forehead in a derogatory gesture that meant 'lake-bottom-sucking scum of Kien.'

Aonar, he of the quiet low voice spoke up: "Enough. This Gathering is convened. We follow the protocol."

Essa was about to announce the agenda when he realized the missing Regent, by name 'Gastina' stood at the step that led to the platform, her son Gasta behind her.

Gastina, if anything, looked regal. Her sharp black eyes took in the scene. Her straight nose gave her face the appearance of a hawk. She was dressed in her finest flowing gown and held a basket. Her black hair fairly sparkled in the sun and held a small white flower. She stepped onto the Council platform and placed a large woven basket of yellow and green 'snaps' in front of Aonar.

Essa smiled and said, "Yes?"

"I want the Council to confirm my son as winner of the lottery and entitled to hold Celiste, daughter of Essa, as his consort before the Traverse."

Chapter 16

There was a time when the Aryan descendants of the twelve Lords and the Beag worked together, side by side to build shelters and fortresses and the apartments inside the pyramids. It was a time before the older generations stopped their young men from courting the females in the Beag tribe. Celiste was barely one cycle old when the Fisherman's War began. She was not allowed to see the injured men. She did however hear her grandparents talking about the sign of evil the Beag carried on their foreheads. She did know the words '*fiorglan*' and '*glantair*' were used frequently to describe her people as 'Pure' and 'Purely Royal.'

Celiste and the people of her village were taller than the short, squat Beag. Some Beag barely reached her shoulder. Her people tolerated their strong, healthy neighbors for their ability to do very hard work in the fields. Celiste's people were thin and somewhat weaker in their back muscles.

The same year Celiste lost her mother she heard a playmate say, "We are Aryas, and royal. You can never do anything with the Beag. They are bastard sons of Kien." Celiste did not understand the word 'bastard.' Many cycles passed while the first and second generations lived and died. By common agreement the two tribes shared the lake and its fish. By mutual agreement they did not catch more than they could eat. Each tribe held possession forever of half the lake. Their engineers worked together to build a long series of anchored buoys that 'split' the lake.

And then, at some point the Great Lake began to walk away from the People's Pier. There were fiery orators who accused the Beag of blocking their marsh, and not allowing the Great Lake to be replenished. Young men among the Beag claimed Celiste's people had diverted water to build an enormous reservoir in the highlands, and claimed their waterfall was almost dried up.

It was not long after these accusations that the 'old ones' among the Aryas pointed out what seemed obvious: the small ridge in the forehead was a mark of impurity. The Beag and their children were descendants of 'Daughters of Kien' who were among the fallen cast out by Enlil after a war on Kien. They claimed the Lord Enki allowed his sons to co-habit with the 'Daughters of Kien' and the Lord Enlil took great offense that the pure line of royalty might be 'polluted.' The royal line was descended from ☓Anu and his official spouse, his half-sister ☓Antu.

"Tis the mark of Kien, to have the ridge above the eyes," said many of the Aryan outcasts. But they grew crops of the field and traded with the Beag for their labor, until the days of the Fisherman's war.

The war began, like all wars, in a misunderstanding.

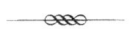

The lake was enormous, and broad. From Celiste's pier, one could just see the tops of small mountains beyond the Beag village. To the east there were small cliffs that drained higher plains into the lake. To the west there was a stretch of bare horizon where the lake flowed to the west before it dropped into an enormous valley that ran an enormous one-quarter of the circumference of the planet. It was a deep valley, clearly visible from space. The lake itself was shallow on the south side, in front of Ibri. Near the territorial markers the lake became deep and deeper still half-way to the opposite shore.

The men of Aonar's village knew where the large fish were: they grew inside the deeper waters. Occasionally the fishermen would catch an aggressive green and scaly 'monster' with the large eyes that they called 'Inanna' because their eyes were so beautiful. The name 'Inanna' honored the granddaughter of the Lord Enlil, rumored to be both wise *and* beautiful.

Therein lay the problem. When an Ibri fisherman brought in a large fish, the Beag who were present at Ibri would jokingly accuse them of fishing in Beag waters. Until the day it actually happened.

Aonim, first son of Aonar, was near the markers fishing for small white fish that fed his village. Out of curiosity he took out a coil of 'four-man' line and attached a hook as big as his hand. He put three white fish on the hook and dropped the line half way to the bottom. His line, he knew, was ultra-strong. Four men pulling in opposite directions could not break it.

Aonim, a fisherman by trade, had a mate and a baby girl at home in the fifth level of their pyramid. They had recently been awarded an apartment with a balcony, an honor accorded Aonim for his work providing fish for the village. He was proud of his role; on this day he was relaxed and looking forward to the arrival of his new baby, a son.

When the 'four-man' line began to snake out of the boat, he did not notice. He was busy pulling in a line with five white fish, unhooking them and tossing them into the bottom of his shallow boat. The line, meanwhile, continued to run out until three coils of the line flipped up and found the handle of one oar. They slowly pulled tight. The line straightened. There was a tug, barely felt but it caught the attention of Aonim. He looked up and saw the line cinching into the wood of his oar. Something had his bait.

He was about to reach for the line to get a sense of the size of the fish when a hard jolt shook the boat. Something big did not like the hook.

"Hooked yourself, did ye?" mumbled Aonim. He saw the line was beginning to rise. Without a conscious thought Aonim realized his boat was moving toward the nearest marker buoy. He looked quickly to his long fishing line and realized it was in the boat. He had unhooked the last of his white fish just before the jolt hit his boat.

'This could be trouble,' he thought.

Chapter 17

Aonim stood up in the boat and grabbed the tight line. He had to pull back on the line and looped it twice around the stem at the bow. *'There. You do the work.'* There was a heavy tug and Aonim fell back into the boat. Much later, thinking about it, he claimed that he was stunned.

The boat made steady progress; it moved with the current but crossed into 'Beag' territory. When Aonim next looked, his boat was half-way to the far shore and it was approaching the home village of the Beag. Two fast skiffs were moving to intercept Aonim; he thought they wanted to help. The skiffs caught him just opposite their village. Aonim saw a crowd gathered on the shore; they were shouting at him.

'Strange,' he thought then realized he was wearing a red shirt with a wide white stripe; those were traditional colors for members of the Ibri fishermen.

The lead skiff rammed into his boat; the man in the bow grabbed his gunwale and was surprised when he realized the boat was being pulled. He pulled a knife out of its holster and made to cut the line, but Aonim swore at him and grabbed an oar. He was about to swing at the man when the other skiff hit his boat and Aonim fell sideways. Struggling to regain his feet, he shouted that they had no right to cut his fish loose.

The four men looked at him for a moment. "Not your fish," said one. Another added, "It is clearly inside our territory." A third man said, "We bring it up." He reached the four-man line and began to pull. They became a strange sight: two men in a skiff pulling; Aonim tying off the line as they gained on the fish. The second skiff fell behind.

Occasionally the men in the skiff would tire; the line would slip and run out while they tried to tighten down on the line. One man cursed the Lord Enlil; the line sliced his fingers. The second grabbed the line and wove it around his wrist; his arm snapped downward into the lake but the line steadied.

Ever so slowly they began to make progress. The line was coming up. The 'monster' was tiring. Looking down they saw fins on its back; it was an enormous Inanna with eyes that flashed when it turned toward the sun. The three men quickly realized they could not land this fish; they began rowing to pull it toward their village.

Aonim fastened his line to the stern of his boat then to the stern of the skiff. Together they pulled on their oars. "It is my fish," he said.

The two Beag men looked at him but said nothing. As they approached the village they heard a commotion; many people came to see this enormous fish. When Aonim saw the lake bottom he jumped into the water and grabbed the Inanna by sliding his arm into a gill on one side. The fish was at least as long as Aonim, and heavier. The two skiff men pulled both boats onto shore then pulled on the line while Aonim maneuvered the fish onto the shore.

The Inanna made one last attempt at escape. It thrashed and lashed its tail and snapped at a little girl who stood near its mouth. Her hand came up and the teeth of the Inanna chomped down on her hand. She screamed in terror. Aonim grabbed an oar from his boat and hit the fish just above its eyes. The fish stopped moving but held the girl's hand. Aonim used his oar as a pry bar and worked the mouth of the fish open. The little girl was still screaming when her father picked her up and left to find some help.

Aonim was speechless. He looked down at the two men who helped him. One was wrapping his injured hand. The other was talking to what appeared to be the village elder. Many in the crowd were talking; several said harsh words directed at Aonim. Inside the mayhem Aonim heard himself accused of theft.

"Theft?" he shouted.

"Yes. You princes of Enki."

"Thieves, the lot of you," someone added.

"No theft," shouted Aonim.

"That is our fish," said an older man. For emphasis, he pointed at it.

"I caught it," said Aonim.

"Did you?" said the older man. "I saw Dergin and Dervla, two nephews to our Captain MarSin; they pull the Inanna up to your boat." He put his foot on the fish and it slowly fell onto its side, tired and worn out from the long struggle. Its mouth opened and closed.

"In our territory," said Aonim with as much force as he could measure.

"In your territory?" asked the old man.

"Our territory, well beyond the markers," added Aonim.

The old man looked at the village elder, called Seth. The elder was a direct descendant five generations removed from his 'great-great-great grandmother, a 'Daughter of Kien' with her short stature and pronounced brow. The old man bowed toward the elder and said, "You see. He lies."

"What ...am I on trial?" said Aonim.

"In a manner," said Seth, the elder. "Where property is concerned, we are relaxed and informal."

"No lie," said Aonim.

"He lies," said the old man.

The elder questioned Aonim and Aonim boldly stated he caught the fish in Ibri territory on the lake. He also believed he was knocked out briefly or groggy and the fish pulled his boat onto the wrong side of the markers. The old man said he saw Aonim's boat on this side of the marker buoys and he saw the two brothers pulling the fish up to the two boats.

The elder looked at Aonim. There was a glint of determination in his eyes. Among the crowd surrounding the elder and Aonim and the fish there were a few words of anger. Someone even suggested 'a community fish roast.' The elder raised his arm and made a fist. Silence fell among the people. Aonim heard the sound of waves; a wind was beginning to push off the lake.

"They are both right," said the elder, Seth. "Aonim believes he caught the fish, but witnesses say that MarSin's nephews caught the fish, by which they mean the two boys pulled the fish in." Several men agreed with his words.

He looked at Aonim and made a small bow of respect. "The fish belongs to us." Seth pointed at four men and told them to cut the head off and put it in Aonim's boat. To Aonim he added, "We wish you no disrespect, but the fish was on our side of the markers, in our territory, when it was pulled up."

Aonim watched four of the Beag when they wrapped the head of the Inanna in an old cloth. They put it in his boat. Aonim waved his hand at the boat with a question on his lips. Seth quietly asked, "Can you tell your tale without proof?"

Chapter 18

It was the proof, the fish-head that led to violence. The men of Ibri village were angry, incensed and livid that their competitors across the lake had 'stolen' what was theirs. To the men, the fish-head was the ultimate insult.

"Can you imagine? They keep the fish and send us the bloody, fly infested head? Are we no better than to eat their trash?"

***

The anger festered for nine turns of the sun. On the tenth turn, while Dorn the dark moon was in the sky, the men of Ibri launched five boats with fishing gear, long handled axes and in one boat sat a small clay pot that held the embers from a morning fire.

They caught Dergin and Dervla fishing alone in separate boats. After they 'surrounded' the two Beag fishermen one man, a distant cousin of Aonim called Markim said "You are on our side of the markers."

"No, we are not," replied Dergin.

"Yes, you have moved the marker into our territory," Markim lied.

"No," replied Dergin. He began to pull in his long line. The line came in with three whitefish and a crab that dropped off short of his boat.

"Thank you …our fish," said Aonim's cousin Markim.

"You know, our elder says, tell them where to go."

"And that would be where?" asked an older Ibri fisherman renowned for his fishing prowess and his stubborn streak.

"Go join the princes and lords of Kien," said Dergin, "…those who seduce their half-sisters and rape the Daughters of *Kien*."

"Yes," said Dervla, his brother. "That's the only way you can have children …by raping my cousin."

Markim brought a long-handled ax out of the bottom of his boat and swung it in an arc. It came down into the bottom of Dergin's boat. Wood splintered and water began to drip, a small leak at first, then a gusher when pieces of the wood broke free.

Dergin began to climb into Dervla's skiff. The low boat rocked and water sloshed over the edge.

"Take your line," said the old fisherman, "…and our whitefish, with you."

"Let this be a warning," declared Markim. Several men laughed. One called the two brothers *'gann Beag'* by which he implied the two men were 'insufficient' to make love to any of his cousins.

———⟨≋⟩———

Thus began the war. There were sporadic fights limited to damage to boats, lines and nets destroyed or the marker buoys moved during the dead of night. It was a 'limited' war until the day about one cycle later when ten Beag marched out to meet the men of Ibri village. They marched around the south end of the lake in order to surprise their enemies. They carried three axes, six fighting 'thumps' and assorted knives. Their Counselor had banned use of the Shar.Ur, known as the 'Supreme Hunter.'

They surprised their enemy: they caught two women bathing in the lake perhaps ten minutes walking time from the village. The women were Gastina and her half-sister Jeannina. Gastina saw the Beag approaching and ordered Jeannina to grab her clothes and run for help.

"I stall them. Bring weapons," she added. Gastina saw the axes and surmised they had other weapons.

When five men arrived ten long minutes later they found Gastina on the ground with a Beag named Ragnar raping her. She had argued and ordered them to leave and threatened them. She had managed to get their fire up. And one man who had a fancy for Gastina had chosen rape as revenge for previous 'wrongs' by her people.

The five men saw they were out-numbered. They stepped out of the brush and ordered the Beag to drop their weapons. No one moved. The man in the rape act continued until he said, with bravado, "There!" He stood up and there was a 'Bang!' from a 'Spitter' and he clutched his arm for a moment then fell backward. He was stunned.

Dergin and Dervla pulled knives out of their boot holsters and glanced at each other. Then they charged at the Ibri men. The 'Spitter' spoke twice more. And the two brothers fell. The Beag stepped backward, away from the two dead men.

"Do not come again," said Aonim. "Or you will be short."

"They are already short," echoed a deep voice.

"We know. You call us 'Beag' or 'Short,'" said Ragnar trying to stand. A Beag took Ragnar's arm and helped him to stand.

"You are Ragnar," said Aonim. The young men glared at each other. "He is a good with the fish," said a Beag.

"Come again," said Aonim. "We make you shorter."

Two of Aonim's friends snorted, barely able to contain their laughter. Aonim reached out to help Gastina to her feet. He turned her away from the Beag so her enemies could not see her embarrassment. Together they walked away from the group.

Ragnar turned and walked toward the Great Falls, with his men in single file behind him.

One of the Beag tapped Ragnar on the shoulder and said, "You cause trouble. Much trouble."

"Someday, Ragnar," said another of the Beag, "…the Great Lake, our Mother, will take you."

"But not today," said Ragnar quietly.

Two moons later the Council approved the joining of Gastina to a young man. They lived together and the village Ibri rejoiced when Gastina delivered a son, some seven months later.

Five cycles (ten years) of the planet around its yellow sun passed away. There were sporadic battles; a few men were injured. The retreat of the Great Lake from its shores became more noticeable. The atmosphere seemed drier.

The anger of each side for the other grew stronger. The Beag men learned how to mash and age corn in large containers. They were frequently seen on the lake, singing ribald songs and taunting Ibri fishermen.

Both communities faced the identical problem: water became scarce. Sleam said the ice caps were growing; the moisture in the air growing less. In their Gathering the elders began to discuss a Traverse, a move of the people back to *Kien* and for some, the long Traverse to their home planet *Nibiru*.

The battles diminished, in the face of a common threat. Celiste's people were cautious. They knew the Beag possessed the *'Shar.Graz'* of Enlil, an enormous weapon. This was the weapon that obliterated an entire city in an instant enormous fireball. Their Counselors, especially Essa, urged patience. They needed to go and request permission of ✕Lord Enlil to be returned to *Kien* or to board *Phoebe* for the long Traverse to home.

Chapter 19

Counselor Gastina repeated herself. "I ask for a ruling from the Council." A few men in the back of the crowd laughed. To them it was apparent that Celiste had rejected Gastan, the winner of the Lottery.

The Council itself was largely ceremonial. In a rare instance the Council might be asked for a ruling. At this 'Gathering' the men, however, waited to hear a report from Deem. The Captain of the *Dara* was their 'ambassador' to the Court of Lord Enlil on Kien. Four ordinary wooden chairs and the padded chair of their Captain were placed at the five points of the star on the plaza. The honor chair stood in front of the red flag with the white band across it; the chair was nearest to *Cead,* the first pyramid.

When Aonar sat in his chair he saw the older women were now arriving to listen to the reports. Essa, as senior among the Counselors asked the people to stand formally. They bowed toward 'Face of Enlil' while Essa asked the people to listen. When he turned toward his chair the only female Counselor, Gastina raised a hand. She turned toward the boulevard and made a slight ceremonial bow and said, "I exercise my privilege ...I ask for a ruling from the Council."

Gastina stood her legs apart with fire in her eye. There was a groan among the men in the plaza. Counselor ShebSin said, "You heard Essa. He introduced the subject of a Traverse when he asked how many of us would remain."

Gastina looked at the old Counselor and knew he should have been replaced by the people many cycles in the past. "I asked for privilege."

"Our decision?" said Aonar.

"Confirmation," she replied.

"Of your son's rights?" said Aonar. "So I heard. There are objections?"

Two men in the crowd spoke up and said "Yes!" loudly.

Aonar scanned the crowd. Three men toward the rear raised their hand to indicate they also objected to Gastan being mated to Celiste. Two of the older women near the platform had their heads down, but they were indicating their displeasure with the idea.

"We will hear the reports. Then we will deal with Gastan's request," said Aonar with determination.

"Get on with it," someone in the crowd affirmed.

"Yes," said Essa.

"Yes," added ShebSin, the oldest of the Counselors.

"And I have ruled," said Aonar. Gastina did not vote. She turned in a flurry of white skirt and flaming red banners and went to her seat. She knew with the seat of Sleam vacant after his death that three votes carried any decision.

"We will hear from the ice-cap team first."

A rustle of mumbled words assaulted the ears of those on the platform. A man of Celiste's age stepped onto the platform. He waited for quiet then bowed to the 'Face of Enlil' then pulled a tablet with a viewing screen from inside his formal coat of dark green. He had a pleasant face, with straight nose and black eyes under his shiny black hair. There was a scar near his chin; the females of Celiste's age believed he was a notable catch.

"I am Sleam.Sin. The venerable atmosphere specialist was my grandfather, Sleam. He believed the icecaps are growing. He wrote this report the day before he died, sucked into the sharp blue maw of a hungry ice goddess who devoured him."

"Oh," said a female in the crowd. Farther back a man snorted. It was hard to tell whether the man was laughing or simply enjoyed Sleam.Sin's description.

"Honor and reverence to the Lords Enlil, Enki, NinMah and others of the Anunnaki," he began to read. He held up his document holder, what some would call a tablet. Among his people there were three tablets; each needed to be sent to *Cead* every cycle to be renewed by the technicians.

"As I said, 'Honor and reverence' and so on," began Sleam.Sin. Then he added, "This is my report. I am Sleam, fifth generation from ӾEnki, sixth generation from the honored ӾAnu, our Lord and Master. We began to install the reflectors on the ice. It was my belief that 500 reflectors would create enough heat to reverse the growth of the ice-cap. We have installed 122 of the 200 that came down from *Cead.* I must report, with sadness that our efforts will go for waste. Even 1000 reflectors will not reverse the dryness of our atmosphere."

He held up the tablet and showed the crowd there was a document on the tablet. Then he handed it to Aonar.

"Do you have anything to add?" asked Essa.

"Sleam was my Counselor. Our team was proud to serve him." He made a bow toward the 'Face.' From the back of the crowd a member of the icecap team shouted, "Tell them our conclusion."

Sleam. Sin looked up, and smiled. "We agreed with Sleam. We were on the ice for 30 turns. In that time the atmosphere passed 13 percent …it is now 12 percent and moving toward 11 percent."

"Which means?" asked Essa.

"The atmosphere will become extremely dry. Our lungs will begin to rebel. The Great Lake will dry up. Our reflectors will make the ice-cap sparkle into the black of space. In time they will be buried in ice."

In the front of the gathering one of the young men from across the lake raised his fist. The older man reached out and gently pulled his arm down. He leaned toward the young man and listened for a moment.

Then the older man raised his arm with his fist open, indicating a contrary opinion and said, "I am MarSin, four generations from ✕Enki who was father of my great-great grandfather, the young god ✕Mar. Duk. My young friend here is headstrong. I speak for your cousins across the lake."

"Cousins? Who said we are cousins?" shouted a young man.

"We will hear what he has to say," said Aonar slowly with emphasis.

MarSin glanced around and saw there were twenty young men standing in a crowd around the young man who objected to being a cousin.

"These are my nephews, Yared and Rey.Gin. They were named for their fathers who died in our perpetual war. They are my honorary aides. They *do not* speak," he added then put his hands on their shoulders.

Both of the young men, to left and right of MarSin, stood a little taller and turned around to glare at the men behind them. Their uncle pulled them back to face the platform just as Deem of the 'Dara' shuttle stepped onto the platform.

"These two young men," added MarSin, "are like sons to me. They want vengeance for their fathers."

"They are not alone," said Essa. He looked down at his scuffed old boots and remembered how Dea hated those boots. *'Use some fish oil,'* she used to say. From the back of the crowd an old fish flew over and narrowly missed Yared. It smacked onto the platform.

Essa looked at the fish, an old whitefish. "They are not alone," he repeated. "No more of that," he said loudly. "They are guests."

"Those of you standing ...sit," stated Aonar with the force of his deep, sonorous voice. He ran a hand through his thinning hair. He watched as MarSin and his nephews sat on a bench. The men who stood on the outside of the platform also sat.

"We listen. We talk. You decide." Aonar was grim.

Chapter 20

Deem came to the middle of the platform and turned to face the members of his village. He held up a rolled document and allowed it to unroll. Everyone could see there were symbols painted on it.

"While we were on Kien, we received word from the team on *Phoebe*." He looked to the sky above where something on *Phoebe* reflected the sun. "The power is minimal. No power to support live beings. We cannot plan to use *Phoebe* to return to our planet."

"Unlikely!" shouted an older man. He raised his fist.

"Irresponsible!" shouted another man.

"Since when has *Phoebe* been minimal?"

"Since maybe 50 years ago," said Deem. "You have to remember. When we made the Traverse the time was perhaps 300 cycles. That converts to 600 rotations of Kien around the sun. We were on Kien for how many generations? Three? Four? Then our grandparents were sent here aboard *Cead* and that was 200 years in the past."

"Our people on *Phoebe*," said Aonar. "Have tried to repair the crystals and induction system. Minimal power is available. Just enough to maintain the defensive weapons aboard '*Phoebe*', no more."

"We thought," said a man in the crowd.

"We were told," said another.

"Irresponsible," shouted another.

"Can we restore the power?" said an old woman in the front.

"The Lord Enlil says no," said Deem in a loud voice.

There was dead silence. No one spoke.

"You know what we think of the *'so-called'* Lord Enlil …do you not?" shouted Aonim, the youngest son of Aonar. He was busy removing a red banner from his shoulder. He dropped it on the plaza and stepped on it. Then he turned his boot, as if to grind the banner into the stone.

"Can we restore the power?" said the same old woman again.

"And what of the Lord Enki? We supported his son," said ShebSin, the oldest of the five Counselors.

"Enlil is the Lord of the Command," explained Deem. "He made me wait four days before he would see me."

"And Lord Enki?"

"He agreed with our Lord Enlil," said Deem. The young man looked up to the east and bowed toward the 'Face of Enlil.'

"No more bowing to Enlil!" shouted Aonim. He looked around to see if anyone agreed with him. *At least, no one disagrees,* he thought. "What is this you hold, Deem?"

"It is the skin of an animal. It records the decision of Enlil and Enki. On your behalf I have agreed to the terms."

"If we do not agree?" asked Essa. He glanced at Celiste where she sat next to the old woman. Celiste tried to smile; her lips barely moved. Essa felt a stone turn in his stomach when he looked at his only daughter. *You will lead our people, my daughter.* The old seer's words echoed across the years.

"If you do not agree you have two options: one is to stay here on this *'dry'* Rock or you can stay in orbit until the next transport in about one year. Enlil continues to ship gold to *Nibiru*."

"Our honored ones are here …and on Kien," said ShebSin.

"The great Lord Enlil does not want us back on Kien," said Aonim loudly. He held a hand up with a fist. The random talk and the loud voices gradually became quiet.

"As ShebSin says. Our honored ones are here," added Essa.

"Lord Enlil makes the decision …and we have to comply?" asked Celiste in a quiet voice. Aonar pointed at his son Aonim. Celiste nodded to indicate that Aonim had the privilege of speaking.

"We should go meekly into the deep dark, all the way back to our home after what …eight generations? I vote 'No!' No one will know us. Our families will have descendants with clear title to royal status. We will be 'outlanders' from Kien," said Aonim with succinct precision.

"Maybe so," added Essa. "I am not leaving."

Celiste looked at him. He was not smiling. Her mouth felt dry; she felt pressure in her chest. "What was the decision of Enlil?"

Aonim lowered his arm. Deem raised the skin document and said, "Hear the decision of the great Lord ✕Enlil."

Someone said, "Get on with it."

Deem began to read. "You are rebels. You sided with Mar.Duk, son of Enki in the rebellion. You cannot be trusted," said Deem and looked up. There was silence across the plaza.

"You will send twenty-four young men to join the troops led by Abram, guardian of the spaceport. You will appoint a woman to have order and justice for twenty-four Beag women in the fields that grow crops for Ur-Shulim, also called Salem. The two squads will be hostages for the acceptable behavior of the rest. Captain Deem shall direct two teams of six on your ship, *Cead*."

"And the rest of us?"

"Those of you of pure blood, descended from the twelve Anunnaki, will work on repairs at Puma Punco in the highlands of the southern planet. Those of you descended from the 'Daughters of Kien' will…" he started, "that is, twenty-four Beag men will begin training with the Army of Abram in the restricted zone near the landing zone in the southern desert. Your term of service will be two years. The remainder of the Beag will be placed on a warm island where crops grow in profusion, where you will pay honorable veneration to ✗Anu, my father. We will train you on the tools to make statues that honor ✗Anu, each to be three times the height of an ordinary male of the clan you call Beag."

There was silence. The short man called MarSin nodded and said he understood. The young male Yared said he believed some of his people would prefer to stay on the 'dry Rock' before becoming slaves on Kien.

"Those are the terms," said Essa. "Our people can go back to a land where there is bright yellow sun, warm breezes, and it rains to feed the plants."

"There is one thing you must know," said Deem. He looked around his neighbors. "There is some kind of unrest on Kien. Mar.Duk, son of Enki, is once again in Babylon and his troops are training. [Endnote[i]]

Chapter 21

The tall young man stood bravely on the plaza. No one told him to use the empty chair when so many respected the old Counselor Sleam. Many remembered Sleam's passion in the face of intractable 'old' beliefs. This young captain was perhaps a third of Sleam's age.

"What did it feel like?" someone shouted.

"You mean …on Kien?"

"Yes. Let's hear," said the same voice.

Deem rolled up the skin document and gave it to Aonar. Then he looked around at the young men and women who would most likely become hostages and soldiers if they landed on Kien. Deem had the straight nose and pronounced cheek-bones of an Anunnaki. The women thought him handsome.

"The pull of the planet is heavy. Heavier than here. The atmosphere has moisture, but not so much as to be oppressive. We were above the mid-line, in land that is sometimes desert sand but there are flat plains with green crops. It does not rain much in these lands."

"Flat plains …little rain?"

"There are water channels. The water comes from the mountains and then is made to spread across the growing land where workers clean the fields of undesirable plants."

"How heavy is the pull of Kien?"

"One half day on my feet and I had to sit down and rest," said Deem before he turned to the empty chair and sat down. "We have been ordered to Puma Punco," added Deem, "a city in the high mountains on a different land mass. I was told the pull of Kien is less, but the atmosphere is lighter, drier."

"Do we have a choice?"

"It is an ancient city. With statues of the twelve Anunnaki who first landed. The gravity is much less. No, you do not have a choice."

"What is your choice?" asked Celiste. She smiled; the corner of Deem's lips turned a small smile. Several men in the crowd chuckled.

"There is an excellent landing field at that ancient city. The natives call it Tiwanaku or Winay Marca, which means 'Eternal City'," he added and then said, "Of course, I will be on *Cead* taking care of its operations."

Perhaps she heard the men in the crowd. Celiste looked down at her feet, which was a common form of submission to the power of men. Her cheeks turned darker.

"We must make a decision," said Essa. Aonar nodded. ShebSin was quiet. The fourth Counselor, Gastina raised an open fist to object.

Chapter 22

Aonar saw Gastina's fist. He knew the question of her son's right to court Celiste must be settled. He nodded at Gastina.

"We can deal with approval of my son's rights, now?"

With slow reluctance Aonar looked first at Celiste then at Essa. He knew that Essa did not like this question. It was Essa's daughter Celiste that was at the center of the question. And her son Gastan was shorter than Essa by half a head. Essa would always have to look down at Gastan if the mating was approved.

Several of the older men stood up. The two 'elder' women in the front began to stare at the stone of the plaza. Two young men in the crowd stood and raised their arms, fists open indicating objection.

"When a young woman reaches her eighteenth year she is now six years beyond the age when she can begin to bring children to the house of her grandfather," said ShebSin, the oldest Counselor.

To Gastina he said, "You can see there are objections?"

"I am descended from Enki. Therefore, I hold royal blood, as does my son. He is entitled to pick a mate and he won the lottery."

Aonar looked at Celiste. Her head was down. Her hands were closed, one over the other, in her lap. Her hair fell and hid her face.

"Did you submit to the lottery, Celiste?"

She mumbled something. Then her head nodded, 'Yes.'

"Were there any problems with the lottery?"

"No," said Essa and ShebSin together. They held the role of joint supervisors. "All the males, and those in *Phoebe, Cead* were in the lottery."

"Winner was Gastan, son of our honorable Counselor, Gastina. He is seven generations from the Lord Enki."

"Do you intend to accept the winner of the lottery?" asked Aonar of Celiste.

Silence draped the plaza. Celiste said nothing.

"Was there a male that you did favor?"

"Yes," said Celiste. She did not look at Deem. Then she added, "We know the rule. We must be paired before the Traverse to Kien or to our home planet." She stopped when Aonar stood up.

"Our honored ancient ones brought their mates," said Aonar. "The men who opposed Enlil were shunned. It was a rule: each male had to have a mate. Each of our honored elders was bound by rule to stay with his mate and to create children to continue the bloodline of the Anunnaki."

There was silence. One of the young men from Beag sniggered. He got a sharp elbow in his ribs from his uncle. Gastan, the lottery winner, stood up and began to walk toward the back of the Gathering. Gastina walked off the platform and quickly caught up with him. Then she turned back and said, "My son wishes to have the approval of the Council."

"According to our protocols we must have a clear majority of the five members of the Council," said Essa. He glanced at his daughter. She was not looking at him. He wondered, *does she want this young man?*

"Are you going to insist on three?" asked Gastina.

"A majority of five is three," said Essa.

"In all my time on this Council there has never been a decision that the people and we did not agree with," said Aonar.

"Until now," shouted a man toward the back. Gastan, the young man with hot blood walked over to him and asked a question. They were seen to be talking and waving their arms just before Gastan hit him hard on his chin. He sat down with a look of surprise on his face.

"This man changed his objection," said Gastan loudly.

Three of the men from the 'Face' carving crew stood up. They were each at least one head taller than Gastan; they wore dark green vests with their muscular arms exposed. There were small scars common to rock carvers on their arms and faces. Their arms looked strong, like small trees.

"We took a vote, just now. We are ready to enroll in the soldier's squad. A chance to drink and pursue ...uh, you know what I mean."

"My friend here, what he means is we have earned our right to be soldiers in the Army of Enlil. We will tolerate no decisions that might have a bad impact on how we are seen on Kien."

He added, "We vote to take our people to Kien." There was general agreement. Several people clapped. Aonar, who held the title of Captain said, "That is our decision."

"Next to the Elamites you three will look like giants," laughed Deem. There was a ripple of laughter among the crowd.

Another man stood up. Then another followed by four more. Then three more. One of them told Deem to note their names. They were the volunteers to be the 'Squadron of Twenty-four.'

"How do you vote? To confirm Gastan as mate to Celiste?"

The men looked around at each other. One raised his hand with the palm open, then another. All the young men voted in opposition.

Essa looked down at Celiste. He saw her glance at the men out of one eye. *At least she cares,* he thought. "Why are you opposed?" said Essa loudly.

"You of all people should know," said the oldest of the rock carvers.

"I am father to Celiste. My only daughter. She has a right to know," added Essa. He indicated Aonar should exercise his prerogative as Captain.

Aonar made a motion. He raised an eyebrow and opened his hands.

"You know why," said the rock carver. Several women present shook their heads. A silence fell over the group. A man in the rear said, "The evil is obvious." A rock carver added, "Gastan is a son of Kien."

An old woman sitting near the edge of the Plaza shook her head. She had been a friend of Gastina in the distant past. She knew, as did Gastina, that the man who raped Gastina was also the man who, as he claimed, 'accidentally' killed Deacair, Celiste's mother.

Several men raised their hands in a fist, agreeing with these statements. Essa saw Celiste turn her head at these statements. She slowly stood up. When she looked at Essa, she saw his puzzlement. She thought, *tell them I accept him.* She wondered how her father felt about having an un-pure son in the family.

To Aonar she said, "The Council has the right to confirm the son of Gastina as my mate." She paused, and then added, "Do it."

Essa, her father, turned to Gastina where she sat and apologized. He told her he had to absent himself from the decision.

ShebSin, the old man, scratched his scalp for a moment then raised a hand with an open palm. Aonar also voted 'No!' Gastina did not vote. She knew that unless there were three votes, there was no decision. Perhaps her son Gastan could persuade Celiste during the long flight to Kien.

It was later that day, with *Phoebe* setting in the east, that Essa asked Celiste why she told the Council to confirm Gastan as her mate. She explained, quite succinctly, that she knew the people did not trust Gastan because his father was, in all likelihood, the Beag who raped his mother.

"I knew there were two no votes. When you decided not to vote, there could be no decision. That allows Gastina to save face." Endnote[ii]

Chapter 23

"They will need your strength." Her father watched Celiste while she wrapped her red coat around her. "They respect you and you hold the rank to be a Director."

She looked at Essa. "I do not need to leave."

"Yes, you do," said Essa.

"Those of you who stay …you can use my strength."

"It will not be pleasant on Kien," added Essa.

"I am stronger than you think."

"And equally determined," laughed her father with a smile.

She looked up at her father and saw the slight smile at the corners of his mouth. He looked so handsome; he wore his age with dignity. His dark black air was a sharp contrast to her light brown, almost tan hair. He had weathered the off-hand comments about her parentage. Her mother never reacted when someone asked about her hair color. Everyone knew the descendants of the Lord Enki and the Lord Enlil had deep black hair. Celiste's hair color made people wonder.

She did not know that her father held a deep secret that would change the direction of her life.

—⸺—

The yellow sun was well above the nose of the 'Face' when Essa and his daughter Celiste stepped out of their residence pyramid. They turned to walk down the boulevard, away from the five pyramids. Essa wore his long coat of hand-woven cloth from their four-legged wooly animals. Celiste wore her long red coat with the emblem of her new rank. After the last Gathering the Council had promoted her to 'Major' status on the request of Deem. The new Captain of *Cead* was aware that her expertise in understanding the atmosphere would be important when they came to deliver their friends to unknown lands on Kien.

Essa walked with his head down, staring at the stones of the boulevard. He wore a hood that cast his face in shadow. Celiste walked beside him with her hand inside his arm, as if he was escorting her to a ceremony. Her green eyes sparkled in the light from the yellow sun but her face seemed grim. They both knew the move of the people up to *Cead* would begin in the next turn. The members of the Beag clan who were going on the Traverse were now camped near the 'People's Pier' and ready to move to the landing strip.

In the south and west a dark gray cloud was slowly spreading out over the lake, moving in the direction of Celiste's village. When she noticed the clouds she nudged her father and he looked up.

"Could be," he said.

"Sometimes the moisture builds up," Celiste noted.

"Been a long time now," added Essa. He knew the village reservoir was half empty and could use refilling.

"Times be what they are," said Celiste. It was an old proverb that served to remind people that the atmosphere on this dry planet was unpredictable, and sometimes violent.

"Yes," said Essa quietly. He looked down at his daughter; she squeezed his arm. He was proud that her training with the old climate Master led to her promotion. "He says what he means," Essa proffered In an old proverb that said bluntly that the males in Essa's family were to be listened to. Celiste's promotion would give her standing on a new world where her rank would help her.

It was a short walk down the boulevard to the first stone that marked the resting place of an elder. There was a long row of stones, some smooth and others rough. Each had a name carved on it. These were the honored Elders who were sent from Kien some 300 years in the past. These were the people who wrote the rules for the Gathering and the protocols for decisions by the people.

In the next section were the second and third generations after the Elders. Celiste's grandparents slept in this section; they both lived in excess of 200 years.

After thirty more steps Celiste stopped. She looked for the odd shaped stone her father brought from the southern falls, smooth but shaped like a round fruit. She spotted it and pulled her father toward the resting place of her mother.

The stone read 'Dea 3. Enoch 7. Enosh' by which Celiste knew her mother Dea was third generation from Enoch, and seventh generation from Enosh who was a son of Lord Seth, a brother to Lord Enki.

She looked toward her village. She saw people hauling cartons of supplies to the landing strip. Off toward the lake she saw the

'People's Pier;' it was largely abandoned. The clouds were closer; there was light rain falling on the lake.

The 'People's Pier' held a sense of desolation; in fact, the water team had stopped hauling water from the lake. Far out on the distant shore one could see four of the slim fishing boats, abandoned. Only the oldest fisherman still continued to go out each day; his wife each day worked to salt down his catch. A part of the green and yellow plant harvest went into storage; part was sent with the water shipments up to *Cead*. The four-legged 'meat' animals would be left for the seventeen who were not going to Traverse.

The *'Dara'* was kept busy taking supplies and small groups up to *Cead,* the transport. Deem, acting as Captain aboard *Dara* saw to the details, storing supplies and cargo brought by the Aryas and the Beag émigrés. He also supervised the training for the twelve assigned to serve aboard *Cead,* eight of whom were new to space travel. Six of the 'Soldier' volunteers were on board to learn how to use high-powered 'Lightning' (the *Shar.Ur*) bolts that could knock a man down without damaging *Cead*. They would be in charge of security during the 55 to 60 days of the long Traverse over to Earth.

Standing near her mother's stone, Celiste's face mirrored the sadness of her people. They were reluctant to leave a land they knew and apprehensive about the 'Eternal City' in the high lands on 'another land mass.' They would be 'a long trip' from Celiste and her field workers.

Her father reached out and put a hand on her shoulder. "I know."

"I do not want…" she began.

"You must go. Your mother and I want you to go."

"My mother," she said and glanced at the stone. "What was she like at my age?"

"A black-haired demon. A maelstrom of discontent. She wanted our world to be so much better than it was."

"Did her energy cause trouble for her?"

"Members of her squad put her up for membership on the Council."

"And?" said Celiste.

"Dea talked to the Gathering. Told them what they needed to repair, and that included relations with the Beag across the lake."

"And?"

"That was the end of her career as a Counselor."

"Did any of the women vote for her?"

"No. They did as their mates commanded."

"And yet she went out with her squad to meet the Beag raiders when they were intent on destroying our collectors."

"She stood up front …ahead of her squad …that was how she was. She knocked two of their men down just before she caught a knife in her side."

"I have seen the report. One of their men disabled. One of ours, injured. And my mother. They brought her back. You were kneeling over her. She was smiling."

"That was my Dea. Always brave."

Celiste reached over and put both hands around his arm. She squeezed slightly and leaned into him and put her head against his shoulder.

"There was something," he began.

He stopped and looked at her. A drop of rain hit his forehead. He looked up and saw the rain was almost upon them. "I promised your mother."

Celiste began to tug him away from the 'Resting' grounds.

"To tell you about your father."

She stopped. "You are my ...?"

"Mate to my Dea for life as we all claimed."

"You say that as if…"

"Your mother's brother is Seth.Dar, a descendant of Seth, a brother of Lord Enki. He came here with a delegation from Enki to review our progress after two generations. I cannot say his name a second time."

"Are you trying to say?"

"We were pledged, your mother and I."

"And this brother?"

"He provided a long feast with wine and a strange weed that some smoked in little burning bowls and then inhaled. He would not allow your mother to leave when the guests left. Your mother said he seduced her and forced himself on her a second time. She was so scared of this mighty Lord from Kien."

"But my hair is not black?"

"My Dea laughed about that. For all his efforts this Seth.Dar will not allow you to claim a bloodline in his family."

She stood and looked at him. The rain became steady and ran down her face. It dripped off the front of Essa's hood. He saw a drop fall from her nose. Her face painted a frown; her eyebrows pinched together.

"Celiste, it matters not. You are a granddaughter of Ningal, who sits on the Council of Twelve. If she retires, you move to her seat. That is why you have Rank 25."

"And now I leave?" she asked in the voice of a little girl.

Essa opened his large coat; he pulled her into it. He wrapped his coat around her and held her. They stood like that while the slight shower of rain passed over them and over the collectors in her village. The rain ran down into the collectors thence into their reservoir.

Several people stopped to marvel at the rain; they turned their faces up to feel the wetness. One or two noticed two people who stood down the boulevard with their heads bowed to the rain.

Chapter 24

When *Dara* lifted off with Celiste and the last of her people, dust and blowing dirt obscured their vision. The small shuttle rose above the dirt cloud; Celiste saw the length of the lake near which she lived. The *Dara* flew past the village of the Beag before sailing down the lake. The water shimmered and reflected crystals of yellow diamonds from a light breeze. Far below she saw a fishing skiff with a solitary fisherman, plying his ancient trade. At the end of the lake the pilot tilted *Dara* so his passengers could see the enormous waterfall that fell down into the massive gorge that crossed their planet. Celiste felt the pull of gravity as the *Dara* began to accelerate.

She found herself pulling her straps tighter. They had all been warned to remain strapped to their bucket seats; when the engines shut down they would begin to 'sail.' Without the straps they could be hurt. The *Dara* flew over the 'Great Forest' of trees. Celiste saw patches of gray, withered trees at the edges and yellowed patches of trees starving for moisture. She found herself thinking ...*the beginning of the end for this planet.*

Celiste said *'Oh'* to herself when she saw the ice pack at the poles; she saw little black dots in rows that were Sleam's reflectors. When she saw the length and area of the ice pack she knew they could not have reversed the 'cold age' ...her term for the drier atmosphere.

The pilot turned *Dara* toward the ice pack and began to descend. There was a flash of yellow sunlight off an object on the hard packed plain near the ice pack. Celiste saw a twin of *Dara* on a flat platform near large circular structures. The pilot tilted *Dara* so his passengers could see the shuttle and the storage tanks. "Shuttle *Enki* ...our transfer base," said the crewman from the front of the cabin. The *Dara* tilted to level and began to climb. Celiste later learned the base was used to send gold and small shipments of limestone up to Deep Black ships for the long haul to Nibiru, the home planet.

Suddenly she sensed more than felt the *Dara* leave the thin atmosphere of her planet. Her fellow passengers strained to see hints of the planet when the pilot turned *Dara*. When the shuttle turned Celiste glanced out the opposite side and saw a black void, deep and unrelenting. She knew her planet circled a yellow sun near the edge of its galaxy; the black she saw was the void beyond.

She felt her chest strain against the crossed straps and looked up. The sound of the triple engines diminished and died away.

A crewman stood and held himself in place with an arm linked around a metal frame near the front of the cabin. "So, at this point you think you ate bad meat yesterday, or too much wine. Keep your bag where you can reach it. You will not ...and I repeat ...will not! ...discharge your stomach into *Dara's* cabin."

He looked around. Several passengers nodded in agreement. They had all attended ground school in order to know what to expect. "And you will not for any reason get out of your harness. Captain Shar will be moving the *Dara* up and down as we approach the *Cead*."

Behind him a door opened. A tall, thin man in the deep red uniform of the Anunnaki pulled himself through the door. He stopped where he could float just above the deck of the cabin. He wore the handsome, masculine face of a sailor, with clear black eyes and tightly trimmed black hair.

He saw several of his passengers leaning to see his feet above the deck. "This is sailing, a condition where there is no pull from the planet."

He smiled. His audience sat in respectful silence.

"I am Captain Shar, of the Anunnaki. There are four of us aboard *Cead*. You will meet Shareen, my mate and our companions Seth and his mate Sud.Lan. We are *Titans*, what some on Kien call the Ti.Ta.An, which means in their language 'Those Who in Heaven Live.' That is their word for the 'Righteous Ones of the Spaceships.' Our role is to maintain our ships at all times. My mate and I have served aboard *Cead* for three cycles, which is six revolutions of Kien around our sun."

He looked at the thirty passengers in the cabin. "We are excited to be going home. We hear they need trained officers on Kien."

"When we leave orbit we will apply the engines for ten days. You will be able to stand on the deck. The engines will be off for 40 days before we apply engines for ten days as we approach Kien. Have a hand on the safety poles, as I do. Always have a hand on the safety poles. Your safety is important. You are rebels. I tell you this once. Have a hand on the poles."

The crewman just behind Captain Shar moved a tablet and held it where the officer could see it.

"Yes," he said. "You will at all times obey the orders of the *Titans* aboard *Cead* and your Captain Deem."

He looked around the cabin. There was a silence that bespoke expectation in the passengers. Celiste saw one young man scratch his head. Then Shar added, "You will be de-contaminated with sprays when you enter *Cead*. That goes for all of us. Then you will be assigned to share a space with two others of your people. You will be assigned an exercise station and time; you will work hard to maintain your muscles and general health."

"Do you understand my orders?"

"Yes," said several of the men.

"Aboard *Cead* you will be extra-polite to Sud.Lan. She is fifth generation from Anu, our revered King. She holds royal blood. Sud. Lan, blessed be her name, is a direct descendant of the Lords Enlil and NinMah, his half-sister. That means she is descended from the *Twelve* who came to Kien so far in the past."

Celiste thought about this for a minute. Then she said, "Why do you tell us so much about those who are descended?"

"You must realize …the Lords rarely show themselves outside their high-walled palaces. Their blood line is strictly protected. They may have an 'official' spouse who is their sister. But it is the half-sister who will produce their heirs. The first son born to a half-sister becomes the legal heir."

"We hear tales…" began a young man seated in front of Celiste.

"About the Lords…" added another.

Captain Shar looked at them for a moment. Then he said, "You will hear about the distrust and anger between Lord Enlil and Lord Enki after we get you situated onboard *Cead*." Endnote[iii]

Chapter 25

Whey they were close the pilot turned the shuttle so his passengers could see *Cead* where it rested in orbit. It was an enormous vehicle with a cloud of energy panels turned towards the sun. Behind the panels the ship was smaller than the panels and gradually grew larger toward its middle. At its stern were three enormous outlets for her engines and a collector for micro-wave energy, about which the émigrés knew nothing.

Around its middle there was a band of lights mounted in the skin that cast light up at long poles. Several of the poles had lights at their ends. Beyond the poles Celiste saw the engine ports and lights of two shuttles; they were copies of the *Dara*. These shuttles were anchored or attached to the *Cead*.

Two shuttles? she thought. *Why did we leave our people?*

Celiste looked around at the other passengers. Near her sat Dren and his mate Drenay. She knew Drenay regretted they had not been able to have children. Their parents went peaceably to their resting place some six cycles ago (*or was it seven cycles now?*); Dren and his mate left no one behind. Dren glanced at her and she smiled back. They were good, loyal neighbors who volunteered to be in the plant growing and cultivating team with Celiste.

When the *Dara* circled the *Cead,* she sailed around the smooth curved end of the *Cead.* Celiste was surprised to see viewing ports; she saw the black outlines of persons watching the *Dara* approach her docking bay. Their progress slowed before a clunk told everyone the *Dara* was docked.

A crewman floated into the cabin and anchored himself to a metal hand-rail near the cabin door. "We will take you three at a time. Aboard *Cead* you will remove your clothes and prepare to be sprayed. When your hair is dry you will receive a disinfectant powder that protects your scalp."

"And our clothes?" asked Drenay.

"You will wear a light cloth uniform of white for those of you with royal blood; and dark gray for you Beag.

"And our clothing?" asked Drenay a second time.

"Will be treated and given back to you."

"We have," she paused, "…small baubles that we cherish."

"Those of us aboard *Cead* have heard about your so-called *baubles.* They will be collected and presented to Lord Enlil as a gift for allowing you to return to Kien."

Drenay turned to look at Celiste while they waited their turn. She opened her coat and revealed a broach of gold on a gold chain. It was the double triangle in the form of a six pointed star that represented their planet *Lehmu,* the sixth planet from the edge of the yellow star's system.

"It has a quality of mystique," said Celiste.

Drenay slipped her hand under the gold star and tilted it upward. She smiled at Celiste.

"You will survive. We will demand that your star be returned."

Drenay looked down at the star, a gift from her mother some ten cycles in the past. Her mother was *'Seventh'* generation after Enosh. Her mother and Celiste's mother Dea had equal rank in the Aryas bloodline.

After they removed their clothes in the disinfectant chamber Drenay refused to remove the star. She wore it proudly.

There was one crewman who laughed. "You rebels are tall and thin, and silent." He watched the women while they removed their clothes. Celiste had muscular arms and strong legs. Her waist was trim; her breasts firm. She felt ...she did not know what to feel about the crewman who stood and watched them undress.

Celiste tried to shield Drenay but the crewman saw the star. He walked up to her and put a hand on the nipple of one breast. "You rebels think you can do as you wish?" he said while squeezing.

"Did you not hear the order?" he spit out. He squeezed her nipple and a wave of pain shot across her face. She whimpered but said nothing. Celiste reached up and unfastened the gold star and its chain. She gave it to the man and he went back to his station. The star was never returned to Drenay.

Chapter 26

They were three, Celiste and her friends Dren and Drenay. They sat in the largest area in *Cead,* the 'Gathering' used for feeding the crew aboard the ship. They were in recovery mode; their exercise period had been strenuous. They had quickly learned that the crew was 'isolated' as if the Ibri and Beag refugees carried some sort of virus.

There were thirty other refugees from Ibri sitting at the small tables. The group of 33 received Burned Black in glass mugs with a mash of corn and wheat in a bowl. The crew member who monitored their group introduced them to a new spice he called 'cinnamon' that he spread over the corn mash.

"He said to enjoy this ration?" said Drenay.

"No bowls," remarked Celiste.

"You mean when they shut down the engines?" asked Dren.

"Yes." Celiste took the eating utensil that had a scoop at one end and used it to bring some of the corn mash to her mouth. "Better than last time," she said without smiling.

"In Ibri my friends would take this corn mash and add the herb that promotes growth before they boiled the mash and allowed it to age," said Dren then added, "They call it *Chicha*. It makes my head fuzzy. My friends…" he began but stopped when he saw Captain Deem approaching.

Deem wore a clean uniform, red with the emblem of the silver circle with the six pointed star inside it. His short hair was trimmed. Under his red tunic he wore black trousers and his boots had been polished with oil. When he leaned over Celiste she smelled a scent that reminded her of the yellow flowers on her balcony in Ibri. "We are wanted on the Command deck," he said quietly. "And bring two friends."

Her face formed a question and he said, "Yes. For a ceremony."

"Ceremony?"

She looked into his eyes and saw a smile forming on his lips and crinkling his eyes. Celiste began to stand up and a frown formed on her face. "The exercises …they create pain."

"That is a good sign. It means you grow stronger."

She looked at Dren, her friend who was perhaps a half-head taller and stronger built. Her face betrayed a question.

"Yes, even the men" said Dren. He laughed. "My mate here," and he nudged Drenay with his elbow, "chastises me for not working harder. I am stronger. But the exercises do cause me pain."

"You will need the strength on Kien. The pull of Kien is stronger," added Deem. He leaned toward Celiste and said, "We are wanted."

She looked at her two friends and said, "We are wanted."

"And you can expect to be presented to Sud.Lan, a Royal."

Drenay said it first. "In these rags?"

Deem smiled. Then he put his hand on Dren's shoulder. "All three. I sent ceremonial tunics to your quarters. I will escort you."

"What ceremony?" asked Celiste.

"It has come to the attention of our Captain that you are not mated."

Her face fell. "We thought…"

"That you could avoid the rule? Even Gastan found an attractive female among the Beag two days before we left. They were mated the same day. That would be..." he began.

"A joining of convenience?" finished Drenay.

Deem laughed. "Of convenience, I guess." He made a motion to tell Dren and Drenay to stand. "We are wanted" he said again.

"What ceremony?" asked Celiste?

"You rejected Gastan," he said and looked down. He was suddenly busy brushing an invisible mote of dust off the arms of his tunic. "And you have always seemed so strong minded."

"Strong minded?"

"Well, yes." The young man took a step back, away from Celiste. He tried to look at her face, but failed. "I mean ...well, I mean ...I think."

"Do not think. I make up my own mind," she said with a frown. Her hand came up as if to swat him in the arm but changed and patted his arm.

"Captain Shar intends to recognize your rank of 25. Same rank your father held, as Counselor. He believes you will be a strong influence on the field workers you supervise."

"Oh," she said quietly. She raised an eyebrow when she looked at her friend Drenay.

"And the Royal, Sud.Lan wishes to conduct a Joining."

"Oh," she said. She saw his smile becoming larger. "You presume much, my captain." She turned away from him. "And what of you?"

"By which you mean? My role after we embark on Kien?"

"Yes?"

"Your people, the Aryas will be in a sacred precinct in the highlands. The Beag will be in another walled section. You will have 20 days to grow used to the atmosphere and the pull of the planet. Then

I will deliver you and your squad. You will have to build your own shelter."

He paused and slowly brought his eyes up to look into her light green eyes. "I repeat. What of you?"

"I will continue as captain of the 'Dara' until I am replaced."

"Which means? You will not be on Kien with me?"

His face displayed confusion. He looked down and took her hand. "With you?" He began to smile, and he brought her hand to his lips.

"Yes, you. You straight-backed Aryan fool of a captain. You are stumbling all over the question you seek to ask me."

"Your father said your mother Dea felt I would be a good mate for her strong-minded daughter."

"I will," she said and slowly raised a hand to grab his arm. "As long as you remember that we are of equal rank. We will make decisions after long discussion, just as we did at Ibri."

Chapter 27

When Celiste stepped through the hatch into Deem's sleeping stall, she was amazed at how much space the young man was allowed. There was a bunk, a shelf that served as a work station, a small stool with four solid legs, a water basin attached to the wall and a padded bed with a padded back against the wall. Deem explained the padded bed was not a bed but a place to sit up-right and talk with another crew member.

"Or maybe your mate?"

"Yes, that would work."

There was a 'Shining' device that made light attached to the wall. Celiste moved to it and looked closely. A half-moon shape produced light; it was attached to a square box with a switch on the outside. "We had these on our planet."

"Yes," he said. "A technician will come by every fifth or sixth day and replace the power supply.

"Ours were mostly dead," she noted. Her father once said, "The reason we are healthy ...our Shining forces us to retire and sleep or stumble around in the dark. The wall opening towards our yellow sun is an essential element of our living style." Celiste smiled when she remembered the times she tried to read documents by the weak light from their sun.

"Oh, I wondered." She reached up to touch the power box. He made a quick "Bzzzt" with his tongue. She jumped back; her action caused her to fly past him. He caught her before she flew into the bunk. She looked into his blue eyes and tried to smile. His face was blank. "I am sometimes naughty," he said.

There was another hatch in the wall. Celiste pulled herself across the space and put her hand on the handle of the hatch. She looked at Deem and he nodded, "Yes. Open it."

Inside the hatch she found a smaller space with a bunk built into the wall. Under the bunk there were two drawers; the open drawer held uniform clothes. On the wall to her left she saw what looked like a bowl attached to the wall; it was as high as her knee. A metal rim flared out around the top of the bowl. Next to the bowl a short hose was held by a metal ring. An oval device of metal was attached to the hose.

"Is that what I think it is?" Celiste looked at him for explanation.

"You know how to squat," he said without looking at her. "In the drawer are towels and cloths for washing."

"And this hose thing?"

"When we have engine power, you can squat. When the engines are off, you will need to use the hose to collect your waste. There is a button on the side of the collector. Push it and an engine elsewhere in the ship will pull your waste into a container where it is treated."

"There are two bunks?"

"I am the last crew member to have a mate. All of the Titans, what the royals call the 'Titans,' they who serve on the shuttles and ships have mates and similar quarters."

"The quarters my friends are sharing …we rotate who is sleeping."

"*Cead* was not built to handle this many refugees."

"Am I allowed to move my clothes to this space?"

"Yes. Move them. I will be on duty for the next day. When the engines shut down, I will be relieved and we can…" he paused for a moment and reached out to touch her hand. Then added, "…get to know each other. You cannot know how proud I am that you agreed to be my mate."

She smiled. Then she watched as he stepped out of his quarters.

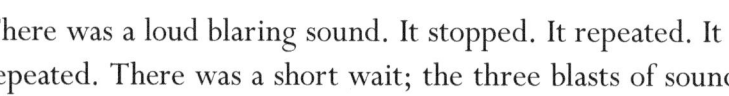

There was a loud blaring sound. It stopped. It repeated. It stopped. It repeated. There was a short wait; the three blasts of sound repeated. Celiste was not surprised. A crewman brought a note that said 'Engines Off Now' and she knew the triple blast had to be the last warning. She moved into her long white gown, a gift from Drenay. There were two pleats in the front that seemed to emphasize her breasts. The gown was soft and clung to her legs. She loved how it felt and said, "Now I am ready."

She moved to her bunk in the small space and lay down. All the refugees had been told to get ahold of a safety rod or anything attached to the ship. Deem said to expect someone to get hurt. There was always a young man who suddenly decided to try his 'strength' in the new weightless condition who hurt an arm or a leg or even his head.

The thrumming stopped. It had never been very loud. This far away from the engine compartment the sound was barely noticeable. Celiste liked the 'quiet' this far from the engines. She noticed when the thrumming stopped; she lay quietly on her bunk. She did not know what to expect. Time passed. Nothing happened. Then she straightened her back and felt herself lift off the mattress. She floated slowly toward the 'ceiling' above the bunk until she put out her hands to stop herself. A gentle push and she moved down into the safety of the bunk.

"What is the big concern?" she said aloud. With her hands she pushed down *hard* on the bunk mattress and suddenly flew upward, right into the 'ceiling' above the bunk. Her head turned and she hit the 'ceiling' with a 'thunk' against her head above her right eye. "Oww," she murmured to the quiet cabin.

With both hands she gently, this time, pushed herself away from the 'ceiling' into the comfort of the bunk. Her right hand came up and she felt her forehead. At that moment Deem twisted the handle on his hatch and stepped into 'his' sleeping space. Through the open hatch Deem saw Celiste had her hand against her forehead.

"Hurt?"

"A little," she said. She began to sit up and held onto the safety rod at the edge of her bunk. Deem held a package in one hand and held onto the vertical pole near his hatch. With his foot he nudged the hatch to close it. He raised the package and said, "We have a gift from Captain Shar."

"We do?"

"It is traditional, on Kien, among the royals and the officers who make decisions and apply the laws of Enlil."

"What is it?" she asked while slowly moving to straighten her body into a vertical position.

"It is a clay vessel that has been hardened in a hot fire. It holds a sacred potion for 'first time' mates. There is a stopper in one end. Captain Shar told me it holds enough potion for four bowls."

"Do you have bowls?"

Deem laughed. "No bowls. With no pull on us, we cannot pour the potion. We have to drink from the container." He removed the clay vessel and placed it in a tube attached to the wall near the 'bed.' He reached out to Celiste. He took her hand and pulled. She came out of her space and directly at him where he wrapped his arms around her when she collided with his chest.

"Oof!" she exclaimed.

She pushed gently against his chest and he allowed her to 'retreat.' In the weak light of his 'Shining' device she was a marvel to behold. She had brushed her hair back and held it with a set of pins. Her hand came up and she touched her neck. Then she slid her hand down almost onto her breast. She looked up at him when he said, "It is time for us to learn about each other."

"Is that what you call it?" she laughed. She seemed nervous.

He held her arms and tried to smile. "My mates..." he began.

"Your mates?" she stammered.

"I mean the officers with whom I share *Cead.*"

"You are not intending to share me; I presume?"

"What?" he said. He knew no words to answer her.

"Drenay told me that mates share a certain physical motion, and that draws them together."

"I have not ever..." he began. She reached down and took his hand and placed it on her breast. "I have not ever..." he tried to say a second time and she placed a finger on his lips. "It is as it is," she said. "I have never been with a man." With her other hand she grabbed the safety pole near the 'sitting bed' and pulled herself and him toward it. She let go of his hand and nodded toward the clay container.

"Let us try this potion," she said.

"My mates..." he began until she started laughing.

"Tell you what?" she chuckled inside her laughter. She told him to take off his uniform and put it away. She pulled herself into sitting on the 'bed' and watched him put his uniform away. He wore a simple cloth garment around his middle. She had seen this cloth item before, on her father Essa and on her friend Dren after they boarded *Cead*.

"This potion will help us relax …I am told," he added. He took a small knife from his pocket and used it to lever the stopper out of the clay vessel. He kept his thumb over the opening, smelled it then gave it to Celiste to smell. She smelled it and leaning back took a drink. Her eyes widened.

"It is not dangerous," said Deem.

"Who told you that?"

"Captain Shar's mate, Shareen." He took the vessel back and after smelling it again Deem tilted it back and drank.

"She said this is the sacred potion, blessed by NinMah, the Mother of her people. It will help us to make…" he began but stopped.

Celiste reached over and put her hand on his leg. He looked down with a look of concern.

"Drenay said I should do this. That it acts to get her man interested in joining with her."

"Well, as you know, I have many responsibilities. I have no interest in joining with Drenay," he said quietly with a sly smile. He reached over and pulled her toward his lips. He kissed her neck briefly, then her cheek briefly, then paused and looked at her lips. She looked up at him with concern.

"How do we do this 'Joining' without floating around your space?"

"I tie myself down. You climb over me and I hold your hips. We can move as much as we desire, or so I have been told."

"So you have been told? By your mates? Your *male* mates, I hope."

"We spend long days up here, with little to talk about."

Deem took two flat leather straps out of the drawer with his uniforms. Each strap held a hook on one end. He fastened one hook into a ring on the deck at the base of the 'bed.' He led the strap over his thigh and back to the ring where he fed it into the ring, tightened the strap and wrapped it around the ring. He performed an identical function with the second strap through a second ring near his other foot.

"Now I am braced," he told her and took a second pull on the potion. She looked at the two straps over his legs. She moved her hand up his leg and said "What do we do with your male member, which as I see, has become stiff?"

"You will crawl over me, stretch your leg onto the 'bed' as you call it, then reach your other leg across me and sit in my lap."

"And?"

"And then we will slowly join with each other."

Chapter 28

They were three, sitting in the 'Gathering' space with small clay vessels held in their hands. The containers held heated water in which ground herbs had been aged before the water was strained to remove the herbs. Dren looked like any crewmember; he wore white work clothes with a cap that covered his hair. His mate Drenay wore a long wrap that she cinched up with a belt. Her hair was pulled back and held by a yellow headband. They both wore the open-toed foot covering with the sticky substance that gripped the decks of the *Cead*. They both were smiling; it was unusual for Dren to be caught with a smile. Celiste enjoyed their smiles.

"Relief," said Dren.

"Is what we feel," added Drenay. She reached over and patted the hand of her good friend. "For three days, or what they call three days aboard *Cead*. We worried."

"About me?"

"Both of you," she said. She reached up and adjusted her headband.

"And then Captain Shar came by, trailed by two crewmen who were being trained," added Dren. He raised a finger and batted a mite of some kind that floated near his nose.

"Yes," said Drenay. "We asked. His response was cryptic."

"What did he say?" Celiste had her hair pulled back and stuffed into a cap similar to her husband's red officer's cap. There was no insignia on the cap; she wore crewman's work clothes and was proud to be a member of the *Cead* crew. Her cheeks began to warm. But she could not stop herself from a small chuckle. Her laughter caused Drenay to laugh.

"Yes, we did worry," said her good friend.

"What did Captain Shar say?"

"He smiles."

Celiste sat and looked at Drenay then at the other Aryas in the 'Gathering.' It occurred to her that the Beag were on a different shift aboard *Cead;* someone wanted to prevent the two groups from mingling.

"He smiles?"

"He smiles. Yes. He smiles." Her elbow moved toward Drenay and she nudged her husband.

"We listened to the talk among our people. They think the expression 'He smiles' is an instant analysis of the pairing aboard the ships of the Titans. These crew members are 'in the heavens' for long terms. They have two shifts each 'day' in which they work one shift and work their muscles the other shift."

"Instant analysis?"

"He smiles means he has 'joined' and is relaxed about the experience or it means his mate also smiles."

They sipped on their herbal drink while Celiste considered their comments. She was about to say *'she also smiles'* when a crewman known as Magan (for Land of Pyramids) came into the 'Gathering' and said in a voice that commands attention, "Please rise for our royal mistress, Princess Sud.Lan, a granddaughter of our revered King Anu."

Celiste and her friends began to rise. Their hands grabbed the round bar at the edge of their table. A tall woman, with regal bearing floated into the space. A device at her waist controlled her distance above Cead's deck.

She was as tall as Celiste's father, perhaps two or three fingers taller.

She wore a long coat of 'royal' red. Her black hair was pulled back and wrapped in a headband decorated with hundreds of sparkling gems. The stiff collar of her coat displayed a circle with seven round gems on a base of gold. The seven gems represented Kien, the seventh planet if you enter from deep space. Around her neck she wore a heavy gold chain that held a circular disk with two wings. It represented Lord ☓Enlil, Lord of the Command.

Her hair was cut short, in the current style. She had a high forehead above deep black eyes that could melt a glacier. Her face was long and thin. A straight, narrow nose sat above thin lips; both were attributes of the Anunnaki.

"My duties bring me here," said Sud.Lan. She looked around and spotted the red cap on Celiste's head. "I seek the one called Celiste."

Celiste touched the brim of her cap as a mark of respect and nodded.

"Two duties, actually," said Sud.Lan "My first duty is pleasant."

She pulled herself towards Celiste. The crewman Magan blocked her path. She raised a hand and smacked him on the arm. "Know your place," she snarled as she drifted past Magan. She used him like you would a post and pulled herself to a stop in front of Celiste.

"There is a rule. I obey the rule," she said. She partially turned and said to her aide, "Even when it means I consort with *rebels*."

Celiste looked up at Sud.Lan. "We are not rebels."

"You are guilty of having grandparents who were rebels. The Lord Enlil has decreed that you all," and here she waved a hand to indicate all the Aryas who were present, "will serve a term of two years until we determine that you are loyal."

Celiste looked up. After a long moment she said, "Yes, Princess."

"The title is not necessary. I am Sud.Lan of the house of Anu."

Celiste bowed toward the woman and said, "Yes, Sud.Lan."

"My duty is to Celiste, daughter by five generations from Enoch, the noble lord who built the Great Pyramid."

"Four generations, my father Essa tells me."

"Your mother was Deacair?"

"Yes."

"Five generations. Your father was wrong." She reached into her long coat and pulled out a small wooden box. "We honor our newly joined 'mates' with this traditional emblem. Wear it when you come to court, if you are ever summoned ... *I doubt you will be summoned.*"

Celiste took the box and opened it. Inside, nestled in a bed of dark red cloth was a device in silver, a circle above a bar above a vertical bar.

"It is called an Ankh. It means eternal life," added Sud.Lan. When Celiste stood and looked at Sud.Lan, the princess added, "It means you hold a position of trust. Your rank is 25. You are, or will be, a Royal among the royals."

Celiste bowed toward Sud.Lan and said "We honor your generosity," as her father had taught her to say.

"That is well. You know your place," said Sud.Lan. She looked up at the Aryas who were watching with intense interest. "I bring shocking details of your planet. Our Deep Black vessel, the *Antu* was approaching our base to recover a shipment. An enormous flash of light and an angry cloud billowed up into the sky. *Antu* reports it was over your city Ibri."

She waited for a reaction. There was none. "That was two days ago." Sud.Lan waited, again.

"The Beag!" shouted an angry voice from the back of the crowd.

"It cannot be," said several of the Aryas in front of Sud.Lan.

"Captain of the *Antu* knew it was a Shar.Gaz, the Supreme Smiter." She gazed over the 90 some Aryas in the 'Gathering.' Many had come just after she arrived. "He told the shuttle to evacuate the Beag."

"Captain of the *Antu* believes it was the Beag. A Shar.Gaz weapon was stolen from our base, three perhaps four years ago."

"We knew it," shouted a man in the rear of the group.

"My father," said Celiste, "reported the Beag had such a weapon."

"The shuttle waited two days. We received their report today. One of the pyramids is split, shifted as if hit by a mighty force. There are no survivors." Sud.Lan turned to leave. Then she turned back.

"The man they call Ragnar, the man with the limp is missing. The weapon had to be set off by hand," she added.

Celiste heard her words, but could hardly believe what she heard. Ragnar, the man's foot was injured when he killed her mother Dea.

"I hope he burned," said Celiste quietly. Drenay came around the table and put her arms around Celiste. They stood with one hand hooked on the table and their other arm around each other. They heard words of violence against the Beag. Celiste seemed to pull herself together then raised her hand with a fist.

Into the sudden silence she said, "We cannot blame the Beag. It was the man Ragnar; I among all of you have reason to seek revenge. I will not dishonor my mother's wish. She said *'No revenge'* and it was her way."

Her friends became quiet. Celiste held a fist in the air. It was a solemn moment; they all wanted to mourn for the grandparents (and parents) they left behind.

Chapter 29

Magan, the crewman 'floated' over to Celiste and her friends. "I know the time is bad..." he said while he scratched the back of his head. "Osiris, we gonna decontaminate the entire ship after you are dumped on Kien." He began then a puzzled expression crossed his face. "Where was I? Oh ...yes. Time is bad. The Beag are waiting to enter. This is their second food period. They sound hungry."

Celiste stood up. She thought vaguely about saying something about her father, their counselor. All she could do was wave a hand at Dren. He stood up and told the Aryas from Ibri it was time to evacuate. From behind Dren came the voice of authority, their Captain Deem. "Most of you are going to grieve. This has been a terrible shock. We have a tradition ...we make a memorial to those we have lost. It will have to wait until we put you down on Kien."

"Thank you Captain," said Celiste in short clipped words. "We will think on how to make a fitting memorial." She looked down at her hands then over at Deem's hands. "Our hands are not clean. We will decide how to deal with the Beag ...they cannot be trusted."

Deem came over to her and put his arms around her. His foot was wedged under a bench; it kept him from 'sailing' when he picked her up. "My love," he said.

She pushed back from him and looked at Dren and Drenay. Their grief was written on their faces. "No, it is my fault. I told Essa they would come back for him and the others."

"But you did not…" began Dren.

"Celiste, listen to me," said Deem.

"We must act."

"No, it is time to grieve."

"No time," she said in a very soft voice. She looked at Drenay with an expression that said, *'I need help.'*

Drenay moved toward Celiste and took her by the hand. Deem told Celiste's friends to take her to his cabin and stay with her. "Do not leave her alone." He would send food and a vessel of fermented grape.

Celiste pulled back from Drenay momentarily. She raised her other hand as if she had something to say, and exclaimed "That's my Deem."

Several men in the crowd raised eyebrows. They were not aware that it was permitted to use a short form of an officer's name. Drenay began to tell Celiste that she could not do that and Celiste spoke up with anger and clarity, "That is his name. He said I could use Deem."

"I meant in private," said Deem.

Several of the younger adults near Celiste and her mate chuckled. The older adults had expressions on their faces that said, "Far too familiar."

From that day forward their Captain was referred to as Captain Deem, which sounded like a pun on the fat ducks that waddle up to the feed trough at the animal feed lots.

⁓❦⁓

There was a ping on the door of Deem's cabin. He said "Come" and waited. His voice was muffled by the heavy metal of the hatch. After several moments the door opened and Shareen pulled herself across the sill and grabbed the safety bar. She wore a red tunic, representing the crew, over a pair of white work trousers. Her short hair was pulled back under a red cap with the *Cead* insignia, a circle with the six pointed star.

"This is not a formal occasion," said the wife of Captain Shar indicating her manner of dress. She looked at Celiste then at Deem. "It has been two days, Captain Deem …you are needed on the Command Deck." Deem nodded at her and placed a strap across Celiste's leg to prevent her from 'sailing.'

"Captain Shar has sent a message. Please convey it to all the members of the group," said Shareen. She handed a velum scroll to Celiste with a small bow.

Celiste began to rise from the padded 'bed' but Deem stopped her by telling her it was not necessary.

"This comes from all of the crew members of *Cead*." Shareen made a small bow and looked at the floor. Celiste thanked her. Shareen looked over at Celiste and added, "We all feel your pain."

The scroll opened upon a message written in pictographic symbols. "It reads," said Shareen, "The Lords ✳Enlil and ✳Enki and ✳NinMah, great and blessed Lords of Kien have declared that a memorial will be held near the Temple of Inanna, Protector of the Dead and the names of those who died with no glory shall be kept forever inside the Great Crouching Lion."

Celiste let go of one end of the scroll and it rolled itself up. Her head was down. A tear came floating off her face and seemed to hover in front of her. She reached up, caught it and placed her hand on her heart.

Shareen waved at the cabin hatch; her movement was a signal for Deem to leave. "I would like some time with your mate."

"Thank you, honored mistress and thank our noble Captain for my mate," said Deem as he pulled himself to the hatch.

"Yes," added Celiste. She watched him float through the hatch.

Shareen pulled herself to the 'bed' and caught a safety bar with which she maneuvered herself into sitting next to Celiste.

"Two days," said Shareen.

Celiste looked at her foot. Slowly she raised her head to look at Shareen. "Is there a new report?"

"They all died. The old fisherman landed and walked into Ibri before anyone could catch him. Our shuttle captain watched him from the west after the cloud departed. The old man entered one of the pyramids. After a long time, the old man re-emerged. He entered a second pyramid. The next time they saw him he staggered across the central plaza. Deem tells me you called it 'Gathering' place. The old man staggered around. Then he fell down and did not get up."

"Captain of the shuttle concluded they are all dead."

"All dead?" said Celiste as a statement, not a question.

Shareen put her hand on Celiste's arm. "We can share your pain, can we not?" She leaned over to put her forehead on Celiste's shoulder.

The two women sat. Quiet painted a sublime landscape across their minds. Celiste saw her father standing near her mother's stone. Shareen remembered her grandfather who died in an accident. "Some time to come …I will tell you of my grandfather Dumuzi who died because of his love for Inanna, a goddess."

"We can grieve," said Celiste.

"Yes, and you have a role to play. Your people look to you for leadership." Celiste said nothing but nodded her agreement.

"When we land you must be the first to cut your hair short. All the men must cut their hair down to the skin. Your people must honor the gods ✗Enlil and ✗Enki. After thirty days we will fly to the land of Osiris and Inanna and the Lord Enki to hold a service for the Dead." Endnote[iv]

Chapter 30

In the quiet of space, the *Cead* moved almost effortlessly until she turned her engines to the path of their flight. The engines grumbled to life and blasted hot gases into their flight path. The ship slowed, avoided the pull of Kien's satellite and found a circular path around the large, blue planet. Aboard *Cead* the refugees were amazed that so much deep blue water could exist. When told there were canyons of water 60,000 cubits deep they were equally amazed.

From space the big planet appeared to slowly move from left to right. The refugees were impressed with the green flowing plains on the surface below. They spotted muddy rivers and white patches of clouds. A crewman told them the *Cead* was stable in her orbit. They crossed an enormous bank of black and gray clouds with angry flashes of lightning.

Deem explained the *Cead* was about to cross more land mass then fly into the shadow of the planet. In the dark they would fly over the largest ocean on the planet while they approached the southern land-mass and its mountains. He provided directions and they began to pick up their small packs of clothes. They then moved in single file through the corridors of *Cead* and into the *Dara*.

They were in the darkest part of the night when Deem told the Aryas from Ibri to take turns observing out the view ports. "We are circling an island. We must wait to approach our landing place until the sun rises on the highlands."

Celiste used the upper deck safety bars to pull herself to the view-port. She looked out on a scene she could not believe. The *Dara* slowly passed a river of fire that spit up into the sky then fell to earth where it flowed and churned around obstacles before it fell into an ocean where it boiled and sent up an enormous cloud of steam.

"The cloud is white in daylight," said Deem to those who waited. "The blazing fire hits the water and turns the water into heated gases."

"Is that a mountain that spews forth the river of fire?" asked Celiste. "Or is it my imagination?"

"Times be what they are," said Deem.

"What do you mean?" asked a man near Celiste.

"That mountain does not always spew forth the river of fire." Deem smiled to himself. "I remember a time …three years ago when the mountain was quiet, timid and shy."

Captain Shar, of the *Cead,* entered the storage cell of the *Dara.* He quickly asked Celiste and her friends to remain seated. He wore a red tunic over white work trousers. His hair was held in place by the oblig-atory red skull cap. He told those present he was proud of how well they had mastered the art of 'sailing' aboard his *Cead.* He also asked if they enjoyed the sight of the 'fire' mountain.

A man near him said, "It must be extremely hot."

"Yes, you know," said Captain Shar. "It is hot. You can place items in the fire and they will be instantly absorbed. Even an item of iron will turn red from the heat and then sink into the flowing stream of fire."

"It is an island. There are no people, no crops. There are long trees with enormous wavy fronds. No one can live there. The god of the mountain gives them no water to drink."

"Is there water in the mountains where we go?" asked a woman.

The captain chuckled. Then he nodded to Deem and moved toward the passage to the command deck. To Deem he said, "Use my description, if you wish."

The young shuttle pilot turned to the Aryas. "We take you to high plains in the mountains where they build a pyramid in a mirror of water."

———— ⌘ ————

The *Dara* rose in its flight path to climb up the mountains. They were steep; snow blankets covered many of the peaks; water flowed in deep gorges toward the sandy desert at the ocean. Coming across the mountains the captain saw his landing spot was about to be painted with the orange of a high altitude sunrise.

Two beams of light split the sky when the sun rose behind three peaks. The peaks were in the distant mountains; a smooth high plain, with no hills, created a level vista The *Dara* turned across a bay. On the shore they saw two small villages. There were irrigated patches of plants fed from canals. The canals were man-made and used to draw water for raised fields of crops. Near a much smaller lake a large temple stood on land raised above the lower plain. Its roof was a series of roofs of thatch that probably collected rain water.

The visual item that caught everyone's attention was the pyramid. It stood inside a small lake. The pyramid stood on raised land; a dike with a paved road served for access to the pyramid. The four-sided structure had six large steps that rose to a flat platform. A long stairway rose from the surface to the platform and a sunken pool of water. From a distance the few people on the roof appeared to be insect size compared to the enormous pyramid.

Each terrace of the pyramid was built to raise the pyramid a height of five cubits. The sunken pool stood on a central area of the roof. Beyond the pool the flat deck of the pyramid stretched for a distance of 100 cubits. The extension, as Deem knew, was used for landing shuttles when they carried the royal lords of Kien.

The *Dara* flew to higher ground beyond the pyramid and set down near a camp of tents and small buildings. Celiste and her friends were led to separate areas where they were asked to use cots inside the tents. While they rested against the heavier pull of the planet, medical technicians came around and listened to their breathing. They also used small silver needles to draw blood from the veins in their arms.

It was explained to Celiste that the Lady ✱Sud.Lan arrived five days earlier and she was in charge of the medical services housed in the large square temple next to the pyramid. ✱Sud.Lan was a goddess in her own right because she had a son with her half-brother Lord ✱Enlil. The people who worked with her were trained in medical skills.

After two days of rest the Aryas and Beag were allowed to wander in their tent areas and take naps when they felt like it. The only surprise came when two tall men (at least one-half cubit taller than Essa) walked into the Aryas camp. They wore short wooden pins on their belts and grim expressions on their faces. They towered above Gastan and came to remove him from the Aryas camp. He vocally claimed he was Aryas, raised by Aryas. The two men said little other than *'You are Beag'* and *'we have work for you in the mines.'* His mate had a demure smile and no brow ridge above her eyes; she said nothing. She followed Gastan.

When Celiste asked Deem about this, he remarked that the blood that was drawn revealed that Gastan was not pure Aryas. He was one-half Beag. "In other words, his father, as we always suspected, was Beag."

"Through no fault of his own," said Celiste. "This is not right. He played with us, he grew up with us, and he hauled water with us." She was silent while Gastan removed his few belongings from his tent and was followed over to the Beag side of the camp. The image of a fire-ball above her small village Ibri flashed through her mind. "But we all know it is a mistake to trust the Beag."

Deem looked at her and saw lines of determination around her eyes. *Can you blame them all for the actions of one rogue man with hatred in his heart?* he thought but said nothing.

On the fourth day after landing both groups were directed to appear near the causeway to the pyramid for a religious ceremony. When Celiste asked about this Deem remarked that it was a local ceremony to honor the gods of the atmosphere in whose name the pyramid was built. Endnote[v]

Chapter 31

A clear sky in turquoise blue greeted the Aryas when they were led by Celiste to the lower ground near the pyramid. The sun rose, that morning, directly behind the center of the three peaks to the east. Brittle cold air bathed the altiplano, the highlands. A light mist was rising from the water around the pyramid. Celiste knew the air temperature was colder than that of the water which created the mist.

"Important, I guess, to the priests of the pyramid."

Along the edges of the lake hundreds of natives wearing multicolored ponchos and woven hats were gathered. Some were playing wooden flutes, others small drums while others twirled a round device on a stick that had four little balls attached with strings. The tenor of the crowd was joyful with expectation. To the Aryas it appeared the native people were shorter than the Beag.

At the base of the stairway stood a group of men who could only be described as prisoners; they stood with their heads down. Several taller men with short whips appeared to be guarding the prisoners.

At the far corner of the pyramid Celiste saw what looked like a woman with her knees drawn up, her head upon her knees and her arms wrapped around her legs. The woman did not move. She sat upon a rug woven with bright red and yellow colors. At the corner of the pyramid nearest Celiste she saw a man in a similar position. Behind the silent bodies there were circular pits and what appeared to be piles of earth. Celiste surmised the woman and man were dead.

On the causeway path there were two priests wearing cloth helmets, with short tunics. They each held a thin bladed ax in one hand. With the other hand they held a woman upright. She seemed to stagger but the two priests kept her from falling. Walking toward Celiste and her friends was a priest with three warriors who carried thin-bladed axes. He was dressed in flowing robes that fell below his knees. On his head a cap with the red fringe of the king held shiny disks that flashed when he turned his head. Celiste and her friends were amazed: his head was not round; it projected to the rear.

He stopped in front of the Aryas and waited until the Beag group had walked down the slope and joined the crowd. Lady Sud.Lan came through the crowd and stopped near the priest. She wore deep red robes with gold amulets on her arms and an enormous gold broach in a circle with seven large white stones. Her headband was really a fringe with gold balls similar to the red fringe on the warrior-king. He bowed to her and she turned to the crowd of refugees.

"You are here to witness the…" she paused and turned to the king. "Our words are not quite the same. A sanctify ceremony, he tells me." She turned back to the priest and asked a question.

"The pyramid is called Saspéir, which means 'in the sky' in their words. It is their word for mountain."

The priest leaned toward Lady Sud.Lan and made a motion to mimic water falling with his hands while he described the ceremony. Her face turned blank while he talked.

"Four of their enemies, the Moche, will be sanctified then buried near the four main corners of the pyramid. The woman joins her mate."

There was silence among the Aryas. Many looked at the woman on the causeway. The two priests helped her walk toward her dead mate.

"They are sacrifices to honor the mountain god who gives rain, wind, snow, …what we need to grow plants," continued Sud.Lan. "The mountain…" she added, "will bring forth water, then blood. It will be sanctified." The warrior-king turned and walked toward the pyramid.

Standing near Celiste a native woman leaned into her and whispered in her ear. "He represents the arrival of the god Veracocha at the lake," said Celiste to the people around her. A light breeze ruffled the water of the lake surrounding the pyramid.

Among the Aryas behind Celiste someone mumbled about 'blood' and 'bodies' and someone said, "Where does the blood come from?"

Sud.Lan glanced around at the pyramid. "It has something to do with the sixteen men at the stairway." The crowd watched as the men were herded up the long stairs. Their chests were bare. Several had bright red stripes with blood trickling down on their backs. When they reached the top of the stairs the men were separated into groups of four. Their hands were quickly tied behind them. Each group was led to a separate edge of the water pool on the top level of the pyramid. Their guards held the thin bladed axes while they used short whips on two of the men who argued with the guards.

The two priests with the woman reached her dead husband. They forced her to recline into the arms of her husband. They began to wrap the rug on which he sat around the two of them. After pulling their legs up the two priests wound long straps around the two of them and applied more woven cloth wrapping them into a bundle. The woman looked at the two priests with confusion on her face. She looked away from them and placed her head on her mate's chest, under his chin. They may have told her what to do.

The king and his three warrior-priests stopped at the foot of the stairs on the west side of the pyramid. One of the priests began to beat on a drum. The other two began a chant. The king stood silent. Observers from the hill behind saw him look up at the sun. It seemed apparent that he waited for something while he stood in the shadow of the pyramid.

Suddenly, rays of the sun lit the stairway. The king began to walk up the steps. His three priests ran to the far corners of the pyramid where the natives could see them. Celiste and her friends heard loud voices and many drums and some chanting from the crowds. All five priests took up station near the bundle at each corner. The priests raised their axes and lowered them in a symbolic move to the necks of the dead enemy in front of them.

Directly in front of Celiste the priest stood near the bundle with the woman. He raised his axe and stopped. He looked up at his king. *No, they cannot do this,* thought Celiste. The king nodded and the blade came down and sliced through the woman's neck. Blood spurted across her dead husband. The priest quickly produced a golden knife, called a *toomi,* and sliced through her neck and severed her head. He gave his knife to the other priest, took the head and held it by the hair while he walked to the stairs and began to climb.

The second priest used the *toomi* to slice off the head of her dead husband. He also moved to the stairs and began to climb. A squad of young warriors moved across the causeway and began to wrap the bundles at the four corners. They lifted the bundles and placed them into the deep round holes at the corners. The priests reached the top of the stairs and stood to each side of the king and raised the heads for all to see.

Water began to run out of the side of the pyramid. Each trickle ran across a step, then disappeared into a drain, then gushed out of the side in a torrent, just as water would run down from the mountain. On the top platform the five priests with axes moved to their particular group of four men who stood near the edge of the pool. Axes swung in unison. Heads popped up and flew into the pool. The dead men fell where their bodies could pump blood into the pool.

"There are other heads in that pool," said a man behind Celiste. From where the Aryas stood the nearly drained pool showed the white craniums of other enemies who were sacrificed to appease the gods of the eastern mountains. At this point the slow trickle of water on the side of the pyramid turned pink, then red then back to pink.

"I think…" began Celiste. "No one could have warned us."

Sud.Lan heard her comment and turned to look at Celiste. After glancing over the refugees, Sud.Lan said, "You must remember. You are on trial until the Lord Enlil decides you are loyal. These priests, here, have control only so long as the native people believe they are lords with the power. The Aryas have power on Kien. Power comes from the Lords and their children. You will do well to keep in mind your place on this planet."

"We are of pure blood," said Celiste.

"Keep that thought," answered Sud.Lan.

From the back of the group came a voice. "Only until the Lord Enlil decides to lop off our heads," said Dren directly at Sud.Lan.

Celiste raised a hand with a fist. The murmuring among her people diminished until there was quiet. Off to their right they heard two Beag in a full argument.

Celiste seemed to consider her words. "We are guests of the Lord Enlil on Kien. We will work to prove his confidence in us."

"We will?" shouted Dren. His mate turned to look at him with a look of both admiration and disbelief. [Endnote[vi]]

Chapter 32

From the direction of the three peaks there was a screaming sound of a hunting cougar, a sound that drew the attention of the crowds around the pyramid. Coming from the clouds they saw the red eyes of the cougar then the bright red belly of the hunter as it flew directly at the extension of the pyramid. Three projections lowered from its belly and a blast of gases poured forth from the beast. The shuttle slowed, maneuvered then set down on the level surface of the pyramid extension, to the west of the sunken pool.

Minutes passed before a ramp at the rear of *Dara* lowered. A crewman walked off. He was Aonim, an old friend of Celiste who volunteered to serve in training aboard the 'spasarthach' or Deep Black ship *Cead*. He was tall and confident, a mature young man whose black hair shimmered in the morning sunlight. His new mate MarLan had a roving eye and it was rumored she was with child when Aonim joined with her.

Behind him down the ramp came Deem, dressed in his best red tunic with his red officer's cap squarely on his head. He looked around the crowds then saw Celiste in her red tunic with the silver broach of her rank. He moved toward the west stairway off the pyramid.

Celiste began to walk toward the causeway. Behind her she heard Sud.Lan announce to the Beag, "I am told 34 of you will serve two years at the mines. Get your things pulled into bags and prepare to leave. Your Captain of the shuttle *'Dara'* comes to get his new cargo."

Celiste walked toward the causeway. Behind her she heard voices from the Beag. In the mix of voices, she believed she heard the voice of Gastan protesting. She thought *It is not correct,* with a level of high-minded clarity. *He was Aryas all his life. He does not deserve...* but she saw Deem on the causeway; her thoughts about Gastan went elsewhere.

Deem took her by the hand and led her to the top of the small hill, past the tent-camp and to a bench next to a tree. He turned her and gently placed her on the bench but remained standing. "Strangest thing," he said.

He turned and looked down the hill. He saw the Beag gathering near the path down the hill toward the causeway. He saw the priests in ceremonial dress moving together toward the east stairway. He saw warriors beginning to drag bodies off the flat top of the pyramid.

"When I asked permission to leave *Cead* to bring *Dara* down, Captain Shar said the strangest thing. He said, 'Where is your mate?' and then smiled that smile of his that says, *'I will say no more'.*"

"I am here," said Celiste.

He turned back to her. "He meant no criticism, I am sure."

"I am here, where you left me."

"He thinks my mate should be on *Cead* learning her duties."

"I was told…" she began.

"He does not know, or does not wish to know."

"I have begun to plan."

She went on to tell Deem about the ceremony that morning, and the brutal way the priests killed the woman. Then she described her plans for raising planting fields and irrigating them from a water canal.

"My squad is 24 of the Beag women, with Dren and Drenay. I have already asked for four men to serve as guards, if you know what I mean."

"Guards?"

"Their men are going to Abram's army; I want guards to protect the women.

"From who?"

"Men who think they are entitled to cavort with Beag women."

"Cavort?"

"I heard Sud.Lan use that term to describe how the Anunnaki lords came down from space to 'cavort' with the daughters of Kien. The daughters were receptive, but naïve, she said."

"That is the attitude among many of the Titans, the 'Righteous Ones' as they say," said Deem. "The Beag exist to serve the Lords. They have no property, no temples, and no places to live with clean water."

"Is that how you feel?"

"There was a time..." he began, but then stopped. He looked at Celiste, first at her hands, then at her lips, then up to her eyes. *How much should I tell my mate?* he pondered, then remembered a shipmate's caution: *never tell your mate something she does not wish to hear.*

"There was a time," he said again. He leaned over to kiss her on the cheek. Then he took her hands. She raised an eyebrow, in a form of question. "I was about to come down to Kien to enjoy myself."

"No more. Tell me. No more."

"But you must understand," he said, ...*even if I do not.*

She put her hand behind his head and drew him to her and placed her lips on his lips and held him and caressed his face with her hands. "We are mates. We enjoy each other. And I have missed you these past six days." She put her hands on his shoulders and pushed him away.

"When my mates came down ...I felt it was wrong to 'cavort'."

She put her finger on his lips. "Enough." *I did not ask you to explain yourself.* She smiled and said, "I will go where you want me."

She looked at him for a moment, and then added, "My father gave me a mission. My role, he said, is to lead our people, Aryas and Beag both."

"I accepted your goal. We agreed when we joined," said Deem. "From what I see, the Lords have no feeling for those who are less."

"You mean those who have no power?"

"I will go where you want me," she said again. "My goal will be to lead and protect those we… that means Captain Deem and his mate Celiste… those we brought to Kien knowing we have to prove ourselves."

"You have rank among the Lords," he commented.

"But I am the granddaughter of a rebel."

"That may be. But among the Lords there have been rebellions and disagreements and then they find a way to remove the irritation."

"You are saying what?" she asked quietly.

"There may be comments. Yes, there will be comments from those who want their world to follow a set of rules. But you are my mate. You can decide where you go."

"And your mates among the Titans will not object?"

"Oh, they will jab me and give me a hard time. But it is in fun."

"And today?"

"We go to the mines. After we deliver our cargo we go up to *Cead* with a cargo of gold. We will have two days."

She looked at him when his hand slid down to her hip. This caused a slight smile to form on her face. "It is as you wish, my captain." [Endnote vii]

Chapter 33

The *Dara* sailed over the jagged mountains of the southern continent then crossed over an enormous ocean of green, dark green and an occasional muddy river. Celiste noticed the mist near a waterfall and remarked how the humidity in the jungle permitted the creation of low-level fog on the river. She watched the jungle disappear, to be replaced with a deep blue ocean that stretched off to the horizon. A white mountain came into view; it floated on the ocean. It had three peaks and sheer sides of white crystal with a blue tint.

'Enormous' was how she described it later. No one aboard *Dara* could tell her what it was, nor how it came to be floating on the ocean. Deem speculated that it must have broken off an ice mass in the far south.

When the *Dara* began to climb Celiste realized the shuttle was about to leave the ocean and cross land. She saw a large mountain with a flat table top where they left the shore of the ocean. *Dara* proceeded to cross jungle that gave way to green plains dotted with animals. She spotted a herd of enormous beasts with tusks and a swinging appendage; they were partially in a river. *Water beasts,* she thought.

She nodded off for a moment then jerked awake when the *Dara* tilted. Looking out she saw a village of round huts with conical roofs of thick ferns. The huts were surrounded by a wall of brush, cut and piled to deter predators. There was a river nearby and several of the 'water-beasts' were engaged in pulling loads on flat barges. The *Dara* moved away from the village and found a stone platform with a staircase. The platform was built with layers of stone, elevated from the ground; Celiste decided that was to protect the shuttle from an angry 'water-beast' or from angry men. *Now, why should I think that?* she asked herself as the *Dara* set down with a bump on the platform.

When the ramp was down the Beag began to walk off the shuttle. They were young men, dressed in the work clothes of fisherman or planters from her 'old' planet. They walked with their heads down; one said 'Two years of service, then what?' as he walked by her. Last to leave the shuttle were Gastan and his brother and their two mates.

She stopped Gastan and asked if his mate knew she would be expected to work in the mines. He said both the women knew; they intended to stay with their mates. From behind her Deem told her to take Aonim if she left the shuttle. Celiste and Aonim followed the workers off the shuttle and watched while a man in a green tunic wrote their names on a ledger and gave them a card with symbols for their mine.

The Beag moved toward a large tent where they received water and food made from grains. Aonim walked over to the kettle and smelled what he described later as the heady aroma of fermented grain. 'Too long in that pot,' he added. When he glanced at the platform where *Dara* sat he saw that Deem had exited and closed the ramp. Deem had a hand device used to deter predators on his hip and he carried a Shar.Ur, the 'Supreme Hunter' that could knock down any animal.

Celiste knew there was a mine nearby. She saw a cloud of dust rising from a pit in the ground. When she waved to Deem and indicated the mine, he waved at her with a motion that meant 'take Aonim' with you. Together they walked to the building near the river. She saw a wheel that raised water that it dropped into a wooden channel where the water washed over steps in the channel. Several women stood nearby. Every few minutes they would scoop out muddy material in a pan and wash it in channel water. Then they took their pan to another wooden channel where other women repeated the process.

One of the women appeared to be much older than Celiste's grandmother when she was her oldest. The woman's hair was thin; ratted and dirty. Her face was unclean. She bent over in a deep cough. She had broken teeth in her mouth. She wore a garment with holes that showed her skin. Her legs were thin; her feet were bare. When she looked at Celiste the woman did not smile.

Celiste walked over to the guard who stood watching the women and said, "Are you one of the young lords, a relative to Lord Enki?"

The man looked at her; he digested her question. "No. I was born in the land of the pyramid. I fought with a guard on the Great River. I must serve two years…I have one-half year before I return."

Celiste looked at her cloak that she wore over her red tunic. She nodded at the old woman and said, "Can I give this to her?"

"No," said the guard with emphasis.

"And your reason is?" said Aonim from behind Celiste. His face formed a frown; he was not happy. In his memory no person had ever said 'No' to an Aryas of Celiste's rank. She wore the gold chain with the circle and six-pointed star on her chest. Perhaps this guard did not know what it signified.

"The rules," said the guard. "Always the rules."

"How do you mean that?"

"She wears the cloak. It will keep her warm at night. But a man, any man, will see the cloak and kill her for it. Around here the cloak is worn by the medical staff. Someone will kill the man to take away the cloak. Then we spend days talking to these worthless workers, trying to decide who killed a man worker. In the end, her guard, that is me, will get punished."

Celiste turned to look at the man. She decided the guard was firm in his decision. She took Aonim and walked to the path that led downward into a small depression. They looked down into a beehive of activity.

They watched a woman push a flat wagon to a pile where she dumped her load of rocks. She wore a simple headband around her hair. Her arms were dark with dirt; her face was wet with moisture. She wore a cloth wrapped around her middle and a cloth with a hole for her head over her torso. She walked slowly back to the opening of the mine.

Nearby men were crushing the rocks with large hammers. Young boys were shoveling the crushed rocks into a large table where the smallest bits fell into containers. Every few minutes the table would be lifted and the remaining rocks were dumped where other men swung hammers to crush the rock.

"Hot work, down there," said Aonim.

"Are they criminals?" asked Celiste.

"This is all they know, or I have been told." He brushed dust off the arms of his tunic and glanced at Celiste. "Lady, you will be covered in dust."

"So we use the 'spraying' room to clean ourselves."

He watched as Deem walked up. His captain looked at Aonim and said, "Are you trained to use the Shar.Ur?"

"Yes, during our last trip to Nippur, at the temple."

Deem gave him the rifle and watched as Aonim made sure the weapon was charged but in the 'off' position. Aonim left to stand guard near the *Dara,* another 'rule' of the Titans who serve in space.

Two short girls came out of the mine pulling a low wagon on four wheels. A large rope attached to the wagon fell across their shoulders; they were intent on pulling the wagon to the rock pile. They wore a simple cloth around their middle but nothing over their shoulders. The skin on their shoulders looked red; their faces were dirty and wet. After they dumped their load of rock they passed by an old woman who made a mark on a tally and gave them a token.

"Those girls?" asked Celiste. "They look like they are …about seven years of age?"

"That would be…" began Deem, "about the right age."

"Where do they come from?"

"The large tent city, off to the east."

"Not what I meant. Where are their mothers?"

"Their mothers work in the mines until they are two months away from delivering the baby. Then they stay with their babies until two months have passed. The mothers, then, return to the mines. The babies are raised to the age of six or seven; then they come to the mines."

"Is this good?"

"Times be what they are." Deem knew Celiste may be concerned about the people working in the mines. "Lord Enlil tried to extract gold from sea water, as the Anunnaki did on Nibiru. It did not work. He directed the Anunnaki to come to this land and dig mines. The Anunnaki had desire for the daughters of men and created these workers. Then the Titans came down and cavorted with the daughters also. The sons and daughters of the Titans now work in the mines." Endnote[viii]

Chapter 34

"We must pay our respects," said Celiste. She knew that the royals among the children and grandchildren of the Anunnaki liked to receive visitors. She looked at Deem and saw his calm, deliberative face and knew she was correct in this matter. She turned from the mine and walked toward the large tent where the Beag they brought to the mines were eating. She walked into the tent and received a round vessel with an herbal drink and a cylinder of baked dough made from ground grain.

While she ate the 'roll' she looked over at the sleeping compound, the small 'village' of round huts with conical roofs. She nodded at the huts and said to Deem, "All these workers in those huts?"

Deem raised an eyebrow, a quick sign of agreement. He had been to Abzu once before, just before dawn. He remembered the surprise on the faces of two big cats that were outside the brush barrier that ran around the village. He saw them turn and run. He saw also a guard getting to his feet. The man had been sleeping.

"Big cat, last year. Caught a young child outside the barrier just after sunrise and dragged her screaming into the trees. Two guards ran after her but lost their nerve when two larger cats with big hair suddenly appeared."

"Big hair?"

"The first cat was sleek. The larger cats have hair that flows out from their heads."

"So they need more guards?"

He dropped his head. He was embarrassed to admit the guard on the *Dara* failed to charge his Shar.Ur, the 'supreme hunter.' He later proposed to Captain Shar that all guards be alert and ready to fire their weapons at any threat to the persons they are protecting.

Celiste did not expect him to answer. The solution seemed obvious. She walked over to Gastan where he sat with his brother and their mates. She pulled Gastan away from the others and discussed their role as guards. Then she told Gastan she would say all four of them had training with the Shar.Ur and with the devices that fire a lead pellet.

A man in a red tunic with a black belt entered the tent. His belt held a short wooden club on one side and a coiled whip on the other hip. His black hair was slicked back; he had the straight nose of the Aryas. He wore a small silver circle with seven spokes on his upper left chest. The man stopped and looked at Deem, then Celiste. When he saw Celiste's silver circle emblem of Kien he brought both hands together and bowed to her.

"My mistress, the Lady Sarai asks that you present yourself in the health facilities."

"Which are located where?" said Celiste while she waved an arm to indicate the vast territory around the mine with its many tents.

Deem gently placed his hand on her arm and looked at her. To the young royal guard, he said, "We will arrive when it suits Lady Celiste."

They watched the guard turn and proceed back to the health tents, past a guard at the entrance to the brush barrier.

"Just say as little as possible," he said to Celiste. "You have rank. That means you already know where to present yourself. And if you do not know then you will punish your guards for not knowing."

She looked at him, raised an eyebrow and mumbled, "O'magadh?"

"Yes, as you say, Oh, Really?"

The guard at the barrier stood a little taller when he saw Celiste in her red tunic. She brushed dust off her arms as she walked. The guard's Shar.Ur was strapped to his back; its presence indicated he guarded a person of royal rank. He brought his hands together and bowed.

Celiste passed him without a word. She looked ahead in a search for the health tent. Then she saw the other guard step out of a tent and she knew where she was going. To Deem, one step behind her, she said, "Do I show my rank with sufficient authority?"

"Yes, my lady," he smirked. "So much so that I almost want to come forward and pat your..."

"Do you now?" she laughed.

The guard at the tent made a deep bow and said, "Lady Sarai asks you to step into the tent. She is watching an assistant deal with two crushed toes on a worker."

Celiste honored the guard with a quarter-bow, where the user leans forward just slightly. He stepped back and allowed Celiste and Deem to enter the tent. Then he stepped past them and disappeared into an inner tent where they heard several people talking. Time passed until it became quiet inside the tent. The wall of the tent was pushed back. There was no ceiling above the area. It was open to the sky; the medical staff had adequate light by which to work.

A mine worker stepped between the three medical staff and picked up a young girl. Her left foot was bandaged. He carried her past Celiste and out of the tent. The medical staff began to wash the table; bloody rags went into a wooden box.

"You honor us," said a lady dressed in a white flowing gown. She wore a heavy gold circle with seven red gems on a thick gold chain. Her hair was pulled up to the back of her head where it formed a waterfall. Her face was *pleasant, elegant and inquisitive,* thought Celiste. Lady Sarai's eyelids were blackened; there was a strong black line under her eyes. Her black eyes bore into Celiste; it was a privilege of her rank.

The three medical staff began to back out of the tent. They took their tools and medicines with them. Lady Sarai watched them until they left, then said, "We are at the end of our work for today. They will go to the hot springs where they will soak and wash and become clean."

She turned and looked at Deem, where he stood behind Celiste. She nodded at him.

He bowed and looked at the ground. "I am Deem, Captain of the shuttle *Dara,* 5th generation from Enoch," he said in a rush. He raised his eyes and looked at the lady. Lady Sarai bowed to him, less deeply.

"This is," he began, "is Lady Celiste, 5th generation from Enoch." When Sarai said nothing, he added, "She holds her mother's Majority as leader of our people."

"That is well said," remarked Sarai. "I am Sarai, 5th generation from Enoch by his wife Ellim."

Celiste bowed to Sarai, a mark of respect. Sarai went on to explain that her mate Abram was Lord Director of an army in Tilmun, the spaceport on the southern edge of the peninsula. The army acts to protect the spaceport and Lady NinMah who holds dominion over the southern lands. Her title is Ninḫarsag and she is a half-sister to Lord Enlil and Lord Enki.

Sarai waved an arm and ushered them out of the health tent and into a larger tent with its sides lifted to allow air to circulate. When they were seated on cushions Sarai spoke to a servant. "She will bring us my favorite herbal drink and a fruit from the land of Lord Enki, land of the pyramid. This fruit grows on tall trees near water pools in the great desert."

"We are honored," said Celiste. She apologized for her mate, that he did not know she was 3rd generation from Seth.

"If as you say, 3rd from Seth, then you are 4th from our Lord Enki."

"Yes," said Celiste.

Sarai considered this carefully. "How do you know this?"

"A grandson of Seth and my mother," began Celiste. She realized what she had said aloud. The royals, she had been warned by her father, did not like to be reminded of their dalliance with royal daughters of Lords.

"As you say," remarked Sarai. She reached out and touched Celiste on the arm. "Keep that information to yourself. I will entreat the Lady NinMah to recognize you as 3rd from Seth."

The servant appeared with three clay bowls on a fancy silver tray with a small gold bowl of fruit. He placed it on the low table between them and backed out of Sarai's tent. After they each held a bowl, Sarai raised hers and said in a toast, "Our Lord Anu, and his beloved princess Antu, may they reign in Nibiru to the end of days."

"May Antu grow in his affection, that she may persuade him to improve conditions for the miners," added Celiste.

"You are an outspoken person," said Sarai. "But then, your great grandparents were instigators of unrest among the loyal subjects of Enlil."

"Yes, you speak truth, my lady."

Sarai looked at Celiste then at Deem. "Your mate says much."

"With few words," said Deem.

The face on Celiste grew calm; the agitation smoothed itself. "Do the workers come to you coughing, with deep rumbling coughs?"

Lady Sarai sat for a long moment.

"Do they sleep on mats in those small huts?"

"Yes, twelve to sixteen in a hut," said Sarai. She thought for a moment. "All those bodies keep them warm."

"I suggest." Celiste said slowly. "Build platforms to raise them off the ground. Get more air to flow in each hut."

Sarai sat with a blank face. "It is not your place."

Celiste continued. "There is a miasma, an evil that swims in their lungs. When they cough they send that evil to their neighbor at night."

"It is not your place," said Sarai a second time. A little color had come into Sarai's face, as if she was mildly angry.

It was perhaps that Lady Sarai did not wish to lose face by admitting she had no authority to change conditions in any of the twelve mine camps. She picked up two flat sticks and snapped them together. Two servants ran into the tent. She nodded at Celiste and Deem. The servants moved to her guests and held out their hands. Celiste looked at Sarai and could not believe she was summarily dismissed so quickly.

"There is another matter, Lady Sarai." When Sarai said nothing Celiste added, "We need more guards. I want you to assign a man and his brother. They were raised as Aryas. They and their mates both know weapons and how to defend a territory."

"Maybe they should go to Abram's army?" Sarai sat and looked at Celiste and her mate. "Teach them to respect the daughters of the Anunnaki."

"I meant you no disrespect."

Celiste began to rise, helped by a servant. Deem was on his feet.

Sarai watched her rise. When she was fully up and beginning to bow Sarai said, "In the matter of the guards. I will do as you suggest.

Before they report to the shuttle tell the four guards to report to my clerk, he of the hideous green tunic."

―――❦―――

While they walked back to the *Dara,* Celiste said, "My mate, how did I conduct myself?"

"You get a royal angry? And you ask me?"

"Times be what they are," she said. Then she added, "You kept your peace when I told you, and the Lady, about my father's revelation that he was not my father."

"Essa was a good man, a good Counselor to our people."

"What do you mean?"

"He is not here. You and I must watch out and protect our people."

"He said that was my role," she added.

"You surprise me," said Deem and patted her on the fanny. "Just now you did not describe Lady Sarai with the anger you are feeling, I think, in your stomach."

"Times be."

"And time will show us both how to talk to a royal."

Chapter 35

The sky grew darker, gradually darker then black as the *Dara* flew up to meet *Cead*. She was small, then larger as they approached. *Cead* fairly bristled with black poles that speared space and enormous engines for the times she moved. The Deep Black ship was on station, maintaining a relationship to E.kur, the Great Pyramid. The crew on *Dara* enjoyed the approach, sailing slowly to 'catch' up to *Cead* but in this case, the ship was keeping station with the pyramid. She was located where she could receive powerful beams of energy from the large white pyramid near the big river.

Aonim and the three veteran crew members were intent on watching Deem's approach to the *Cead*.

Celiste, strapped into her chair, looked down and saw the pyramid in the distance. It was a large building of stone, covered in white limestone that added brilliance to its solitary stature. A small black pyramid, called a 'BenBen' capped the pyramid. It stood near two smaller pyramids. The three pyramids echoed the pattern of the stars in the Hunter's belt. They stood near what Celiste thought resembled a cat, an enormous cat.

"I am told the head resembled the first pharaoh, Ptah," commented Deem to his listeners. "He was Ea, the first Anunnaki to land in the far distant past. He later became Enki, the Lord of Abzu."

"Many titles," noted Aonim.

"The royals seem to glory in their titles and descendant position from Anu and Antu, the royals on Nibiru," said Celiste. Deem glanced at Aonim then back at Celiste and said, "Perhaps we should not be critical."

"Perhaps." What Celiste thought to herself was *Perhaps you should not be in awe of persons who allow warriors to behead their enemies or who allow slaves to live in squalid conditions.*

Deem began to focus his attention on *Dara's* approach to the docking collar on *Cead*. He maneuvered the shuttle to his right, then back to his left when he saw that he over-corrected. "Flying backwards can be a challenge," he commented.

Deem focused on *Cead* as he maneuvered to dock. The ship was enormous with metal poles spearing the dark and five viewports on each quadrant. There were three power cones that push the ship with exhaust gases. Just outside the power cones were three circular dishes that receive power from the earth base, the power plant in the pyramid. *Cead* was 'on her back' while she received power from the pyramid.

Celiste knew that the command deck on the shuttle had a view screen which allowed the pilot to align his entry port at the rear of the shuttle with the entry port on *Cead*. Deem explained the access port on the *Dara* was at the rear because the lead edge of the shuttle took the worst of the heat when re-entering the atmosphere.

"We will be joined to *Cead* for about one day. We have to unload our cargo and have our engine power renewed," explained Deem.

"Those tanks in the cargo hold? They hold water for *Cead* and an explosive gas that empowers the 'engine' of *Cead* when she is moved."

When her face seemed blank Deem read her expression as regret. He realized she wanted time with him.

"You are wrong. Aonim and *Dara's* crew will be in training and working with a technician to learn all the quirks of re-charging our fuel cells."

"Which means?"

Deem began to smile then thought he should maintain decorum in front of Aonim and the other three members of the crew. "You and I will be busy for one day to learn the rules of the Titans, those *'who observe from space'* and report the movements of armies on Kien."

It took a moment before she realized he said, *'one day'* and she began to smile.

Chapter 36

Descending from the black of space Celiste marveled at the pilot's ability to fly with the nose of the *Dara* pointed up. White-hot flames flashed past her viewport. At one point she saw Captain Shar point at a small display where a line indicated the horizon and another line indicated the relationship of the *Dara*. She saw him make a small correction; the two lines became one.

The shuttle rotated. Celiste found herself looking back into the deep black. She felt herself pushed into the cushion of her chair when the shuttle's two engines began to slow their descent. Time slowed; the engines droned on with their roar and crackle. Then they went quiet. Time slowed again; then the pilot rotated the shuttle. The horizon moved up, then down, then up in a motion as the shuttle fell.

"We call this motion 'leafing' like a falling leaf," said Shar loudly.

Dara came down in a flash of white smoke. Her lead edge became red then bright white as she heated the atmosphere into white steam. Captain Shar put her down on the landing platform at the top of the Temple to Inanna, a short distance from E.kur. It had been a quick trip to the land of the Lord Enki.

The older Captain Shar sat at the controls and smiled. "T'was about time for me to fly a shuttle again."

His passengers smiled, quietly. They knew Shar's navigator was in charge of *Cead* which no longer received energy from the pyramid. Shar wanted 'Captain' Deem to meet the engineer who directed pyramid operations.

They made an impressive group when they left *Dara*. Captains Shar and Deem wore their best red tunics with badges of rank on their right upper chests. Both men brought their mates to observe. Aonim stayed behind to guard the *Dara*. The two women were resplendent in flowing white drapes belted at the waist under red loose covers.

Celiste wore a type of sandal which she tied to her leg. She wore her red cover over her white gown. She applied black oil to her eyelids with a black line under her eye. The line ran half-way to her ear, just as Sud. Lan wore hers. Her hair was pulled back and bound inside a headband of red and white. The silver circle with white stones sat between her breasts. She wore a new emblem, a silver star. Captain Shar explained that it signified the rank of majority, or 25 rank among the Anunnaki.

They preceded single-file behind Captain Shar and his mate, down a long stairway inside the temple. That stairway brought them to a paved path that struck out across the plateau toward the enormous white pyramid shining in the late morning sun. The path led them through a wall into a courtyard where they were stopped by a tall guard who was one-half head taller than Shar and Deem.

Shar spent a long moment explaining they were a delegation summoned by Lady ⚔Ninki, mate to Lord ⚔Enki. The guard smiled and bowed. He turned and led the group through a stone portal into a courtyard with high walls. Sitting in the shade was an aged crone dressed in white robes that fell to her feet. Her head was down. The guard held out an arm and stopped Shar and his party.

"She sleeps," said the guard. "Stand in silence."

Celiste saw the old woman's head bounce. *She is half asleep.*

"Middle of the day," said Deem.

"This is an honor, to be asked to present ourselves," explained Shar to his fellow 'observers' from *Cead*.

One of the men standing near the old lady made a sound in his throat. She raised her head and looked at him.

"My pardon, my lady," the man said quickly.

Lady Ninki's face was carved with deep ravages of time. Her eyebrows were gone. There were purple veins in both cheeks. Her lips were painted a bright blue. When she raised a hand Celiste saw her finger nails were long and curved, painted in the same blue as her lips. She looked at her nails then seemed to realize there were people waiting at the other end of the courtyard. To her minister she said, "What is happening?"

"Captain Shar of the *Cead* and his captain to be appointed, name of…" the minister said while staring at a papyrus scroll, "…oh, yes, Deem."

Lady Ninki stopped examining her nails and waved a hand at the group. Shar and Deem approached the guards with their heads down. The guards parted; the two men stopped. The lady's throne was elevated; when seated her head was slightly above the heads of her visitors.

"Can you believe it?" She stopped and looked at Shar and Deem.

When they said nothing, she repeated herself. "Can you believe it?"

Her minister finally interjected and said softly, "Say 'No, mistress'." He brought a hand up and pointed at his ear, telling them Ninki had a problem hearing.

"No, mistress," said Captain Shar loudly.

"So short, I say. No one around here pays me any attention," Ninki said loudly to her minister before she turned to Shar and Deem. "There was a time when our sons were two heads taller than…" she began but her head seemed to acquire a bouncing rhythm of its own.

Her minister stepped to her side and presented a papyrus scroll. He then unrolled it and said, "Captain Deem, the rank of your mate Celiste is confirmed. Lady Ninki understands Celiste holds a majority and will direct a growing operation with 90 workers. Lady Ninki confirms the appointment of Deem to the rank of Captain of the *Cead*."

Deem suddenly stood up taller. His face acquired a blank expression. He began to say, "Lady Ninki, I am…"

But the minister interrupted. "We are finished. Lady Ninki has signed this decree. Honor the Lady by backing to the portal from which you entered." He raised an eyebrow; the captains knew it was time to leave.

Captains Shar and Deem and their mates backed away from the throne and Lady Ninki until they were outside the gate. They began to turn just as a guard came out and asked for Lady 'Ka-List.'

He indicated the gate and motioned that she should re-enter. She stepped back into the shade. Lady Ninki motioned for Celiste to approach.

"How do you say it?"

"My Lady?"

"Your name, dear."

"Ah, my father preferred *'Say-Leest-Ay.'*

"Thank you." She sat and looked around to her minister.

"What was it?" she said loudly at him. He bowed, slightly.

"Tilmun," he said equally loudly.

Lady Ninki turned to Celiste and said slowly, with great pauses in her words: "Tilmun …Land of the Missiles …a dangerous place …you will be far north of Tilmun …near the deep lake they call White Salt, or some such name. Listen to me, my dear."

Celiste turned her ear toward Lady Ninki; she indicated she was listening. A small frown formed on her face.

"The son of Lord Enki, named Mar.Duk, is tired of the desert and the palms and the big river. He wants to build a temple at Eridu, south of the temple of Lord Enlil."

Celiste stood and watched Ninki. A small spittle of saliva formed at the corner of Ninki's mouth. An eyelid drooped.

"There will be war. Mar.Duk refuses to retreat from Eridu. The land belongs to Enlil. Enlil's army in Tilmun is growing. Mar.Duk is gathering men to build an army. You are sending some of your people to join with the Army of Abram in Tilmun."

Celiste bowed toward Ninki. "Our people thank you."

The old lady nodded, once. Then she looked at Celiste and said, "What name did your mother have?"

"Deacaire, we called her Dea," answered Celiste.

"Good. If you get a message from Deacaire, then move your people into the mountains." The old lady paused then said, "Do you understand?"

"You honor me, Lady."

"Do you understand?"

Celiste bowed toward Lady Ninki and said, "I understand." The old lady crooked a finger at Celiste and urged her to come closer. When Celiste was close Lady Ninki handed her a silver ankh, the half circle on the top of the 'T' that once represented the great island that was flooded when the stars fell.

"It is a mark of trust in your position. Wear it when you meet the Council."

Celiste took the ankh and removed her silver circle with the six white stones and gave it to Lady Ninki. "This is our emblem for our own land, the sixth planet, Lahmu, the planet beyond Earth. My father told me Lahmu was called the sixth because it was the sixth planet when you approach from the Deep Black. Keep us in your thoughts. We will build a new city," she added.

Chapter 37

At the side of the pyramid stood the engineer who promised to introduce Deem to the source of energy that supports *Cead* and the other two Deep Black ships of the Anunnaki. In the background stood the two smaller pyramids built on the style of E.kur, but shorter. The middle pyramid seemed to be taller, but it was an illusion. The engineer was a short man dressed in long robes with a cloth wound around his head. He introduced himself as Enoch, the son of Enoch who went into the heavens.

"These other two pyramids will soon be tuned to produce energy."

"For what purpose?" Deem mumbled, his head lost in confusion.

"The Lord Enki wants more power, to supply his flying boat and to provide new fuel for all the shuttles now in use."

"Is that necessary?" asked Captain Shar.

"We are told to expect a Deep Black ship, the *Osiris* which brings three new shuttles with weapons mounted into their lower sides."

"Will these new pyramids send energy to the shuttles?"

"If they can find the place to properly station their vehicle," said the engineer. "Come with me," he added to Deem.

The two captains, their mates and the engineer Enoch moved toward the shadow cast by the pyramid. They walked to the mid-point of the base on the eastern side. "Observe the shadow," he told them.

The group looked at the shadow. With a stick Enoch drew a square in the dirt on the plateau. Then he drew two lines from the east corners of the square. The two lines came to a point.

"When you are in correct position, the length of the shadow to the point will equal the length of the height of the pyramid. If both sides of the triangle are equal, then you are at the right elevation. You must rotate to the mid-point of the southern side of the pyramid."

"Captain Shar understands this," he added to Deem. "Then you signal to my command deck inside the Temple of Inanna and we will adjust the power sent to you by E.kur." He looked at Deem.

Deem nodded to him. Enoch said "Tell me what I just explained."

Deem repeated back to Enoch the instructions and noted that if the sides of the shadow were not equal then the *Cead* would not be directly in front of the power output of the pyramid.

The engineer Enoch nodded his agreement. He turned to Captain Shar and raised an eyebrow. "We hear you are training Captain Deem for a reason?"

"Yes, I have fulfilled my contract with Lord Enlil."

"And you are...?"

"Going to be released. Soon."

"Ah..." said the engineer. "You will return to Nibiru?"

"No."

Captain Shar paused. He looked at his lady, then at Deem before he added, "There is an island in the north ocean, the land of the White Wall. It is cold, damp and is a land of star observers. Crops grow in a short growing season. There is rain and snow in the cold season. My lady and I are looking forward to our new home."

As they walked away from Enoch, back to the *Dara* atop the Temple of Inanna, Celiste said, "What did he mean, new home?"

"There will be a time when he will retire." [Endnote[ix]]

Chapter 38

Descending through a cloud bank Celiste marveled at the pilot's ability to fly blind in gray clouds. At one point she saw Deem point at a small display where a line indicated the horizon and another line indicated the relationship of the *Dara*. She saw him make a small correction; the two lines became one.

The shuttle rotated. Celiste found herself looking back into the deep black. She felt herself pushed into the cushion of her chair when the shuttle's two engines began to slow their descent. Time slowed; the engines droned on with their roar and crackle. Then they went quiet. Time slowed again; then the pilot rotated the shuttle. The horizon moved up, then down, then up in a motion as the shuttle fell.

"This is called 'leafing' like a falling leaf," said Deem over the noise.

Celiste saw brown rock and black shadows of mountains below her. The mountains began to retreat when the shuttle descent slowed. They flew down a valley; sharp angular cliffs passed by. Then a small village appeared. Deem turned and pointed down. Celiste saw a few roofs and many shells of houses without roofs. She thought, *what happened?*

Beyond the village Celiste saw green fields that were divided by small canals of water. She briefly saw one or two workers. There was a 'spit' from a forward rocket and the pilot turned the shuttle slowly and in the far distance she saw the Great Lake, the source of salt used for trading and for cooking. The shuttle turned; another 'spit' slowed their rotation. The lake was behind her and she surmised the pilot was about to set *Dara* down.

The maneuvering jets kicked in. An enormous blast of sand and dust roiled up and surrounded the small shuttle. Their forward progress seemed to slow to a stop; a bump told her *Dara's* feet were down. Deem turned and said, "We wait. There is an air current that will blow the dust away."

Celiste sat and waited. Gradually she began to see square boxes built with mud bricks; a few had a window to one side of the empty door. On higher ground she saw an older building that could be a temple. Flat white limestone faced in her direction. There was a circular tower at one corner. A cloth of two colors, red and white, hung from a pole at the roof of the temple. She saw a woman stand and look at the shuttle. The woman turned and disappeared, probably back into the temple.

Deem turned in his seat. He looked out her viewport and said in a low voice, so the crew could not hear, "This is your village. You must walk in as if the Lord Enlil himself has sent you."

"I must, you say?"

"Use your rank."

She smiled. "From now on I will call you Deem."

Her comment drew a blank face. Then he nodded, "As you wish."

"How far is the lake I saw?"

"About two days walking," said Deem, and then added, "It is called Yām ha-Māret, but some say 'Sea of Death.' It is not healthy."

"And these broken down relics?"

"The village is Arad. The fields grow beans, onions, radishes and lettuce for Salem, the spaceport to the north."

She looked out the opposite viewport. She saw green fields with tender shoots bending in a soft breeze. In one field she saw a crew of six women working. They were 'planting' tubes that brought water over small dikes, into the fields. *They control how much water, I think.*

She looked at Deem and reached out to pat his hand. He smiled, almost leaned in to kiss her. "And you?" she said quietly.

"We return in four days. Dara goes to the highlands to get your workers and Dren and Drenay."

She unbuckled her straps and stood up. It felt good to stretch the muscles of her legs. She pulled her long cloth coat around her and tied a strap around her waist. Celiste reached up and touched Deem with her hand. He looked into her eyes. He saw her determination and her sadness.

"It's only four days," he added quickly. "Time enough for you to get settled and prepare for my arrival."

"Is that a promise I hear inside your quiet words?" *To herself she added, where am I going to get a platform and padding to make a bed?*

Deem said nothing. He turned and waved at Aonim and said, "Lady Celiste expects to show her rank. Carry her bags."

Aonim turned toward her and said with a smirk, "Yes, my lady?"

They stepped off *Dara's* ramp and walked toward the village. Deem came first with his Shar.Ur strapped to his shoulder. He wore his formal red uniform with the six-pointed star on his tunic. Behind him Aonim and a crewman brought her two bags of possessions. Celiste came last with her long cotton coat that protected her from dust.

They walked up a well-trodden path that led from the fields to the houses of Arad. Celiste looked down when she realized some of the fine dirt was inside her toes. From between the houses two men with long curved swords appeared. Then a woman with the regal bearing of the Aryas appeared. She was dressed in a short wrap that reached her knees. Her hair was pulled back and protected by a long swatch of red and white cloth wound around her head. She had the straight nose, black hair and high cheekbones of the Aryas. She did not smile.

When she stopped she said something to the two men. They stopped and stepped to both sides of the path. Deem stepped sideways and his two crewmen did the same. This left Celiste in mid-path, directly opposite the other woman.

Deem made a small bow in the woman's direction and swung an arm wide, pointing vaguely in Celiste's direction. "Lady, I have the honor to…"

"Yes," said the woman.

"Pree…sent…" he tried.

"Yes," said the woman.

"Lady 'Say-Leest-Ay' who is…"

"Yes," repeated the lady.

Deem stopped. He stood straight and turned to look sideways at Celiste. She minutely raised an eyebrow and cleared her throat.

"I am…"

The lady ignored her and turned to Deem. "Are you the pilot?"

Deem turned away from the lady. Celiste unbuttoned her long coat and exposed her red tunic and emblems of rank. To the lady she said,

"You will address me. Yes. He is the pilot."

"Then he should know that I will retrieve my maids and my clothes and we can leave."

"With my permission," stated Celiste with blunt accuracy.

The woman looked at Celiste, then at Deem and said, "I was told 30 days in this dismal place. It has been 45. I am ready to leave."

"You will leave when I grant you the right to leave," said Celiste with a certain amount of hot pepper inside her voice.

The lady looked stunned. She said nothing.

"You are?"

"Narai, daughter of Sarai and our Lord Abram."

"And your role here in Arad?"

"Directing the rebuilding. We made no progress."

"And why are you proud of, as you say, *no progress?*"

"These women have no pride, no sense of purpose."

"Explain please," said Celiste in two words of a demand.

Lady Narai looked down at her feet for a moment and seemed to realize she was making a royal with rank stand in the sun. Her voice went up with urgency when she said, "Please. I am solely aggrieved that you stand here. Come into your temple. My maids will wash your feet."

"Explain yourself," repeated Celiste.

The lady looked away. She glanced at Aonim and the crewman and waved them toward the white stone temple. To Deem she said, "My Lord?"

"I will stand with Lady Celiste," said Deem.

"Explain yourself," said Celiste once again.

"You must understand. I take responsibility for my failure," said Narai while she looked boldly into Celiste's eyes. "There was a full squad of men here. They planted the onions and beans and radishes that this dismal hovel sends to Salem. An old shipment of barley seed went into the ground. No lettuce. The men planned to grind and ferment the barley. Two of the men joined with our women. The rest, shall I say, were of a lustful nature and abused our women. They were all taken away to serve in the Army of Enlil."

Celiste said nothing.

"We have struggled to prepare your quarters. The washing pool is clean and your quarters are private. An old woman prepares our food. I have dismissed the two priests who were making a shambles of the temple."

"And where do the workers sleep?"

"Three of the old ruins have been dug out. There was one cubit of dirt and debris inside the ruins. We were about to build roofs when the men were taken. The fields are growing. My half-sister Eglan waters the fields."

"But you have done little to repair the small hovels?"

"Yes, my lady," said Lady Narai.

"You will stay. You and your maids can serve me for the next ten days. We will make progress in building roofs or you will stay longer. Am I making myself like a crystal that shines beyond doubt?"

The lady said nothing. She busied herself brushing imaginary dust off her gown. She nodded at her two guards then led Celiste and Deem into the old streets of Arad and to the temple.

Chapter 39

The reflection off the distant lake was brilliant and blinding, a white hot beam of sunlight reflected off the water of the lake in the early morning. The fields in front of Arad were quiet. In the hour before dawn a misty dew settled on the plants. Each morning Celiste and Eglan and a few of the women walked out into the fields to feel the dew. They had never seen such a wealth of water sprinkled on the young plants, almost as if by magic.

In the eight days while Celiste waited for the return of the *Dara,* Lady Narai helped to organize teams to build roofs on the old shells of houses. Her two guards did some of the heavy lifting. Narai and her half-sister Eglan insisted on an afternoon review, when the squad leaders reported on the day's progress and plans for the next day. Celiste found herself in an unusual situation: when the squad leaders asked for a day of rest, Celiste was firm in her determination to continue building roofs.

The squad leader in the fields, Eglan, began to train workers in how to 'gently' water the fields. She explained how the canals had to be cleaned. She demanded that one worker be present to monitor the tubes used to drain excess water from the low side of the fields. She led teams with hoes to clean the vagrant plants that always grew inside the row crops like radishes and onions.

"They enjoy this work …out in the fields," Eglan commented.

Celiste watched the 'field squad' walk past on their way to the washing house. They all smiled at the *new* 'Lady' of Arad.

"Why do they smile?"

"They stand on their feet, unlike in the temple at Salem." Eglan smiled at the last woman passing by and waved her on to the washing house.

"These are temple women?" Celiste's jaw dropped.

"They earned much in tribute for the temple," began Eglan. "But you know they provided a service to men?"

"This is new to me," said Celiste.

"They were promised men," said Eglan.

"What? …here? Instead they find an almost abandoned village, the men removed?" said Celiste in disbelief.

"They held a lottery for the two guards."

"So you will tell me two of the women are happier than the other three?"

"Yes, my Lady."

"And Lady Narai's maids?"

"My sister has rank in the temple. Her maids are each a priestess in their own right. They have mates."

"Their mates are not here?"

"No. But by custom the absent priestess must assign a slave to service her mate."

"So the priestess assigns an ugly slave?"

Eglan stood for a moment. A frown formed on her face. She looked at Lady Celiste, then up at the white stone of the temple. One eyebrow seemed to droop as comprehension dawned across her face.

"We did not have slaves," noted Celiste.

"How did you…?"

"Each male was required to have a mate by the end of his eighteenth year."

"What about unmarried females?"

"They joined their sisters as 'Wife Number Two' and the problem was solved."

"I think you tease me?" asked Eglan.

"Oh?"

"We have no ugly slaves," noted Eglan with an enormous grin.

When Celiste asked about Eglan's title, Lady Narai went into great details to describe her two brothers and four sisters. Eglan was the last-born sister and she was not entitled to hold a title.

Eight days passed quickly. Lady Narai and her maids built a platform and 'created' a sleeping pad for Celiste's bedroom. Her two guards were adamant they were not wood-workers; they spent their time shaping wood for the roofs on the 'hovels' as Celiste called them. Celiste, by her own admission, was worried. Four days had stretched to eight. She wondered about the *Dara*. She studied the skies and waited.

Late on the eighth day as the sun began to fall into the mountains to the west, the *Dara* came with a loud scream down a nearby gorge. She blasted past the small village and flew almost to the lake then came slowly back to Arad. After she set down the ramp dropped. A long minute passed then Deem appeared. Behind him came Dren and

Drenay, the childhood friends of Celiste. A line of women with bags of possessions followed.

Celiste watched the women walk toward the village. The two men who acted as guards escorted them into the courtyard near the temple. Last to step off *Dara* were Gastan, his mate Sinar, her brother Shen and his mate Shenar. They carried bags for clothes and one long bag that Celiste assumed was a weapon. Gastan and Shen stopped in front of Celiste and made a small bow.

"You honor us. We received training," began Gastan, and added, "We are beyond belief gladdened to be off *Dara.*"

Celiste looked at Deem and said, "Pilot, you are here."

"I am," he said with a large dose of anxiety. Then he added, "We went to Abzu, the gold mines. These four asked to be assigned as guards. The lady told me to take them to you."

"That was seven days in the past," said Gastan.

"Then the *Dara* was directed to the highlands. We delivered twelve Aryas and 24 Beag to the army that is being trained in Tilmun, near the spaceport and health facilities in the southern mountains."

"That was five days ago," added Gastan.

"The Lady of the Two Mountains, Lady NinMah had your request," said Deem. He gestured toward Gastan and Shen and noted they received two days training on the 'Shar-Ur,' also known as the 'Supreme Hunter.' Then he added, "Their 'Shar-Ur can turn a man inside out. They have sworn to use it for defense only."

"If we are attacked," said Celiste.

"Only if the Lady tells you to use your weapon," added Deem.

Gastan and Shen and their mates, who stood three paces behind them, made a bow from the waist and said, "When the Lady tells us."

Celiste raised her right hand as symbol and stated: "The Lady Celiste declares it to be as you said. Let no man say otherwise."

She then touched her friend Drenay on the arm and indicated it was time to walk to the temple. When Celiste walked past Deem she glanced at him and said, "That was three days ago?"

He smiled. He knew she would ask. He had 'promised' four days and here it was the end of the eighth day. "We went to the highlands in the mountains, where the air is dry. We bring you the Beag who were assigned to work in the fields."

"Assigned?"

"What do you ask?"

"Assigned? I thought volunteers; their mates serve in the army."

"Ahhh…" he began. "I see."

"I think not," Celiste said. Then she added, "I will have to personally check your eyes later," she noted with a rather large smile.

The twenty-four women stopped in the stone plaza in front of the temple. The women waited. Celiste told them they were there to work on the fields. That meant building the hovels into useable protection from the elements, which meant roofs.

"There is a large building near the stream; it is our washing house." From among the women Celiste chose the oldest and assigned her to the Washing House. "Men must receive permission only when there are no females present."

Then she surprised the group. Gastan and Shen held a serious weapon, *one that killed at a distance,* she added. No one was allowed to touch that weapon except the four who brought it. She thought for a moment and told the crowd that Dren was now Keeper of the Laws and the guards. She explained by saying that Dren and his guards would be expected to observe the laws. Disobedience to the laws --- punishable by death. Theft or rape --- punishable by death. "Sharing your bed with any person who is not your mate --- punishable with death," she stated bluntly.

When Deem later asked, she told him a few of the women had encouraged 'evil' behavior by ignoring Enlil's proscription against 'bad' behavior. Deem chuckled and said, "You mean like the Titans who came to Kien and 'knew' the daughters of men?"

"They were not '*Joined*' to those women …were they?"

"No, I imagine they were not," he answered.

Celiste stood and watched Lady Narai assign the women to sleeping quarters. She heard the Lady accuse them of being dirty. Narai told them to head for the washing house. As the women moved away Celiste said,

"Deem, what about you?"

He looked at her with a blank face covered with light red dust.

"You mean did I ever?"

"Did you, you know, come down to Kien from the *Cead*?"

"They left me behind. I was always assigned to maintain the ship's position. A few found mates among the Aryas in Salem or Eridu or Shur.Rup.Pak. Our Captain then performed the Joining ceremony."

"That is as it should be," said Celiste.

Deem coughed, and then cleared his throat. He took out a thin white cloth and blew his nose. "Do you wonder why I did not?"

"Come down and shall we say, visit?"

He glanced at Celiste. "I did not have an urge," he said.

"And now you do, have the urge, I mean?"

"You are somehow turning my words back on me," he laughed.

"You must have no worry in that area," Celiste said and reached out to pat his face. "You have proved yourself to me," she added with a smile.

"We are joined," he said quietly, as Dren approached.

"We shall have our own ceremony *once again,*" she said in a quiet voice, and then louder she said, "as soon as I give Dren orders to search those mountains for a large cave."

She smiled at Deem then turned to explain her comment to Dren.

Chapter 40

The sun continued to climb into the northern hemisphere of Kien while the plants reached maturity. When it became evident the radishes and onions needed to be harvested, Eglan reported a wagon and two of the pulling beasts was needed. Lady Narai also noted the need for salt and a new plow to open more fields for onions and radishes. Celiste considered their request for a moment then said,

"We only planted one crop each year. The cold made it difficult to get a whole crop. We never even asked about a second crop."

"We get two perhaps three crops," said Lady Narai.

"How do you know?" said Celiste, perhaps without thinking.

"All my life I have lived in Salem. My older brothers served on the gates as guards. When I visited them we talked about what was entering and leaving each day."

"My brothers always took a few of each crop as tribute to the city. In quiet moments we ate what we had."

Lady Narai stopped and looked out over the fields. Eglan turned and walked toward the washing house. Narai turned to Celiste and said quietly,

"You must remember. You are Aryas. You know these things. Do not, and I repeat, do not query a royal ever in front of the Beag. We hold high status because we know the answers and the magic and the fury of our shuttles and power of our tablets."

"Yes," said Celiste. Her cheeks felt warm. *This woman has the onions to give me directions? She is nothing but a dried radish.* She enjoyed the comparison. *I will say nothing.* She smiled to herself.

Lady Narai glanced at Celiste and added, "We cannot and do not trust the Beag. We are Aryas. We are pure. They are not. They are the unlawful children of our Titans and our, how shall I say this? ... our brothers and cousins who like to dally with the daughters of Kien."

They are not that different, added Celiste to herself.

<hr />

The sun was high overhead when Dren walked back into the plaza near the temple. He was followed by two Beag, Gastan and his brother Shen. Gastan carried a Shar.Ur strapped to his back. Shen had a bundle tied to his back and he turned toward the river and the 'old' cook house.

"We found deep red beets in the higher lands," Dren told Celiste. She watched Shen walk toward the house they repaired, with the tall brick chimneys. A current of pale smoke drifted upward from the two chimneys.

Celiste looked at the dirt on Dren's face and smiled. His tunic and trousers were covered in pale brown dust. His boots were equally dirty. Gastan stood tall with his Shar.Ur and said nothing.

"What is your report?" she said to Dren.

"As you asked, we found a large cave. It is in a higher valley that requires climbing. We saw a large cat in the area. The cave showed evidence of small bones. The cat lives there."

"And water?"

"There is a fast moving flow within quick walking of the cave." He hesitated then added, "The stream becomes a pool just beyond the cave then drops over a rock cliff."

Celiste nodded. She decided to act. To Dren and Gastan she said,

"Go to the cook house and eat. Tomorrow you both will escort Lady Narai to that large village called Sodom, at the south end of the Great Lake. We need a wagon for crops, four pulling beasts, salt and two plows and seed for onions and radishes."

Dren's jaw dropped slightly. He stood there for a moment.

"Lady Narai is going to pay a tribute to Arad, our village. Her tribute will be four pulling beasts, a wagon, salt, two plows and more seed and a four-legged meat animal."

"Excuse me, my lady," he began, "In return for what?"

"After you return from Sodom you will escort the Lady and her two maids and our first load of radishes to Salem. She has served long enough in our village."

Gastan snorted. He turned away from Celiste and Dren. His shoulders bounced, as if he laughed.

"And you two," snarled Celiste, "will never present yourself to me or another royal in this condition, ever. If you do, I shall have you whipped."

Dren looked at her with a blank face.

"And you, Gastan. You have had your hands on one of the unattached women two or three times. You will stop such behavior. This is your only warning. You are demoted. Give the Shar.Ur to your brother Shen and tell him my order. Perhaps he can keep you out of my anger."

Dren and Gastan stood for a moment with blank faces. Dren began to bow toward 'Lady' Celiste and Gastan followed suit. She turned and walked into the temple; she began to think of it as 'her' temple.

———— ⁂ ————

Five days passed before Lady Narai returned ahead of four enormous horses for pulling and two wagons and plows. The next morning Dren helped Narai's 'maids' to climb into the wagon among the bags of radishes. They took bags with clothes and food and Lady Narai's formal clothes and her personal items used to prepare her face and hair. She walked onto the plaza in a long flowing cloth coat. Over the long coat she wore a short coat with a hood over her hair. Her face barely showed but the black oil on her eyelids seemed to give her a sinister appearance. Two of the guards helped her climb onto the back of the wagon.

Her maids had prepared an over-size chair with two pillows and she sat slowly down while she tested the chair. She looked regal despite being surrounded by bags of radishes. Her maids sat on top of the radishes. Dren and Shen, with his Shar.Ur on his shoulder, sat at the front of the wagon. At the last moment the old lady who cooked for Lady Narai brought out a bundle with cooked onions, beans and the newest addition to their daily menu, a ground wheat product formed into rolls and baked.

Lady Narai said nothing to the cook. One of her maids said, "We thank you," to which the cook replied, "Not me. Lady Celiste ordered me. These rolls are for the 'great' lady Narai."

The maid smiled. Dren raised the leather ropes on the pulling beasts and urged them to begin moving. Lady Narai looked with disgust at the cook and said, "Perhaps someday you will learn to prepare food beyond boiling the goodness out of it."

Under her breath the cook said, "Yes, I boil, you leave." She smiled.

When Dren returned from Salem he told Celiste that the cook mashed and mashed a mixture of the purple weeds called 'spurt' into the rolls she sent with Lady Narai. When Celiste asked why, Dren replied the cook wanted the 'great lady' to enjoy squatting, in haste, next to the road.

"Ah," said Celiste laughing. "We will call those rolls the 'Cook's Revenge'."

Chapter 41

Celiste sat at a small table in her sleeping quarters when Deem walked in. She wore a thin white tunic that fell to her knees. She had not bothered to tie the belt. Deem had used the 'washing house' to clean himself while the women were banned from the house. He wore a white tunic. that reached to his knees.

Celiste glanced at his attire while she used clear oil to remove the black oil around her eyes. A shiny bronze disc on the wall served to reflect her image. She saw Deem out of the corner of her eye and said,

"You have legs that are fit for a Titan."

"Daily I strive to work my muscles."

"But?" she said.

"But what?"

"Your tunic is entirely too short."

He thought for a moment then answered, "Entirely to impress you. You must want the other women to admire me. I build your reputation."

"There is another item I want you to *build*." She slid her hand up his leg until the curve of his hip stopped her.

"I know. But I have a question. Why did I bring twelve clay vessels; each amphora is about two cubits tall?"

"They are going up into the mountains. They will hold water. I am preparing if there is a war. Lady Ninki warned me."

"Could there be a war?" he asked.

"What have you heard among the Titans?"

"Captain Shar says that Lord Mar.Duk has built a new temple in Eridu, and Lord Enlil is furious. Mar.Duk has flown the 'Disc of Ra' to and from Eridu several times. We do not know what he is bringing to Eridu but there is a suspicion he has armed his army with Shar.Ur. The Lords think Mar.Duk has discovered the location of the seven deadly weapons that Enlil brought from Nibiru in the distant past. They are in Tilmun.

"Should I be worried? How will I know?"

Deem walked over to stand behind her. He put his hands on her shoulders then moved his hands down her side until he could slip his hands under her arms. He cupped her breasts and said, "Enough. If you need to leave, I will come and get you."

"Unless you are ordered ..." she began but stopped.

She turned slowly towards him until she could put her hand on his leg. She brought her hand up and covered his left cheek. With her other hand she unfastened the belt of his tunic and spread the cloth to both sides. Then she kissed his stomach.

"I wanted to see you *build* a sword for me. Now I want you to use your very hard sword to ...we will decide later." [Endnote^x]

Chapter 42

When the Lady Celiste walked out to the fields in the morning, she usually wore a pair of light colored trousers under a tunic of white cloth. Someone gave her a hat of straw in a cone shape that she tied under her chin. On her blouse she wore her emblem of rank, the silver circle with the seven white stones.

On the day after Deem returned the two 'partners' walked out to the fields with empty sacks and digging sticks. They were determined to add to the harvest of radishes from their fields. Deem wore nothing on his head; on his hip a leather pouch hid a 'shooter' that fired a lead pellet. When Celiste asked, he said,

"Not very accurate, except at close range."

"Not what, but why do you wear it?" she asked.

"You are a royal."

"You are afraid of me, is that why you wear that weapon?"

"You are the royal, descended from who? Some old guy?"

She put her hand under his arm when she stepped over a row of radishes and nodded toward the area they were going to pick. Some of the women working with Eglan were farther out in the field.

"You have rank. You are entitled to a guard."

"That is why I waved off your guard," he added. Deem reached over to put her hand on his arm just as they reached a white stake in the row.

"Right here," she said. "Eglan marked the row for us."

Deem looked at his stick. He knew how to use it. She chuckled to herself and said in a low voice, "Can the mighty Titan work in a field?"

"I imagine I can, if you can."

"But I had more practice back on our planet. You were always off somewhere, fishing or chasing creatures in the forest."

"Is that how you think of me?"

"Ah, my love," she began and stopped.

A man she did not recognize was approaching the field from the direction of the Great Lake. His face was haggard; his hair dirty and snarled. He carried a sack over his shoulder; his feet were covered with mud. When he reached the radishes he walked down the row, which brought him toward Celiste and Deem.

When he was 25 paces from his mate Deem raised a hand to stop. The man took two more steps then stopped. He looked at the two of them then bowed, and said, "Can you tell me where to find Eglan?"

"We might," said Deem.

He looked the man up and down and said, "Who are you?"

The man made a small bow toward Deem, then said, "And just who do you think you are?"

"I am Deem, pilot of the *Dara* which you see over by that large building with the two smoke towers. I am partner to the Lady Celiste."

"Well," said the man. "You are certainly full of yourself, just like my officer in the Army of Abram, as it is called."

"Who are you?" he paused, "Before I lose my patience with you?"

"Well, my lord, I am Ashur, 'partner' as you say it to Eglan, my beloved mate."

"How do we know this?" said Celiste.

"The woman speaks," said the man Ashur, incredulous.

"Chew your lips," said Deem using an old expression from the dry planet on which he was born.

"The woman is Celiste," she began, "the woman of rank who will have you whipped for your impertinence."

Ashur stood and looked at her, then at Deem. "As you say."

Then he bowed slightly and added, "I stand in your shadow, my Lady." This was an old expression used in the Land of Enki, near the Pyramids. "And to you, Lord Deem."

The man put his sack on the ground. He stepped into the next row of radishes and stretched his back. "I paid a man to deliver me. He put on a load of salt in Sodom and when I awoke the next morning, he was gone."

"Gone to where?"

"Back to the Army in the Land of Tilmun, where the Lady NinMah has sway and holds Command of the Landing Fields near her mountains."

"How do you come to leave the Army?"

"We received a message. My beloved is with child."

"She is?" stammered Celiste.

Deem turned to her with a raised eyebrow. "I did not know," said Celiste while she pushed her straw hat away from her face. She turned and pointed to where Eglan worked with six other women.

They watched the man walk toward Eglan and the women who were digging the 'unholy' weeds. Deem glanced at Celiste then back at the workers in the distant field. Without looking he said, "You said, *'My love'* to me."

"Yes."

"Can you say it one more time?"

"Yes, I can."

"Well?"

"And what shall I receive?" she asked in the voice of a little girl about to receive a gift from her father.

"What do you wish to receive?"

"You, my love."

Deem turned to look into her eyes. "Your words say much."

Celiste raised her hands to his face and cupped his cheeks. She leaned into him and kissed his nose.

Deem looked quickly in the direction of the field workers but no one was watching the two of them. He paused and put his hands on her shoulders and said, "And you, my love."

Celiste turned her face down. When she looked up at him there was a drop of wetness in the corner of one eye.

"There is pain in my heart," he added.

"Yes. Will it always be this way, that you are here when the sun goes down behind the mountains and then you leave after the sun rises in the east?"

"My love …there I said it again," and he added, "when Captain Shar moves to his northern island and leaves '*his ship*' as he calls it, I will have to decide."

"Between your beautiful ship *Cead,* the first Deep Black ship to arrive here at Kien, and me, a lowly female with her feet in the dirt?"

"Yes, that will be the dilemma. Almost ten years now on *Cead* and *Dara* and I know everything about both ships."

She said nothing. She lowered her face again.

"I envy that man and his Eglan. And Dren and his mate Drenay. I hear she also is with child."

"It is the planet," she answered with a laugh. "Being on your back to make a baby must work."

He looked at her. Something said, 'Stay' but he felt a pull to get moving in *Dara*. He leaned forward and kissed her on the forehead. She looked up at him and said, "So, go!" To her, 'Go' felt like a swear word.

Chapter 43

That evening Eglan brought one of her field workers to Celiste with a complaint. The woman, said Eglan, was complaining about back pain while she worked and two of her friends reported she had been sick several times in early morning. Her friends probably wanted to make conditions better for their friend.

Eglan reported that she believed the woman had slept with one of the guards. Dren, standing in back of the room in the 'temple' added, "No, none of my guards."

When Celiste said, 'How do you know?' the director of the guards said, 'well, I asked them,' to which several of the women present laughed.

Celiste looked at the woman Nanar. "Can you continue to work in the fields?"

The woman probably thought she was being offered a reprieve and said, "No, my lady, the bending gets my back to making twinges."

"Are you weak in the morning?"

"I get confused and walk in the wrong places."

Someone in the group standing behind the woman said, "She gets confused easily and sleeps with the wrong man." There was more laughter.

"Is that true?" said Celiste. She stared at the woman.

The woman said nothing. Celiste repeated herself.

The woman said, "Do not be harsh, my lady."

"Is that true?" said Celiste for the third time.

"Yes."

"Do you remember the punishment?"

"He was not my mate. I have no mate"

"Did he have a mate?"

"I did not enjoy his attention. When I said, No! …he ignored me."

Celiste considered this situation, and asked again: "Did he have a mate? It was a man was it not? From this village of Arad?"

"Yes, my lady, to all questions."

"Will you tell us his name?"

The woman stood quietly and looked at Celiste then around at the group in the room. Her eyes did not stop on anyone. The person she sought was not present.

"My lady," said Eglan. She was nominally in charge of the field workers.

Celiste said "Do you know the punishment"

To which Eglan replied, "I do."

"How should I rule?" asked Celiste. As in any army the field hands had a person, Eglan, who gave them directions. Her opinion carried weight with Celiste's decision.

Eglan thought for a moment then lowered her head and without looking at Nanar said, "We all know the penalty is death."

The group of women, with the guards standing outside their circle, became quiet and looked at Lady Celiste. Someone quietly said, "Mercy."

"There is a problem, here. I do not know the name of the man." She told Nanar to stand directly in front of her where she could see her eyes.

"You will tell us his name," She said in harsh sounds.

"No, my Lady. He is the father of my…"

"That is what Eglan and I think. He will be a father." She looked across the small gathering of women and then paused.

"Well, we have a dilemma." Someone in the crowd said, "Mercy." Celiste looked at the gathered women and said, "Here is my decision."

"You will be sentenced to two years in our other post, the cave up the valley. For now, Drenay will go with you." When she looked at Drenay she saw only despair. "Dren and two men will haul bedding and cooking pots and storage pots of our crops up to the cave. You will begin to make the cave useable."

From the back of the group Dren said, "What of the large cat?"

"The cat will decide if Nanar should live. She will deal with the cat before Drenay is permitted to enter."

In the morning, when Dren, his mate Drenay, and Nanar left with supplies loaded on the village wagon, he knew his role was to get the wagon to the base of the path that led upward to the valley cave. The three rode the wagon for some distance then began to walk when the hills became steep.

They walked for the better part of a day. The vertical valley ahead grew slowly. The sun was about to fall behind the mountains when they neared the mouth of the valley. Scattered green trees stood on precarious perches on the rocky slopes above the path. There were large rocks and the occasional falling stone. The stream from above moved quickly past the narrow opening as it fell toward the village of Arad.

In late afternoon there were deep shadows in the valley. Sun bathed the brown and black rocks in the higher cliffs. Dren tied his horse to an old gnarled tree and gave the women the lighter loads of bedding to take to the cave. Then he realized they could not make it before nightfall and they camped near the wagon.

"What did my Lady mean 'to deal' with the cat?" asked Nanar.

"You will deal with the cat," remarked Drenay.

"How?"

"I will give you a spear. You can drive it out of the cave." Dren looked at her then added, "Be strong. It is possible the cat has already left for higher places in the mountains."

He looked at Drenay and she added, "I believe the Lady may have known the cat may have moved."

"Your words, they mean …"

"You had to be punished. Lady Celiste could not punish your child could she?"

Chapter 44

In the late afternoon, two days after Dren and his companions left, Eglan brought a new complaint to Lady Celiste. From what she could see, Sinar, the mate of Gastan, was showing bruises on her arms. That morning Eglan saw her cringe when a woman touched her side under her arm. When she asked Sinar how she felt, the woman said nothing. One of her work mates noted that Sinar had been sleeping with her mate for the last ten days.

A second woman said she heard loud voices and what sounded like a person being struck with a hand.

Eglan and Celiste chose to talk to her mate Gastan privately. When they talked to him, he said she had fallen down, and added that she was clumsy. When Eglan pressed him to explain, he began to say,

"She was hurt when she was with…"

Gastan stopped and stood quietly. He looked around, as if looking for a way out of the large room in Arad's temple.

"With who?" demanded Celiste.

The man stood silent. He looked at Celiste briefly, then at Eglan. Then he began a long dialog:

"A man is allowed to dream, is he not? To dream of one day holding his son? To dream that one day his son will join his father in working together? I have that right, do I not?"

"That may be true," said Celiste. She looked up when the old woman who cooks for her appeared at the door. She waved her away.

"That may be true," repeated Celiste.

"What of it?" added Eglan.

"It is my right," said Gastan. He stood a little taller. "So, when my friend asked if I would share Sinar with him, I asked for a large bag of dates that he brought from Sodom. He agreed."

"For what purpose?"

"A double purpose," said Gastan. "The man has two sons already. I knew he could provide me with a son. And I could travel to Salem with a load of onions and trade the dates for a weapon to protect our village."

"Is it your role to acquire weapons?" asked Eglan.

"No, mistress." Gastan stood and stared at Celiste. He did not look down and his face began to show color. Then he added, "My mate Sinar does as I tell her. I ordered her to sleep with the man."

"His name is…" began Celiste.

"I do not chose to…" he began before Celiste added, "You will be whipped. Ten strokes in front of the women. And the other man will receive twenty strokes before he is hung. If you do not name him, you will receive his twenty strokes on top of your ten strokes and the women in this village shall enjoy watching you hang."

Gastan stood while the meaning of her words sank in. "I am stronger than you are, Lady See-Leest-Ay," he said with a snarl.

"The whipping shall be carried out in the morning." She stopped and looked at Gastan.

"He is gone. He lives in Sodom."

"You will have ten days to recover from the whipping then you and Dren and four others shall go to Sodom and bring the man back to me."

When Gastan said nothing, she added, "If you fail, you will suffer the fate that I have decreed for the other man."

Eglan mentioned the matter of Nanar and the un-named man. Celiste looked at her as if she was puzzled, then added,

"If I find out you are the man who spent time with Nanar..."

"You will do what?" asked Gastan quickly.

From the back of the large room, near an opening, came the voice of Deem. He was dressed in his red tunic with his black cap. He wore a belt that held the leather pouch with his 'shooter' on his hip. "You will show respect to the Lady," he said when he began to cross the room.

Gastan began to back away from Celiste and Eglan, moving in the direction of the far opening to the outside. He said nothing.

"You are too merciful," said Deem.

Celiste looked up at the tall man with the straight nose and smiled. She shook her head. "He knows what will happen."

"If you be lenient," added Deem, "they will come to know you are weak. They begin to disrespect you." When she said nothing, he added, "This is not Shin'ar, where the lords make the rules and dispense justice."

"I am Lord in this forgotten hovel of broken houses."

"Yes, you are." He smiled.

"I showed mercy where it was necessary, with Nanar who is sentenced to two years' service in the mountains."

"And with Gastan?"

"The whip for abusing his mate. The other man will hang."

She said no more. She could not hang Gastan. It was the other man who violated the law against 'knowing' a woman who was not his mate. Celiste looked up at Deem and smiled. He made a small bow to Arad's mistress. Eglan bowed and left. A small breeze entered the cavernous room and ruffled the wall hangings.

There were six chairs made of roughly hewn lumber with leather to fit the user's backside. Deem walked to one and plopped into the chair.

Celiste walked over and looked down at him. He was her mate but there were times when she felt he was a stranger. It had been ten days since his last visit; ten days was a long time when you have strong feelings for your mate.

"What do you hear of the anger of Enlil toward the son of Enki, this one called Mar.Duk?"

He looked at her and began to slowly pull himself out of the chair. "My friend Shar and his mate have been reading a tablet they claim is a copy of a tablet written by Enoch, the builder of the Great Pyramid."

"And?"

"I will tell you later. I am heading for the washing house."

"Is this how you disrespect a Lady who asks a question?"

"It is only because I respect you," he said and added, "that I will be presentable when I make my 'report' to the Lady Celiste."

He turned and walked toward the doorway that led out to the washing house. She smiled and her tongue caressed her lips. *Deem makes a false impression. Perhaps he is...*she began ...*trying to pretend there is nothing between us. How do I get him to admit his love?*

Chapter 45

The first thing Deem revealed to Celiste when he returned from *Dara* wearing a clean uniform was news about troop movements in Shin'ar, the valley between the two rivers.

"What you know from past trips is this: Lord Enlil has a temple at Nippur, a site north of Eridu where he controls the flights of his shuttles to and from his spaceport, Sippar. I have been there once. His temple in Nippur has a large flat space on top of the temple. It is perfect for a shuttle landing and easy to protect."

"The Lord Mar.Duk has decided to make his capitol at Babylon, an ancient site destroyed in the first and second floods. Lord Mar.Duk has not asked permission from Lord Enlil to re-build Babylon. Enlil is furious that he was not asked. This breach of relations prompted the building of an army when Enlil realized Mar.Duk wants to control the landing zone in the desert peninsula they call Tilmun."

Celiste was seated at the small table in her sleeping room that she used for preparing her face. Her maid was cutting her hair to a length the women called 'first knuckle,' the length of the end joint in her thumb. Celiste had made public statements about short hair being easier to wash, even though the opportunities to wash hair were rare.

Her maid was a Beag field worker that hurt her leg in a water canal. Celiste gave her 12 days of work in the temple to recover. She finished cutting Celiste's hair, brushed it slowly, then left the room.

Celiste stood up. The soft white robe she wore reached to her ankles. The robe showed the soft curve of her hip while it hid the rest of her charms. To Deem she said, "Do you see this robe? It was a tribute from Dren and Drenay. He found it in the marketplace at Salem."

"He has been busy, that leader of guards."

"Do not be …" she began, then added "envious. He was here. You were not."

He smiled at her then walked toward her sleeping platform while he unbuckled his leather belt. He sat and removed his boots. She took steps toward him while she unlatched the wide belt at her waist. Her robe fell open briefly; she pulled it across her body.

"I knew what you just told me."

"The tablets of Enoch tell of a time before the Great Flood."

"What was this flood?"

"A mass of water hundreds of cubits deep; it covered the earth."

"All the earth?"

"Except the mountain tops."

"How did that happen? Does Enoch say?"

"The planet of Lord Anu passed by. The Lords knew it was coming. Lord Enlil wanted to punish the Sons and Daughters of Kien, the children of the I.gi.gi (the Watchers) who came down to mate with Daughters of Kien. The Titans were evacuated. They saw the death of their children from the heavens; there was much turmoil and weeping."

Celiste stood; she was quiet. She had been using a short brush to clean her scalp. She turned toward Deem with a look of distress on her face.

Deem turned away. He saw the 'maid' return with a small brush to sweep the deck. "Should this maid be here?"

The maid straightened up and said, "As my mistress wishes," and bowed toward Deem.

"She is a friend," said Celiste. "I trust her. She hurt her leg."

To the maid he said, "Go and ask the cook for her best herbal drink, cold, three of her baked rolls and a slab of meat. We will eat here."

He watched the maid leave. When she was out of the room he explained the text of Enoch's tablet.

"There were wars. In the distant past. Mar.Duk was Commander of Abzu and the mines. He wanted control of the Land of the Pyramids. He built an army and marched north. He made demands. One of the Counselors, as we refer to them, named Dumuzi met with Mar.Duk and some kind of accident happened. Dumuzi died."

"A royal died?" she asked with disbelief across her face.

"His mate was Inanna, goddess of the Land of Pyramids where she is worshipped as Ishtar. She urged attacks and built a force to attack Mar.Duk. The battles spread across several years. Mar.Duk was imprisoned inside E.kur, the Great Pyramid."

"Imprisoned?"

"Lord Enlil could not find reason to kill Mar.Duk." [Endnote xi]

———— ∞ ————

"Our Lord, the one they call Enlil, decided to destroy the seed of mankind by allowing the Great Flood to over-whelm our lands which were not elevated above the oceans." [Endnote xii]

———— ∞ ————

"Enoch states Lord Enki pleaded with Enlil for the lives of any who were righteous. Enki was especially fond of the king of Shu.Rup.Pak, his brother-in-law, one called Utnapishtim. Enki told him to build a large boat and to put his family and all the seeds of living things in the boat." [Endnote[xiii]]

"Then the flood came?"

"Yes, it killed most of the Beag upon the earth."

"And the Aryas? Those who were fathers to the children?"

"The Aryas gathered at Sippar, Enki sent all the shuttles. In the days before the flood, they gathered aboard the three Deep Black ships. Enoch says many of the men cried and were in great pain when they saw the death of their mates and their children."

"But Enlil was satisfied; his command was honored?"

"That is why the Aryas call him Lord of the Lands."

Celiste shook her head; she rejected the obvious idea that the Lord Enlil had the right to watch the death of the children of Kien. "But then they had to rebuild their cities?"

Eridu, Nippur and Sippar were rebuilt. But the land to the north came to dominate Shin'ar. Inanna supported a king named Sargon and he became dominant in the Land between the Rivers. Inanna is known as the Goddess of Love, but she is a seductress of men."

Chapter 46

On the path up to the cave, Nanar carried an old spear. It was a sturdy pole onto which a sharp spike of forged iron had been grafted. She had pulled her long hair back and wrapped it. She wore both of her coats as extra protection. She felt her legs were exposed; she thought the cat might attack her legs.

The air was brisk; the day was clear as she walked slowly up the path. The heat of the sun felt good in her hair. She was about to turn a corner around a large boulder when a ground bird, large enough to eat, suddenly jumped into her path. Nanar reacted on instinct; she threw her spear.

Her spear bounced off a stone in the path. The tip came up and struck the bird in the neck. She ran forward; the bird struggled. She put the spear across the bird's neck. With her foot on the spear she reached down and broke the bird's neck. Coming around the rock behind her, one of the women said,

"What will you do with that thing?"

Nanar looked at the limp bird for a long time. Then she smiled. She asked for a cutting knife and began to cut the bird into pieces. She threw the feathers over the edge of the path.

"Throw a piece into the cave. Wait a while. Throw a piece into the cave mouth and outside the cave. If the cat comes out I will prod it to move into these mountains."

It was late in the day when Dren, Gastan and four guards walked into Arad, after a long five-day trek to Sodom and back. Their faces were covered in dust; their hair matted; their clothes carried mud. Behind them came a stranger with a rope fastened around his neck. Dren pointed at the post in the center of the plaza in front of Celiste's Temple. Gastan and the guards tied the man with each arm on one side of the post. They ran a rope through an iron ring and pulled his arms up until he stood on his toes.

Dren pointed at two of the guards and they took up station at opposite sides of the post, their backs to the prisoner.

Another guard brought a pack over to Gastan and opened it. He gave a jug to Gastan who took it to one of the guards. The guard sniffed the jug and took a long swallow. Gastan took the jug to the second guard and he also took a long swallow. He gave the jug to the two remaining guards and retrieved a similar jug from the pack.

He gave the jug to Dren who also sniffed the contents. "Three days older, would you say?"

"Aye, we have earned this drink," said Gastan.

Dren raised the jug, took a drink and spent some time considering the contents. He swallowed and said, "Aye, you are correct."

One of the maids who serve Lady Celiste walked up to Dren and said, "My mistress wishes you to visit the Washing House then she will meet you and Gastan here at the post.

The sun was touching the mountains when Celiste and two male guards stepped out of her temple. She wore a black gown to signify her intent to administer the law. "Your name is?" said Celiste to the man tied to the post.

"Water."

Celiste looked at Dren then at Gastan. "How long with no water?"

"Two days," said Gastan.

She looked at Dren then at the small crowd that was growing on the plaza. She looked down at her emblem of office, the silver ring with seven white gems, and said, "No water?"

"My lady," began Gastan, hoping to please her. "He comes to be punished. He deserves his thirst."

"So he does."

She looked at the jug in Gastan's hand and pointed at the prisoner. Gastan opened his mouth to protest and stopped. Celiste pointed at the prisoner. Dren said, "That was to be Gastan's reward for the long trek yesterday and today."

"Gastan does not deserve a reward."

"Yes, my lady," said Gastan quickly. He held the jug where the prisoner could drink from the open mouth of the jug. He watched as the man drank until the jug was empty, and Gastan backed away from the man.

"What is your name? The Lady Celiste demands you answer."

The man said nothing. He leaned in and wiped his forehead on the post. Celiste saw his silence and said to Gastan, "Apply the whip."

Gastan unhooked his whip from his belt and snapped it back toward the witnesses. He flicked it forward to gauge the distance. "I am ready," he said in a soft voice.

"You will tell us your name," said Celiste. She nodded at Gastan and the whip flew smartly across the plaza before it bit into his back. She nodded again and Gastan applied the whip. The man jumped a little, as if stung by a scorpion. She nodded again and again the whip attacked the man's back.

"Malor," said the man.

Celiste held up a hand to stop Gastan and his whip. "So tell me, Malor, how many dates did you pay to Gastan?"

"A large bag of dates," he said.

"Did you hit Gastan's mate, Sinar?"

"It was an accident," he said with strong conviction. Celiste nodded at Gastan and once more the whip bit into Malor's back.

"Stop, I ask you ...my lady?"

Celiste held up a hand to stop Gastan. "We stop," she said then added in a soft voice, a voice to convey hope, "Tell me the truth now, did you sleep with Sinar?"

"Sleep? No, mistress. She would not let me sleep," he made a guttural sound. "She kept pestering me for, you know, more of me and then she climbed on top and really seemed to enjoy herself."

"Do you know the penalty?"

"I buy what I get," said Malor. "I always pay."

"In this case, you have bought yourself a rope."

The man looked at Celiste for a long moment while he absorbed her words. "Can there be mercy?"

"No, you have convicted yourself out of your own words." She turned her back to the man and walked to Gastan. She pointed at the Temple where an arch formed the entry. "You see the iron ring above the entry?"

Gastan nodded.

"Then hang this piece of Beag trash, slowly, after you cut off his male member as a warning to any man who might do likewise."

"Mistress, did you forget? I am Beag," he snarled.

"You caused this spectacle. You finish it."

She turned away from the gathering. As she did she glanced at Dren, the only Aryas male present on the plaza. Dren did not smile but he nodded toward Celiste.

She walked into her temple to the farthest room; she almost did not hear the man's screams.

"The Titans," said Deem when they were alone in her sleeping quarters, "are making frantic plans to lift some of the Aryas out of the areas where the two armies will someday face each other." He untied his belt and removed his red tunic and lay down on their bed. He raised a foot and Celiste came to untie his sandals.

"Is there a reason?" she asked.

"Yes. The Shar.Graz. Both armies have the Shar.Graz."

Celiste looked at Deem with a blank face. Her hand found its way onto her stomach. She turned her head to look into his eyes.

"It is called the Thunderer, although it explodes into a brilliant sun of glowing white that stings the eyes before the cloud turns blue and black. The cloud expands and grows while it brings death to a large area."

"Would they use it?"

"Captain Shar says Lord Enlil believes it may be hard to defend the spaceport in Tilmun, which is Mar.Duk's objective."

Celiste came over to their bed and sat next to Deem. She placed her hand on his knee and said, "We have people in the southern army."

"They are Beag, after all," he said and moved his hand onto her arm.

"Some of them are trustworthy."

"Like that man Gastan?"

"No, he is the worst example. I do not trust him."

She moved her hand up his arm and onto his chest where she twirled her fingers through the hair on his chest. He smiled up at her just as she said in distraction, "We must warn them."

"Warn them?" he mused. "You do not trust them."

"We must try. Their mates are here, in my village."

"And you must?" he asked.

"I am Celiste, daughter of Essa. I must."

"Can we do that tomorrow?"

He enjoyed the comfort of her bed and the feeling of the planet's pull that he could not feel when aboard *Cead.* He thought, *Celiste, you are Aryas always. But I know how to make you smile.*

He reached up and put his hand behind her neck and slowly drew her down to his lips.

Chapter 47

"It is strange how these royals prepare for war," said Deem when he walked off the ramp at the rear of *Dara*. The day was almost over; the sun was behind the mountains to the west.

"Five days this time," said Celiste in a quiet voice. She stood next to him, head bowed. She had walked in from field work in the onion fields.

Deem smiled and said, "Yes, my love."

He debated the question, *Should I tell her about the troops of Mar.Duk's army who have moved south toward the Land of Tilmun?* But he thought ... *this is not the time.* He was dirty after five days of almost constant flight and needed to visit the Washing House.

He turned toward her and saw his mate in her white work clothes, with dirt in the knees of her trousers. When she removed her conical hat he reached up and plucked an onion stem from her short hair. There was a smudge of dirt near her nose; freckles were scattered under her eyes. She licked her lips; he thought about kissing her. Standing here outside her Temple in full view of her women field workers, he decided to avoid the trouble such an action might cause.

"You said it was strange?"

"Yes, I loaded the tablets of Enoch in Akkad, where King Sargon has a scribe making new copies. *Dara* and I moved the tablets to the Great Pyramid. They were loaded on a barge and sent down river. Princess Inanna told me they would be placed in long boats and sent beyond the Great Sea to a new place of safety."

"Were the tablets stored in E.kur, the House of the Gods?"

"At one time. The princess referred to them as 'Tablets of the Ages' that told the story of the Lords and their wars before the flood."

"There is a reason to move the tablets?" she asked.

"There must be," he responded then added "the Princess tells me there are storm clouds on the horizon. Such an unusual expression."

"Is she easy to look at, this Princess Inanna?"

"Her beauty exceeds all the deep red color of the sky just before the Sun falls off the earth." Deem smiled to himself then realized what he had said to Celiste.

"She is beautiful, then?"

Deem put his hands on her shoulders and said, slowly, "Her beauty is but a dim reflection of your beauty. You are more beautiful than the red turning into pale red just before the sun revisits the earth. Your beauty out-shines the light blue of our pale sky in early morning."

Celiste's lips formed into slight smiles. One eyebrow went up as if to ask, *who told you to flatter your mate?*

Deem reached into his bag of equipment and produced a gift made of papyrus. The sheet was folded over itself into a square. A wax mass over the center of the square held the logograph of Lady Ninki. He held it out to Celiste and said, "This came to me from Lady Inanna. She made me promise to put it into your hands."

Celiste looked at the folded document and her face betrayed her sense of concern. She knew what this message might be.

"Make yourself presentable. We will open this together with Eglan and Dren in my Temple."

She saw Eglan among the women and waved her over. Celiste told Eglan that she and Dren were expected to be in her Temple room after Captain Deem was presentable.

She said this laughing with a hand open, as if 'presenting' Deem.

His face was blank before he also began to laugh. "Are you presentable?" he quipped as he began to walk toward the Washing House.

Over time the Central Room of the Temple began to acquire a mystique, as if the people who lived in Arad knew the Temple held sacred mysteries. When Celiste, Deem, Dren and Eglan arrived, they stood near the new stone altar in the center of the meeting room. The walls had acquired large wool banners, made by two women using a loom and wool spun into long strands. One of the banners depicted Celiste arriving; the *Dara* sat in the background. Deem, when he saw it, politely teased Celiste. He laughed and said, "Where am I in this banner?"

She laughed and smiled while she said, "Are you the goddess of this small village, this Arad?"

The altar was behind a sunken fire pit where coals heated and burned herbs. If the priestess (Celiste) wanted the community to arrive, she would add chemicals that made the smoke white. There were six chairs in a circle around the sunken fire pit. The four friends, however, stood.

"We sent three wagons of food and three more large containers for water up to the cave. Four of the women have worked hard to get those supplies up to the cave," added Celiste.

Dren chuckled. "I hear gossip that Nanar was brave," said Dren He scratched his hair above his ear. "She says the 'ferocious' cat swung his vicious claws at her and she thrust her spear."

"Are her words true?"

"Let's say they are. I was far back but I saw her throw the spear. It hit the ground and whacked the cat in the rear. The cat ran up the path; it stopped. Nanar stepped around the large boulder and shouted at the poor cat. It turned and walked away, as if to say, *'I go, you not make me'*."

"She and Drenay have moved the food to the back of the cave," added Dren with a note of pride.

"Yesterday she wanted to know why so much for only two women?"

"A friend warned me," said Celiste. She did not say that it was Lady Ninki, the aged and somewhat infirm mate of Lord Enki.

"Warned you?" said Eglan with a look of concern. Her hands went around her swollen belly. "My mate should know about this."

"He does not know?" said Deem with a wicked smile.

"You mean, about the baby?" she laughed.

Celiste told Deem that Eglan's mate Ashur had been in Arad for the past thirty days. "Of course he knows," she laughed.

"About what?" added Dren. He was confused.

"The Lords Enlil and Mar.Duk are at war," said Celiste. She raised the folded papyrus and held it for her friends to see. She placed it against the edge of the altar and cracked the seal. She unfolded the crinkly item and found a single word inside … 'Deacair.'

She showed it to Deem who passed it to Dren and Eglan.

"What does it mean?" asked Eglan.

"We must take all our women and move to the cave."

"Do we have time?" asked Eglan.

"Two days it takes," added Dren. "One day to the valley, one up to the cave."

"There is other news," said Deem. "I was not going to tell you this," he said to Celiste. "I was afraid for you. I want you to come aboard *Dara*."

She looked at him and said, "What news?"

"From *Cead,* we saw two strikes from the Shar.Graz. Off to the east where it could only have been Lord Rama. There were two bright as sun blossoms over the horizon. We think Lord Rama hit Mohenjo-Daro and Harappa, the two cities of the Hittite kings aligned with Mar. Duk."

"Oh, this is…" began Celiste. "I have no words."

"There is worse…" added Deem. "Today I flew over Sodom. I saw a large camp. There is a large camp of troops near the south edge of Sodom."

"That is a terrible place," said Dren. He smiled and added, "Perhaps the troops are to punish the wicked men in Sodom."

"How do you mean?" asked Deem.

"You cannot see their depravity from the air. The men have a fondness for boys," responded Dren. His eyebrow went up in a look of chagrin.

Celiste looked at Dren for a moment then added, with slow words, "That man Gastan. I sent him to the south. I told him to tell our men to resist the orders of the 'old' Royals and find protection in the mountains."

"He did not listen," said Dren. "We have a message. He formed a troop out of 'his' men and is leading them."

Celiste blew air out of her cheeks. Eglan turned away and said something like 'hard to believe' but her friends knew she meant the opposite. Deem shook his head and walked around the altar to put his arms around Celiste. She looked up at him.

"We are going to the cave."

"I know," he began. "While I was in the Washing House, Aonim brought a message. I am ordered to the southern spaceport."

"When you are there can you persuade Gastan and his men?"

"To do what?" asked Deem without a smile.

"I do not know…" Celiste looked at Dren, then Eglan, then back at Deem. "Perhaps to tell the Beag who trust him to take their camels and head for shelter in the mountains?"

"Can you trust Gastan?"

"We can make the effort. If he betrays us …what will happen?"

Chapter 48

"My love," he said quietly.

Celiste stood with her head nuzzled under his chin. She felt her feet getting cold. Dressed in her white gown, she knew she would prefer to get into the heavy blankets of her sleeping platform. She tightened her arms and pulled him closer. She felt his hand run down her back until his strong hand cupped her bottom. This was a signal; he wanted to climb into her bed.

"My love," she said into his chest. There was so much she wanted to say, but could not. *There are other pilots who can fly Dara?* she thought while he held her. *Such as Aonim; you trained him well.*

"Come with us in the morning," she said and placed her hand on his stomach.

He leaned back so he could see her face. He reached to the small table and raised the belt that held his 'Shooter,' the small pistol. "I want you to have this."

"My love," she said again.

"Wear my 'Shooter.' It gives you authority."

"Come with us," she said again.

"No, you are coming with me," he said slowly, barely hoping she would say 'Yes' but knowing she would stay with 'her' people.

She moved her hand up his back until she could pull him toward her mouth. She leaned up and into him and caught his lower lip between her teeth and said, "I am the Lady Celiste, mistress of Arad."

He laughed.

"And I command you," she mumbled while her tongue explored his teeth. She withdrew her tongue and meshed her lips with his lips ever so softly and slowly. He hummed something, an old lover's tune.

"And now I command you to join me."

"Where would that be?"

She laughed. She reached behind her and pulled his hand off her hip, to her waist. "Where we usually join each other."

"Ah," he mumbled and dropped his belt on the stone floor of her bed chamber. He began to unfasten the flap on his tunic. "I must go in the morning."

"I must lead my people," she stated flatly.

She watched his reaction. He shrugged out of his tunic and tossed it to the floor. She added, "If I could I would go with you."

"I know," he said. His face had no expression.

"But for tonight," he began.

"I want to be under you," she softly caressed the muscles of his chest. He stood a little taller.

"And then the second time…"

"Second time?"

"I want to be on top." She took his hand and pulled him toward the bed. He unwound the cloth band that held his trousers and let them drop. She stopped with her back to him and pulled her white gown up over her head. She held the smallest jug; she removed the stopper and dabbed drops between her breasts. The scent of cinnamon surrounded them. She backed up and reached for his hands. She took his hands and moved them to her waist then up over her stomach she moved them ever so slowly while she hummed and said,

"Yes, my love. A second time. It is time we make a baby."

Chapter 49

All four wagons were loaded. The four horses that belonged to Arad were about to haul their cargo up the long winding trail to the west, toward the path up the valley to the cave. Each wagon had been assigned six women who knew their task was to move the wagon if the horse faltered. They had thrown their bags of possessions onto 'their' wagons.

Three of the guards stood at the head of the caravan. One of them wore the village's main weapon, the *Shar.Ur*, known as the 'Supreme Hunter.' They waited and watched the women prepare. The one called Ashur nodded toward Eglan and said, "My mate. Her stomach grows."

"We know," laughed Shen. "My brother Gastan was smiling from ear to ear. He left ten days ago."

"He smiled?" said Shen.

"Yes. He smiled when he looked at your mate."

"My mate?

"Is there something she has not told you?" quipped Ashur.

Shen stood still while he looked down the line of wagons to where his mate was helping with a wagon. Then he looked up at Ashur and saw Ashur with a grin that could swallow an entire onion. He laughed.

"Perhaps we are better off that Gastan, his high holiness, has gone to join the army," laughed the third guard.

They watched Dren, their guard captain, as he stopped at each wagon to check on the women. When he reached the last wagon he talked to Celiste. He waved an arm at the guards; his motion meant for them to begin. Shen turned to the nearest wagon and said, "We go."

One of the women took a long switch and snapped it on the rump of their horse. He turned to look at her as if to say, *'What?'* but took a first step forward and the wagon creaked. With his second step the wagon began to move. The six women walked along beside the wagon. The guards turned toward the path and led the way.

At the rear of the caravan a load of onions, hidden under a mat of straw, waited for Lady Celiste. Her badges of office were inside a small box at the bottom of the onions. It was hoped the straw would keep the onions cool. Celiste and her maid spread blankets over the straw. The women of the wagon then placed their small bags over the blankets.

The second and third wagons began to move. Celiste looked up and saw Talinda, mate of the caretaker of Arad coming out of the temple with a folded and wrapped package. Talinda presented the package to Celiste.

"Your two red tunics and white trousers for the fields," she said.

"Have you considered your decision?"

"Yes, my lady. We stay. There are floors to wash; clothes to wash; we will enjoy the quiet.

"And your mate? Where is he?"

"He returns from Sodom in two days, my lady."

"Very well, then."

Celiste put the package with the other small bundles that nestled in the blankets above the onions. She saw they were being left behind and told Dren to get them moving. When the wagon began to move she turned to Talinda and said, "You and your daughter will be careful?"

"My mate, two days, the three of us will look after Arad."

Celiste nodded her head. She thought of Deem and Aonim aboard *Dara* and the twenty-four Beag in the army with Gastan and her own twenty-four brave women, some of them with child, walking ahead of her. In her mind she saw the long path under a hot sun. She enjoyed the heat from the sun; it was a pleasure she never experienced on her birth planet. She remembered 'Old Sleam' and his attention to the atmosphere and the vagaries of the winds. She remembered the cold on the ice pack when they built 'Sleam's Reflectors.' She remembered the feel of rain on her face the day she parted from Essa, her father. *What could I say about him?*

We will build a stela, here in Arad, she thought. In her mind she saw her friends helping to sanctify a stela with the names of those who died from the Shar.Graz bomb that exploded in her village, beloved Ibri.

She felt tired. This past night would be a memory she would hold and cherish. She tried to remember Deem's arms around her. She could taste his kisses on her lips, his kisses on her neck.

Shen, the man she rescued from the ore mines suddenly said, "My Lady, your eyes?" then added, "Your eyes are leaking water."

Celiste reached up and touched her eye. She brought her finger around to her nose and saw dampness, and smiled.

"It is a new pleasure you and I never felt in Ibri." She paused then added, "My grandmother talked about these. They are called tears."

"Yes, my Lady."

Celiste watched the brave, older Talinda walk toward 'her' Temple. She scanned the horizon and saw few clouds. She felt satisfied; they were prepared.

At the end of a long day the caravan made camp at the opening into the mountains. They formed a square with the wagons and posted guards outside the camp. Dren and Shen built a cooking fire in the center and the women boiled onions and some of their last supply of meat. It was tough meat, as some said, but they believed the boiling would make it tender.

"It was an old cow to begin with," said one of the women.

"Another of Gastan's foolish decisions," said another.

"We are not all foolish," said another referring to the twenty-four Beag in their party. The wind from the valley became stronger just before a loud roaring was heard coming from the valley ahead of them.

The roaring became louder. Celiste could feel the sudden increase in the wind coming out of the valley. "It's a blast of mashed air," she shouted at the women who were looking toward the valley.

Chapter 50

The wind diminished during the night. By day break there was only a soft breeze flowing down through the rocky cliffs that guarded the valley and its canyon. The women boiled beans and onions for a meal and washed as they could in the swift stream that flowed out of the valley. Dren and his men helped load bags of supplies for the backs of the women. The entire caravan knew they faced an uphill climb with a weight on their backs.

After the women left the men took the Shar.Ur and pointed it at the head of their oldest horse. The weapon whined for a moment before a flash of light cracked the air; the horse dropped onto its side. Dren and his crew began to carve the horse. Lady Celiste had asked, politely, that more meat be hauled to the cave.

Going up the path Shen took the lead, the women followed. The narrow path followed a mind of its own; it meandered up and around boulders then down and around other boulders. Always, the path rose upward. The sun was high over-head when the first of the long line reached the cave. They were welcomed by Drenay and Nanar. Both women displayed enlarged breasts and long gowns tightly stretched across their bellies.

Drenay was quickly told her mate Dren was coming up the path. Nanar showed Shen where to store his load of firewood while Drenay led the women to the area for storing supplies. Six of the women were assigned to finish filling the large water jars. The long string of tired women brought their first loads into the cave. Celiste arrived at the end of the 'walking caravan' as she described it.

After resting the men who struggled up the path with loads of meat, already attracting black flies, turned to the path and walked down for a second trip. The women followed.

They made the return trip up the path in less time. They carried smaller bags of supplies and their clothes. Dren brought an enormous pile of blankets up the path. Celiste hauled a load of onions wrapped in one of her blankets. Two men came up the path slightly bowed from the weight of firewood on their backs.

The path was in shadow when the long 'caravan' reached the cave. Above them, the sun was beyond the mountain tops. A long shadow was cast across the flat land where stood Arad and across the eastern sea. In the far distance the shadow was beginning to paint darkness on distant mountain tops. Celiste was at the end of the line, behind the men with the firewood. Directly ahead of her a flat boulder blocked the path.

A brilliant white flash lit the valley. The flash was intense; the stones and trees in the valley cast black shadows. Celiste was frozen; she saw her shadow outlined on the flat granite rock. She began to turn to look toward the source; she stopped. The bright white light was beyond her experience; she felt humbled.

The light began to fade. Celiste heard Dren call her name and she told him she was around the boulder. She turned toward the source and saw an enormous black cloud climbing into the red light from the setting sun. There was white lightening and red flashes within the cloud; it grew and boiled into the heavens. She remembered the old seer: *'You will see the black cloud of death rising with anger and darkness.'*

Dren walked up beside her. "What is it?" he asked.

"A black cloud of anger. Deem warned me they might use the Shar. Graz, the weapon that is lifted into the sky on a blast of fire and falls onto an enemy. It is called the 'Brilliance of Enlil' for the whiteness of the light.

"Is that Sodom?"

"Yes."

As she said this a second white flash appeared. It was over the horizon, beyond the mountains south of the great lake. A moment later the mountains to their south were back-lit by three white flashes that sent white light into the sky, illuminating high, thin clouds.

"Where is that?" asked Dren.

"The Land of Tilmun, the great southern peninsula, the restricted zone." She realized there must have been an army moving south toward the Army of Abram to force the use of such devastating weapons.

"I was told to avoid the *Black Cloud.*"

Who knew about the cloud?" Dren was puzzled.

"An old woman. She said my father would be ...gone."

"We should be inside the cave, mistress?"

"You go. I am behind you," she shouted. *Time to walk* flashed through her brain. They began to move quickly toward the cave. The men with the firewood were entering the cave when an enormous 'Boom!' thundered up the canyon past their cave. Celiste found herself at the entrance of the cave and saw a woman below her, lugging a water jar up from the stream below the cave. She shouted at her to hurry.

Standing there, at this elevated site, she realized the valley opened to the east, as if she stood at the head of a funnel. If wind came from the East, it would be compressed by the walls of the canyon. She looked down the canyon and saw a wall of black boiling and roiling from the direction of the eastern sea. She knew, without being told, that she must get out of the path of that cloud of death. She looked down at the woman with the water jar on her shoulder and shouted at her to drop it and run to the cave.

The woman looked up at her with confusion. This was the woman who spent her free time in Arad making pots and jars from river clay and tending them until the fire hardened them. The jar on her shoulder was probably one of her creations.

Celiste saw the top of the black cloud, where it was illuminated by the setting sun, approaching the opening to the valley. She shouted once more but the woman continued to climb at a steady pace. Celiste turned her back to the cloud and rushed into the cave. She shouted at her people to get down.

An enormous rush of air passed the cave entrance. Some of the air suddenly increased the air pressure on everyone's ears. Then the sound of small rocks thrown against the canyon walls made a rippling sound in the canyon. The air pressure diminished and the blast of air passed up the canyon.

Celiste climbed to her feet and walked to the cave opening. There was no sign of the woman with the water jar.

———— ∞ ————

"Lady Celiste, what must we do?" asked Eglan.

"Stay in the cave until this black air has passed."

Celiste turned to see most of the women in the cave were looking at her. They believed she must know the answers. Celiste nodded at Dren and took him aside.

"We have water for four days. No one leaves the cave for four days," she said and added, "Post a guard. No one leaves."

To the women she explained that the black air outside was dangerous. They were to stay in the cave for four days and in the canyon for five days total.

Dren and two of the guards built a fire just outside the cave mouth. The fire was in the fire-pit Drenay used for cooking. One guard was assigned to stand just inside the cave mouth and to feed the fire during the night.

Toward morning, when the eastern sky was barely pink, the guard heard a 'swish' overhead and looked up. He saw a flash of silver, possibly reflected from *Dara* when it turned to circle overhead. *Dara* did not land; it climbed into the sky and flew east over the black cloud.

In the early morning, the wind changed direction. The soft current came out of the mountains and down the canyon. It was a scrubbing wind. It scrubbed the canyon and its rocks and sent a blast of air through the canyon mouth. Beyond the canyon the air cleared and it appeared the lingering black cloud was moving off to the east.

Later that morning Dren told Celiste that he could see their village Arad from the edge of the path. There was no apparent movement in the village, but then the distance was too great to see any details.

In late afternoon, before the sun touched the mountain tops 'behind' her canyon, Celiste walked out quickly and looked to the east. She saw the black cloud was climbing up the mountains beyond the eastern sea.

When she returned to the cave she told the women the black cloud had gone to the east. She then turned to Dren and asked what was beyond the mountains.

Dren was puzzled. He thought for a long moment. He looked at his mistress with confusion. He was not sure of her intentions in asking what was beyond the mountains to the east.

"The cities of Lord Enlil, Lord Anu and Lord Mar.Duk, the one they call Babylon," he said finally. "You mean?"

"Your mate Deem was talking about the cities that were rebuilt after the Great Flood. The gods declared that each city was the sacred precinct for one of the gods, there is even a temple called Erech, built to honor Anu and his queen Antu when they visited Kien from their planet. [Endnote[xiv]]

Chapter 51

"One of the women heard a whistle sound when the blast of heavy air went up the canyon," reported Dren.

Celiste waited. She wore a puzzled expression.

"Farther back in the cave," he added.

Sinalan walked over and added, "I told Shen there may be an updraft."

She wore an old dress this day, instead of work trousers and a light caftan. The women knew they would not dig onions and radishes this day. Sinalan took pride in her appearance; her hair was braided and coiled around her head. She saw Celiste looking at her head and added, "We could not sleep. We worked on our hair."

"The updraft?"

"Shen used an old hammer. There was a hollow sound. He hit the rock a mighty blow," added Dren.

"And?"

"A piece of rock hit his shoulder. Shen is 'damaged' shall we say?"

"Not that badly," added Sinalan, Shen's mate.

"And?"

"We have an updraft. We will move the cooking fire into the cave."

"Thank you," said Celiste without smiling. Later that day she took Dren aside. Her message was simple: *We cannot afford to lose any of these women or the men. We have an old village to re-build.*

∞

In the east, beyond the Eastern Sea, the mountains on the horizon became visible near the end of the day. The ominous black cloud was gone, passed beyond the mountains. The sun shone down on Arad, the quiet town. The sun shone down on the camp site used by the women when they evacuated Arad. The entire valley, from west to east, was quiet. There were no birds, no animals.

The first blast of the 'Brilliance of Enlil' was south of the Eastern Sea, the one they called *Yām-ha-Māret* (Sea of Death). The blast destroyed a once proud village. The walls of houses were crushed by a mighty weight. The defensive walls were pushed in by the force of the explosion. Their temple crumbled. The people who lived there with pride and contempt for the laws of Lord Enlil, the men who practiced an evil act with boys, all died. The village was quiet. The same fate was suffered by Sodom.

A crack formed in the southern wall of the sea; water poured into the low lands beyond. The waters covered the ruins of the once proud village. The waters rose and rose until Gomorrah was seen no more.

The army was moving. They were south of Sodom when the missile hit and obliterated the men, their wagons, their train of 'busy' women who follow an army always in search of work. Their hopes and fears for the future were wiped off the cosmic slate of the universe in one brash, ugly and painful moment under the white hot flash of Enlil's missile.

"My mate Gastan?" said the woman. She wore her best dress and her short hair fell straight to her ears. Her face was the face of a Beag with a very slight brow-ridge above her eyes. She had the brown eyes and light brown hair of a Beag; she was definitely not of Aryas stock. Her birth name La.Ra.Ak meant 'brightening glow.' When Lara walked up to Celiste and Dren, she bowed to both and made a slight smile. "I am here to ask about my mate."

"Your form is not correct," said Dren. "You should say *I ask the Lady Celiste to favor my humble request for information.*"

The woman stood taller for a moment. Her eyebrows formed into a frown. Then she bowed to Dren.

"Master Dren, I wish to ask…" she began.

"Yes, Lara, I understand."

Celiste reached over and patted Dren on the arm. "See to the cooking fire and ask the cooks to warm some herbals for Lara and Lady Celiste."

Dren nodded and walked toward the fire where it burned inside the newly built fire pit. Celiste took Lara by the arm and directed her toward planks that sat on top of empty storage boxes.

They sat and Celiste said, "What of your mate?"

"What can you tell me?"

"You know I sent him to the army in the south?"

"Yes, he told me that much."

"It was punishment," added Celiste quietly.

"I heard gossip from several of the women. They said nasty words to strike at me with their tongues and their vicious eyes."

"The ill wind blows from the east," noted Celiste.

"One of our men said there was a flash?"

"The mountains were lit by three flashes."

"Were they like the one that brought the Black Cloud?"

"Yes," said Celiste. *This woman must know the truth, or should I help her hold onto vague hope?*

"Gastan was directed to find the thirty-six Beag men we sent down there to serve two years in the Lady Ninmah's army. She is the goddess of Tilmun, the land beyond those mountains."

"Yes?" said Lara. She watched while one of her friends brought two small bowls of hot herbal potion. She took her bowl and smelled the herbals and raised an eyebrow.

"Gastan was directed to take his men into the mountains for their safety." Celiste watched while Lara took a tentative sip of the herbal.

"So he is alive then?"

"I want to say …Yes."

"He was not a good man," said Lara. "He beat me."

"There were reports," said Celiste.

"And he abused two of my friends."

"What are you telling me?"

"Of the three of us, we voted last night." Lara took another sip of the herbal and tasted her lip with her tongue trying to decipher the taste.

"You voted?"

"We voted. We do not care if he is alive. We prefer dead."

Celiste saw Dren nearby and waved him to come over. "Take Lara to her sleeping station. She needs sleep."

When Lara began to ask, Lady Celiste told her the herbal potion contained an elixir to help her sleep. Then Celiste apologized and said she feared Lara would be distraught if she knew her husband was dead. Lady Celiste then moved to her sleeping pallet and placed her head on a rolled up blanket. The smell of onions was strong. She began to smile to herself and hoped the herbal was strong. Three days without sleep was one too many.

Chapter 52

Day five began with a bang, or a whimper depending on your perception of the tension in the cave. The rising sun was only a weak suggestion in the eastern sky when the groans of Eglan became louder. The entire cave knew she was about to present her mate with a baby.

The two women who were helping Eglan became frustrated with Ashur and told him to slice a pile of wood into shavings and be prepared to heat a blanket to receive his child.

After the sun cleared the mountains in the east, the women began to tell Eglan she should scream. They knew she was trying to keep her pain inside; she should let it out. Everyone in the cave knew she was trying to be brave. It was time to stop the groaning.

One of the women said, "Now!" forcefully. Eglan screamed with a force that knocked small dust mites off the roof of the cave. One of the women placed a white cloth under the head of the baby and helped it to depart from its mother.

She held the baby by its ankles and smacked it on the rump. The baby made an intake of breath then cried loudly in protest. In the momentary silence following the baby's scream, the people in the cave smiled at each other. The woman turned toward the cooking fire and told Ashur he was the father of a baby girl.

———⊶⊷———

Mid-morning the sky was a brilliant blue color. There was a slight breeze from the west; a small bird came down the valley and found a site to build a nest inside the gnarled branches of a stubborn pine that refused to let go of its precarious perch on the rocky slope of the canyon.

Into this quiet scene came the sudden 'swish' of the shuttle *Dara*. The vehicle hovered near the cave until a guard stepped into the cave opening. Then *Dara* flew down the canyon; it stopped near the wagons of the women's camp. The guard stepped out of the cave opening to watch the flight of *Dara*. He saw the vehicle hesitate briefly over Arad before it flew to the Eastern Sea, the one they call 'Dead.'

When *Dara* returned she hovered above the cave opening. A small package with a colored cloth attached fell onto the path outside the cave before it bounced and rolled down the slope and stopped above the river. Moments later a much larger package, a cloth sack wrapped inside a blanket fell onto the path and rolled a few feet.

The guard brought the large package into the cave and untied the cords holding the bag. He held up a slightly red fruit called an apple. The women quickly gathered around him while he counted 80 apples. Then he looked up at Dren and told him about the small package on the slope.

———⊶⊷———

Celiste opened her eyes, but slowly. After Eglan's baby was born she felt tired and meandered into a nap. She smelled onions and remembered where she was. She tried to remember her dream about 'sailing' aboard *Cead* when she and Deem joined for the first time. Her dream faded into obscurity. She listened to the cave and heard silence.

When she turned her head she saw her friend Drenay sitting three cubits away from her, watching.

"We were told to let you sleep."

Celiste said nothing. Under her large blanket she stretched and felt the small pains of unused muscles and began to sit up.

"We have apples," said Drenay quietly.

"Apples?"

"*Dara* brought apples."

"And?"

"We wish to eat one. There are two for each of us."

Celiste nodded and Drenay slowly lumbered onto her feet. Her baby was close, the women believed. Her stomach was swollen tight inside her gowns. She wore a light blanket to keep warm. Drenay walked toward the gathering of women and said, 'Yes!' with a bounce in her voice.

Her mate Dren brought an apple to Celiste. He watched her admire the apple before he handed the small package to Celiste. She looked at him with a question in her eyes. Dren said 'It fell' meaning from *Dara*.

"You, me and Shen, outside," she said while climbing to her feet. Then she added, "No, wait!"

He turned back toward her; she opened the package. Celiste unfolded a message painted onto a papyrus sheet. She scanned the sheet until she saw the name at the bottom, then gave it to Dren. Her face was blank; her eyebrows marched together into a frown.

The name at the bottom read 'Aonim' with the symbol for Captain. Dren saw more than felt her shoulders slump. "You thought…"

"Yes, from Deem."

He looked down at the message: *Stay in cave until ten days. Your camp, two horses dead. Arad, three dead. The camp near Sodom is a vast empty field of ash. Cities: Gomorrah, Sodom, Zoar nothing. The sea covers their evil. All the Lords, families evacuated from Shin'ar. Aonim, Cpn.*

"Arad, three dead," said Dren stating the obvious. "Talinda, her husband…"

"Yes," said Celiste. She looked up at Dren, with expectation and fear in her eyes.

"You told me yourself that he trained Aonim to take over the *Dara* when he became captain of the *Cead.*"

"An evil wind from the east," said Celiste.

Dren looked at her.

"It means nothing good can come from the east. Shin'ar is the land of the four rivers that come down to the eastern sea."

Dren made a small nod of his head. But a frown formed.

"Deem told me the Titans saw Enoch's Great Flood happen."

Dren stood and looked at her. Her eyelids came up sharply and she shouted "Stop eating! Now!"

The women turned to look at her. One said "Stop?"

"Yes," shouted Celiste with authority. "Take all the apples and carefully wash them in the river. That is my order from this day forward."

The sun was behind the mountains to the west when Celiste stood near the cave opening, watching the mountains to the east turn dark blue then black. *You Lords,* she thought, *have the power. The Black Cloud came and you ran to the shuttles. Are you safe in the sky? How could you abandon the sons and daughters you, yourself …yes, created?*

One of the twenty-four women who worked by her side in the onion fields walked up and put her hand around Celiste's hand. Together they stood and watched the canyon become dark. They saw the flash of a bat as it fluttered by their cave.

"You are worried? I think?" said the woman called Layla by her mate.

"It has been fifteen days. He never stayed away this long."

"Dren tells us that Deem no longer has the *Dara.*"

"Captain of the *Cead* is my guess," said Celiste.

Layla squeezed Celiste's hand. It felt cold. There was a visible sheen across her forehead. There were little beads of sweat across the visible top of her chest. Layla reached over and touched her side and felt moisture through the cloth.

"I bring wind from the east," said Layla. When Celiste said nothing, she added, "Margon, the guard, is sweating. There are blisters around his stomach. He ran a hand through his hair and some of it came away in his hand. He asked me to apologize to you for him. He does not feel able to stand his work shift in the cave mouth."

Chapter 53

Celiste looked down at Margon where he was wrapped in blankets. His hair was matted and wet. His pale face tried to mask the pain in his stomach. When he turned his head more hair pulled out and fell onto an old blanket he used for a pillow.

"You were a guard that first night after the bright explosion?

"The enormous flash and black cloud? Yes."

"You were in the cave opening?"

"Yes, my Lady."

"We were all so tired. Dren thinks you were on duty all through the night. We forgot to send a replacement."

"Yes…" he began but something turned a vice in his stomach and his face turned white. A small groan escaped his mouth.

"Were you inside the entire night?"

"No. I was not," he mumbled between clenched teeth.

"You were not?"

"My mate was bringing water when you came and shouted at us to get down. She was on the slope to the river. You fell and I covered you to protect you."

"I fell?"

"Your voice had the sound of panic."

"And your mate?"

"She was gone."

"The air was black and full of small pieces of stone and sand and I do not know what else. I told everyone to stay out of the cloud."

"Yes, my Lady, you did." He coughed once, then choked on some saliva in his throat then coughed again. "I went out three times. Looking. Calling. The third time I went up the path with a torch.

"How long were you out?"

"A long time. Shouting her name. Looking. The sun was about to rise when I hurried back. You saw me come back. They were all sleeping."

"But you were in the canyon, breathing that air?"

"I held a cloth over my mouth."

"But not all the time?"

"No. I had to shout."

"I am sorry, Margon. There was a bad miasma inside that black cloud and you breathed it in."

"I know I am about to leave. Promise me something?"

"If I can?"

"Send a squad up the canyon and find her body."

"Her name was..."

"Surliann."

Celiste bit her lip. The woman's name meant 'foul weather' on their home planet. The name was equally applied to 'foul' mates.

Margon coughed again and a little blood leaked from his mouth.

"She was not that way. We only knew each other a short time. She was kind. She made pots and bowls in Arad. She was proud of her work."

"I will remember. We will erect a stone to you both."

The hint of a smile formed at one corner of Margon's mouth. He turned his head toward the wall and coughed. His hand moved and Celiste took it to mean, *'Thank you,'* and moved away.

———❦———

She felt cold. Two blankets were wrapped around her. Her feet felt cold. She touched her forehead. It was warm and damp. Layla came up to Celiste and gave her a small bowl of water. Celiste gulped it down.

"Drenay is with the pains."

"It is about time for her to produce a baby from that enormous belly of hers," said Celiste with a smile. "Who is with her?"

"Lara and Eglan and my big, brave bumbling mate, Shen."

"Shen? What is he…?"

"He is showing Dren how to allow Drenay to squeeze his hands through her pain. It is like some of the pain moves to her mate."

There was a long, slow scream from the isolated area of the cave. Three blankets were stretched over ropes to form a privacy wall. Celiste glanced back toward the blankets.

"We have a new Aryas arriving," she announced forcefully.

"That is right. I forgot both parents are Aryas," said Layla.

There was silence for a long period, broken by the sound of a slap and a baby's plaintive wail that grew into an outright cry of protest.

From behind the blankets Lara announced, *'It's a boy!'*

"And his name shall be Drensin."

When Celiste glanced at her, Layla added, "She told me."

"That is as it should be. You and Drenay are good friends."

Layla stood for a moment looking down the cave to the blanketed area. She saw from the sheen on her forehead that Celiste was running a fever. To herself she thought, *Same fever that Margon has,* but said nothing in the vain hope that perhaps her diagnosis was wrong.

"The Lady Celiste states..." began Celiste in a stentorian voice of authority, "we shall celebrate in Arad, our new babies."

Then she sat down quickly. Her stomach felt like the early stages of rebellion and dissent. In fact, she felt like she ate bad meat. She thought to summon Dren, her second in command but remembered where he was.

The woman who provided care to Margon for the last eight days and stayed by his side straightened up and dried her hands on a towel. She stepped around boxes and large water jugs in order to walk toward the front of the cave. When she reached Celiste, she said, "He has departed."

Celiste thought for a moment and turned to Layla and asked her to record her words in the log of events of Arad: "It is a cycle. A man we cannot lose, dies. A baby boy joins our little village."

Chapter 54

'Lady Celiste in distress.' There was word of mouth around the cave. The women knew she had a fever and rambled. For three days she cursed and swore, in the best traditions of the Aryas. Several times they heard her swear at Deem, shouting that he had no right to leave her here.

When Dren tried to talk to her, she rambled on about onions and radishes and wheat and *get that muddy dirt off your knees.*

On the twelfth day her friend Layla washed her face, as she had for several days. Layla reported to the rest of the women that Celiste's face was dry and she seemed to be sleeping, even snoring lightly.

The next day the sun was high overhead when Celiste opened her eyes and slowly struggled to sit up. When Layla approached, Celiste said simply, "There has to be food?"

Layla went and retrieved a bowl of stew from the cooking pot. The taste surprised Celiste and she raised an eyebrow.

"There is rabbit. One of the men set traps far up the canyon when he saw small tracks. The black cloud did not affect the rabbit."

"Good. I eat."

Celiste looked around the cave. Half the women were outside on the washing crew, hanging blankets on ropes strung between stakes. The remainder looked at her.

"How long was I asleep?"

Layla smiled and said, quietly, "Three days."

"I had this dream, just now, I think."

"A dream?"

"Yes, I was walking in an enormous field of onions. It stretched to the horizon where we had pens of sheep and a few horses. We are going to expand our fields. There are people who eat onions and radishes and sheep to the north of us, in Hebron and Jericho and Salem."

Layla smiled.

"And I felt angry in my dream…"

Layla put her hands together and began to rub the knuckles. Her hands appeared to be recovered from the work in the fields.

"Lady Celiste, I will tell the others. You should rest." Layla began to smile and her smile broke into laughter. She reached over and touched Celiste on her temple in a mark of respect.

"Any word? Or message from Deem?"

"No, none."

"That man is going to pay a heavy price when next I see him."

Layla opened her mouth to speak, but stopped. She smiled.

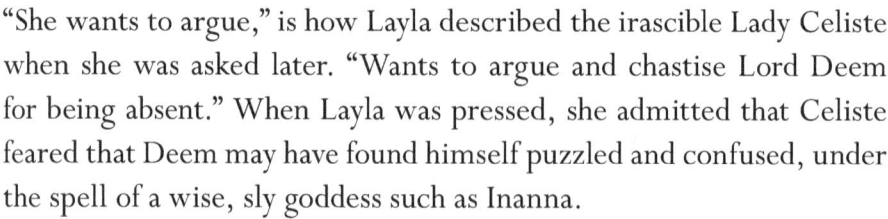

"She wants to argue," is how Layla described the irascible Lady Celiste when she was asked later. "Wants to argue and chastise Lord Deem for being absent." When Layla was pressed, she admitted that Celiste feared that Deem may have found himself puzzled and confused, under the spell of a wise, sly goddess such as Inanna.

Celiste tried to bring herself to describe the beauty and soft smiles of the goddess Inanna, who they met near the Great Pyramid. It was obvious the goddess had never been in the sun, nor toiled in a field. Her skin was flawless and darker than the skin of Deem. Her white teeth reflected the beauty of the light reflected off the white limestone sides of the Pyramid.

Layla kept her own counsel, as a friend should. But Layla was older and had seen this behavior in the past in other women who did not know, yet, that they were carrying a child.

Layla did relay the wishes of Celiste to the women. Three women and one of the guards volunteered to make the trek to Arad to bring back vegetables. They were told to fan the vegetables in the storerooms to get the dust off their surfaces. Have as little contact as possible. And wash the vegetables in the river before they bring them up from Arad.

❦

"The maneuver was tried eons ago, on Nibiru," said Captain Deem to the four crew members on the control deck of the *Cead*. They were seated at their control stations, with their padded chairs swung around so they could see their Captain and look down on the blue and white vista of Kien.

Their vista included seas of deep blue or light turquoise where the mighty clouds did not obscure the waters. The four crew were joined by Aonim of the *Dara;* they never grew weary of admiring the depth of the oceans. Kien was so unlike Nibiru, with its golden shield sparkling in sunlight when it approached the Sun.

"We will enter the atmosphere by using the steering rockets. Slowly down until we begin to rock. We will rock back and forth as does a leaf falling from a tree. At 5,000 cubits more or less I will turn our engines directly into our path and fire the engines. We will burn engines until we are 300 cubits above the water."

"And the shuttles?" asked the first officer.

"They will catch *Cead* when our motion becomes neutral and lower us onto the spit of land near our final site."

It was a decision of the Council of Twelve, he explained. Some of the workers in space and on Mars wanted a lower gravity environment where they could acclimate to Kien's heavier gravity.

He went on to describe how the engineers were to build two air locks on the upper shell of *Cead* that could be jettisoned if *Cead* went back into space. Their goal was to use the stronger power of *Cead* and its crystals to filter and precipitate more gold from the seawater. The new crews would use suction devices to 'bring' sea-bottom into the *Cead* to be filtered.

"All four shuttles will be at their stations in one day," said Aonim. He reached out and tapped Deem on the shoulder. It was an old mariner's 'nod' to the captain that meant 'good flying.'

"The shuttles need all their power, and a little magic, to lift *Cead*."

"No magic involved," laughed one of the crew.

"True," said Deem. "Once *Cead* is in place we can begin to make water for our tanks and prepare for our guests.

On the day Captain Shar and his mate left Cead for 'their' island in the north ocean, Shar heard about the new mission for *Cead*. His remark would not be repeated by *Cead's* new captain. "Using a vehicle built for the heavens *as a boat under water?*" Captain Shar shook his head. [Endnote[xv]]

⸙

"Tired of this cave, are we?" Celiste laughed.

Dren, Eglan and Layla stood around Celiste where she sat on a stool with a blanket over her legs. They, as did all the women, hoped it was time to return to Arad.

"We go," added Celiste, "when our squad is back. Lara and the two women and the guard can tell us what they saw. I suspect we will have to clean the roofs and walls of dust, and the floors inside also."

"I have a decision about Lara. She brought both babies to join us. She earned the right to guide us in our health. I want her to go to Jericho and seek training in the healing arts."

"She is not Aryas," said Layla with a frown, "and you have more than once displayed distrust for those of her kind."

"That was before this land was destroyed."

"We are the entire world," said Dren. "We do not know if Jericho still exists."

"For it not to exist …that is possible." Celiste looked across the cave and saw 'her' women were packing their few belongings. "These women have a role. They will make babies. Their mates will rebuild our world."

She paused. "I think I can trust Lara."

Chapter 55

"That miserable excuse! He left me with something I do not wish to have," said Lara, then added, "...before Gastan left."

"How do you know?" asked Celiste.

"Shortly after the sun rises, I get up. My stomach is in revolt. This morning at our camp near the river what I ate came back up."

"That is a sign," said Celiste thinking about Eglan's description of her mornings in the early days.

Celiste helped her loosen the thin ropes that held her load of onions, radishes, and a sack of barley. Lara's small squad returned from their long walk to Arad early in the afternoon. The other two women and the guard were talking to the other women about what they saw in Arad.

"The bodies were swollen," said Lara.

She watched Celiste smell the bag of barley. One eyebrow went up.

"The guard Sem says mix some herbs with it, boil it good, then put it in a large jug to ferment, then add wheat ground into a paste."

When Celiste frowned, Lara said, "Or something like that."

"Tomorrow, twelve of the women will go to Arad. The rest of us will stay here for seven more days."

Lara looked at the crowd near the cooking fire, where the women were animated and excited about 'walking down' to Arad.

"I want to go with them," said Lara.

"You and I will stay here for seven days. We must be careful. You are with child," added Celiste.

"And you?" said Lara with a raised eyebrow and a smile.

Celiste looked away for a moment. She watched the crowd of women and three guards while they milled around the cooking fire. One guard was busy eating from a bowl. The two women in Lara's squad were munching on an item that had no name. Wheat had been ground and mixed with herbs and let to sit until it became a spongy mass. Then dates and apple chunks had been inserted and the mass baked in a makeshift oven.

Lara asked her again, "And you?"

"I stay. I must be careful."

Celiste turned back to Lara and held her hand for a moment. *Your mate Gastan is no loss if he does not return.* Then Celiste released Lara's hand and smiled. She recalled Lara's reaction to her discovery of her condition.

"Your child …it will be a treasure."

"You think so?"

"I do."

Celiste looked out the mouth of their cave. The far side of the canyon was still in sunlight. A black shadow in the shape of the mountain behind her cave was slowly crawling up the far canyon wall.

"It will be dark soon," said Celiste.

"And you will stay here for seven days?"

Celiste turned back to Lara with a small smile and tilted her head toward Lara. "You must not say anything to the other women."

"About what?"

"I am having the sickness in the morning."

Lara looked at Celiste then over to the group of women at the cooking fire. Lara gently squeezed Celiste's hand and gave her the quiet smile of a co-conspirator.

Chapter 56

"It is appropriate," said Drenay.

"That we stay?" remarked Celiste.

"Yes."

They stood and watched the twelve women and Dren and one guard when they walked down the canyon. The women carried small bundles of possessions, blankets and clothes. Three women carried empty water jugs to fill and haul into Arad. The guard carried their only effective weapon, the 'Supreme Hunter' as he called it.

Across the valley the sun reflected off the eastern sea and created a yellow and white landscape. High thin clouds streamed over the valley, pushed by a high wind from the west.

"Do you think it is safe?"

"The black cloud was here for what, sundown to middle night?"

"There could be poison," added Drenay.

"Dren and the women will camp for three days by the canyon mouth," said Celiste. "At the first sign of illness he is to begin the return to our canyon."

Drenay reached up to pull the light blanket tight around her baby boy. He slept with a small smile on his lips, as babies do. She looked down and touched his pink cheek gently.

"There could be poison," said Celiste. "Dren knows they must dust and wash everything and dispose of the wash water in a hole where it can be buried."

"The squad you sent with Lara. They told me there was very little dust or dirt on the buildings in Arad."

"The strong wind," Celiste said while she watched the last woman in the long line turn the last corner in the canyon trail and disappear from sight. "Still, there will be pockets of black poison on the roofs, in the corners."

"And the poison?"

"If it is still there, we will move over the mountains toward Hebron and find a new town or build one."

'death roams the street, is loose in the road; stands beside a man, none can see it.' (A Sumerian Memorial of Eridu).

On the fourth day, Dren and his squad of women moved into Arad, walking slowly and checking for black poison. They found small piles of dirt blown into corners between buildings. The buildings were clean, scoured by the winds from the west. Two of the women set up the water jugs on a stone altar near the small river. They worked to clean and scrub the Washing House; Dren insisted the women wash themselves each day.

On the fifth day away from the cave, *Dara* arrived. She came down gently, if such a word can be used, across the river. When her captain, Aonim was asked he said he did not want to blow dirt back toward Arad. Landing in a field of wheat seemed like a sensible plan.

Dren and three women came out to meet Aonim. They took bags of apples, dates, figs, beans and lettuce back to their cook house. Dren remained behind, half expecting to receive bad news about Deem.

"No, my captain is well. He is with the *Cead* in the eastern sea south of Eridu and Ur," remarked Aonim. "He asked me to bring as much news as might be helpful to your squad. How are the women?"

"Twelve are here. Twelve up the canyon at the cave. We are being careful. One of our guards and three caretakers here at Arad died from the black poison," added Dren.

"The women are busy, working in Arad and up at the canyon?"

"You mean are they well?"

"Yes, I mean..."

"We have delivered two babies. They are showing the usual growth. There is one 'mother-to-be' at the cave."

"And that is?"

"Lara, the mate of Gastan. He 'caught' her when we were aboard *Cead* on the traverse to Kien."

"That is indeed ...unfortunate."

Dren saw the pallor of gray crawl across Aonim's face. He knew what it meant. Dren waited a moment before asking.

"Gastan was told to take his squad of 36 men into the mountains. He marched them to the landing site and built a camp near Ninmah's Temple."

"We saw three flashes of brilliant white light beyond the mountains south of here. Down in the Restricted Zone."

"Lord Enlil decided to destroy the Landing Zone. Apparently Lord Mar.Duk wanted to capture it; he wanted to be ruler of all this land. Gastan and his men are dead, pulverized as one observer described it."

"Sand builds hills," noted Dren.

"Yes, that man Gastan was a determined sort."

"I will tell his mate."

"Thank you. Tell Lady Celiste."

"I shall," said Dren with a small bow to Aonim for the information. He looked at Aonim then back toward the small village of Arad and added, "Thank your Captain for us."

"The Captain is fully occupied. They brought the *Cead* down. It will be living and working quarters for some of the Titans and some of the Royals. At least half of the royal Anunnaki have been brought to *Ninti*, the 'Lady Life' before she leaves for their home planet."

"Working quarters?"

"Oh, you do not know. *Cead* is in the sea near the long ago location of E.din. The pilots and crews wanted to live where the pull of the planet is less. They can harvest crops and fish and supply themselves in the sea.

"Why are the Royals leaving?"

Aonim went on to tell him how the great Black Cloud crawled over the mountains to the east and killed everything in Eridu (Enki's Temple) and Erech (Anu's City) and Nippur, where Enlil directed the comings and goings of the shuttles and deep space transports. Mar.Duk declared his city Babylon to be his capital. Enlil returned to the Land of Osiris after expressing grief for his destroyed temple at Nippur.

"They fled the cloud in a state of terror, those who are so quick to let the slaves in the Abzu mines die," said Aonim.

"You know about the mines?"

"You forget ...we took you to Abzu after the highlands allowed you to adjust your breathing."

Dren nodded and added "I remember."

Dren watched the women and their cargo step out of the slow current of the river. "Good to wash."

"That is a standing order. Wash to get rid of the black dust."

"We have been lucky. Only one person dead at the cave. A man, his mate and their daughter died here at Arad. Our horses died at our camp."

"Yes, I saw them dead. Nothing compared to Eridu or Nippur."

"What did you see?"

"Many dead in the streets. Cattle dead in the stalls. Sheep dead and bloated in the sheep-holds."

"So the Lords and their ladies left their temple cities?"

"We hear some news from the stricken. Ningal, in Ur, went into an underground chamber. She complained that only cockroaches could live in that hole. One of her slaves pointed out to her that she was still alive to complain. She had the slave whipped.

"Enlil we took to the Great Pyramid; it is called *Ekur*. His mate, Lady Ninti we took to Abzu in the south. Lady Inanna, the one they also call Ishtar, complained all during the trip that she had to leave her jewelry behind in Babylon."

"We are much obliged for your information," said Dren.

"And your Lady Celiste?" with emphasis on '*Say-leest-Ay*.'

"She is well."

"Good. I will send word to Captain Deem. [Endnote[xvi]]

Chapter 57

A brilliant blue painted itself across the dome of heaven while Ra rode his chariot across the morning sky. The sun shone down on fields of onions, radishes, barley, melons, beans and lettuce. Despite the nuclear disaster, the fields planted in early spring by Celiste and her squad flourished and grew and turned a deep green in the early summer.

The days grew warm. Light breezes caressed the mountains to the west and brought strong winds down the canyons. Arad basked in the sunlight; a light rain washed the buildings. Celiste kept her women busy; they used digging sticks to rid the fields of weeds. The women enjoyed the sound of the two new babies who let everyone know when they were hungry.

The three men, their remaining guards, found mates among the women. There was some jealousy among those left alone when their men did not return from the Restricted Zone. Celiste, when she was told of this, issued a rule with the force of law. She ruled that Dren and two men would go to Hebron to recruit men for the women. She also ruled that 'those left alone' will not talk nor entice the men who have mates. To break this rule could result in banishment.

This day would be remembered in the future for the brilliant blue sky and the dark animal who wandered into their onion field and began eating onions.

———

Ashur, Eglan's mate stood next to Shen, the guard on duty. They stood atop a small building where they could survey the fields. Ashur regaled Shen with stories about his baby girl and her behavior during the dark night. Ashur was grateful his baby girl was beginning to sleep all during the dark; she woke up hungry at first light.

To Shen the black mass appeared to be a small bear, crawling into the onion field at the far eastern corner of the field. There was long black hair on its head; its body was covered with a short fur. Then the animal turned and Shen saw its hips had no fur; it was a man of dark skin with a fur wrapped around his body.

When he asked Ashur to look his friend stared at the black mass and agreed that it was indeed a man with long hair. They both wondered why he crawled on the ground. When Shen saw two women at the north end of the field turn in his direction, he decided he must get the Supreme Hunter and go to prevent them from contacting the dark man. He asked Ashur to inform Lady Celiste that there was a man in the onion fields.

———

Shen dragged the man, forcing him to walk out of the onions and into Arad. They stopped; the man fell to his knees. Shen said "Here he is."

Celiste looked at the man where he stood with a light rope tied around his neck. He was bent over; his long black hair had streaks of gray; his hair hung down over his face. His hands and feet were covered in the light tan earth of the onion field. A ragged fur with small holes covered his body. His skin color was dark; his brow had a prominent ridge. There were blisters on his nose.

"You …up …up," said Celiste with a gesture to stand up.

The man tried to bring his head up. His shoulders went back. His face was covered with gray hair. He stood with effort. His eyes looked at her briefly then back at the ground. His legs were not straight; they remained bent.

"Up," she commanded.

The man bent his back, tried to straighten himself. His head came up slightly before he looked at Celiste a second time.

"He was injured, I think," said Dren from just behind Celiste.

She looked at his legs where they bent at the knee.

"Too dark for Beag," said Celiste.

"He is Adamu, born after the Anunnaki Lords rebelled and demanded workers for the mines," said Dren.

"What is he…?" she began but stopped. She looked at Dren and Shen and Layla and the three women who formed a circle around the man. She bent over to look into his face and said, "Who? Who?"

The man reached up and pulled a thin rope from inside his wrap of fur. The rope was threaded through an old wooden plaque. It held the symbol $\bar{R}.\widehat{\omega}$ which puzzled Celiste. She pointed at $\bar{R}$, the man said, "Ren."

She pointed at the symbol of the double horns and he raised one eyebrow. Dren moved forward and leaned in to stare at the symbol.

"Double horns, sign of Osiris, the Bull. The other marks say twelve, that means twelve generations from Osiris."

"How do you know?" asked Celiste.

"I asked the Lord at the second mine we visited," said Dren. "Much later Deem warned me to not ask many questions, as he put it."

"This man is from…?"

"The mines of Abzu," finished Dren.

Celiste waved her hand in front of the man's face. He took his eyes off the leather sandals on Dren's feet and looked up at Celiste.

"How?" she said loudly and waved her arm around then pointed at the ground. The man looked at her for a long moment. Then he pointed in the direction of the eastern Sea and said, "Sleep. Sleep. Two sleeps. Lord tell me walk toward my shadow"

"He came from the east," said Dren.

"What did you see?" said Celiste.

The man looked puzzled and said, "I work, Mistress. I work."

She pointed to her eye and mimicked looking around.

The man raised his hand and moved it, as if across a flat landscape. He stopped the movement and said, "Dirt, Mistress. All dirt." He looked up at her and added, "Bones. Heads. No skin."

She looked up at the eastern Sea in the distance. Sunlight bounced off the surface. The glare seemed to turn the sea and the land to the south into a white miasma.

"Do you suppose?" she began. Then she looked at Shen and told him to take the man to the river and wash him and throw away the decrepit fur thing he wore. She told two of the women to bring some trousers and a wrap from the house of the caretaker who died after the explosions. When they left she told Layla and the two women to go to the cooking house and prepare simple food.

"It is a waste," said Dren.

"Why?"

"Shen said his mouth voided itself of the onions he ate. There was blood in his half chewed onions."

To the man Ren she said, "How many days?"

When he did not answer Dren waved his arm across the sky and raised one finger, then two, then three, then four.

The man suddenly bobbed his head. "Four," he said. "Four crossings the sky."

Celiste nodded her head. "Yes, four days," and meant four days he walked from the ruins of Mar.Duk's army. She looked at Ren and said, "Your mate? You had a mate where you worked?"

The man nodded his head and held it down while he looked at the flowing gown Celiste wore. He raised his head to say, "Mate. She work. She give..." and he held up one hand to indicate 'five' ...workers. She die."

"So your mate had five children ...no, workers?" The man did not reply. Celiste told the man Ren to go with Shen. She saw two of her squad walking toward the river with clothes and soap and a large towel and directed, "Do not touch him."

The man Ren began to turn. Dren suddenly shouted stop and walked over to Ren. He bent over to look at the backs of Ren's legs. Dren took a long moment to inspect the back of the man's knees. Then he waved a hand at Ren and told him to "Go" with Shen.

Dren watched the man walk toward the river. His legs were bent. Dren did not look at Celiste until she said, "What?"

"His legs are bent for a reason."

Celiste said nothing.

"They cut the muscles in back of his knees. To keep him from running."

Celiste said nothing. She turned away and looked back at her small village with its white temple shining in the afternoon sunlight.

"Do you suppose...?" she began.

"Lady Celiste, I do not suppose. I know. One of your..." he paused, trying to find a word, "...rulers, or Great Rulers, *or his scribe* chose that man. They put him down where the Brilliance of Enlil destroyed the army of Mar.Duk. He saw skulls and bones and dead vultures."

"They wanted to know..." she began. Dren finished with "...if he would live."

Chapter 58

Mid-summer. Days of high heat. The field workers began to pick the largest of the onions and radishes, leaving the smallest plants to continue their growth. The barley they brought to the oven where it was baked until a hard brown then ground to fine powder and allowed to age in a large clay pot with water. The field workers began to bring in melons and beans to be eaten as they matured.

The men were sent to dig silt out of the main canal when the river level began to drop. There had been little rain on this side of the mountains but the river out of the canyon continued to provide what they needed.

The man called Ṝen lived for another six days. He ate what he could between bouts of enormous cramps in his stomach. His screaming woke the entire village several times in the long black night.

The shuttle *Dara* came down just after sunrise on a crystal clear morning. Aonim marched stiffly, as if afraid of the ground and the buildings and stopped in front of the tall wooden doors of Lady Celiste's temple. He was informed the man Ṝen was dead, by one of the women.

Aonim stood and waited. A woman brought him a glass of light green juice. When informed it was 'juice from a large fruit' he sniffed the juice and returned the glass to the woman.

The woman stood and smiled at Aonim. By now five other women had arrived. He glanced at them and they also smiled. Time passed slowly for the captain of the *Dara*. When Celiste stepped through the door of her temple, she was radiant with energy. Aonim later described her as a beam of sunlight that outshone the early morning sun.

She wore a long flowing gown that reached just above her sandals. Her dark hair was lighter, bleached in the sun. Her hair was long now, uncut but wavy with curls each side of her face. Her stunning face reflected the weight of the decisions she had made. A woven shawl wrapped her shoulders and covered her stomach. Celiste's blue eyes cut through Aonim when she examined him. She noticed a twitch in his hand.

"You must eat. We have fried fish and boiled beans."

Aonim bowed toward Celiste and thanked her but refused her invitation. By way of explanation he said he was told not to touch anything. Celiste reacted with "You tell them we are alive here."

Are we dying? No, she thought. *All these years …I am still not Aryas. My hair and eyes are not black like this so-called Captain.* Through clinched teeth she said, "You tell them we are alive."

She looked at Aonim to see if he understood her words, then added, "Your marker, that worker you set down in the devastation, has died."

"I am to bring his body to Abzu. The doctor wants him."

"So be it," said Celiste through clenched teeth. "We do not want to do anything contrary to the wishes of the Royals who fancy they are gods."

Aonim looked at Celiste with a raised eyebrow. He looked puzzled. Then he added, "I am to tell you Deem is at Ekur, the great white pyramid. He sent you those apples and dates which my crewman Ragnar is bringing off the *Dara.*"

Celiste made a small bow as a sign of appreciation. Ragnar, the crewman from *Dara,* passed by with two large sacks. He walked to the women who stood nearby and began to talk to them. One of them reached out to caress the fine-spun quality of his uniform jacket. He glanced at Aonim; his captain pointed at the *Dara.* The message was clear.

"Will you take a message to Deem? My words, only?"

Aonim nodded and she said in a quiet voice, "Captain Deem, if you intend to remain a pilot, do not return to Arad." Aonim raised an eyebrow for a second time, but nodded yes, he understood.

Celiste then directed him to take a load of onions and radishes and Dren to Salem, for trading. She dismissed Aonim with a wave of her hand and turned to step into her temple, where the cool air gave her a chill.

She wrapped her arms around herself and rubbed her arms against the chill air inside her temple. Then she bowed her head, and said a silent prayer to any god who would listen. After a short moment she looked up and saw Eglan watching her from the far corner of the main room.

When she crossed the room Eglan said quietly, "Was there word of Deem?"

"Yes," Celiste began with bitterness on her tongue, but quickly looked through a high window at blue sky and remarked that they should get their tasks finished before the heat of the day rolls in.

When Eglan was asked later by two of her friends, she noted that her Mistress seemed to be sad or quiet or angry or all three. She also noted that Lady Celiste was hiding her belly under the shawl she wore.

A cool breeze meandered down the canyon and enveloped Arad in a blanket of cool relief. In the mountains heavy gray clouds began to dump their cargo of rain into the mountains. In the village Arad it was a blessing. Their river from the canyon had shrunk to half its size. The water would be welcome for the fields and somewhat cooler for washing.

It was several days since the visit of the *Dara* before Lara decided to ask about Deem. Her question brought silence. Celiste stood and looked out across the valley to where the Eastern Sea was covered by gray masses of cloud. Out of the silence Celiste said, quietly,

"Could he tell? Did I look thin?"

"You mean?" began Lara.

"You were off to one side. Could he see my little bulge?"

Lara was silent, trying to formulate an answer. "Men are somewhat like a heavy cream about these things. Slow to pour, sweet when they need to be."

"He will tell Deem I am the mistress of Arad?"

"Aonim is an obedient servant of the Aryas."

"He has changed. He was radical before we came to Earth. Now he has power, of a sort," added Celiste.

"Some men are hot like fire," said Lara. "They burn your fingers."

Celiste smiled, then stood silent for a long minute. She looked out across the fields, then at the three women who just returned from the fields. Her hand touched her stomach with a caress.

"We will build what we want to build. We will get more men. We will have more babies. We are Aryas."

When Lara remarked that she was mixed blood, not pure Aryas, her mistress said, "We can make a better world; a world better than the Royals and their 'so-called gods' has created, with its wars and Black Death."

Chapter 59

The Great Pyramid was now called Ekur, the Temple of Lord Enlil. The ancient lord and his lady (Ninti) had returned to the land of the decrepit crouching lioness called the Sphinx when Nippur and its people died from the Black Poison. The damage from an explosion inside the pyramid was repaired and the pyramid now beamed masses of energy up to the Lord's shuttles and the two Deep Black vehicles in orbit above Kien.

The third Deep Black vehicle, the *Cead* was now serving as a base for Titans and some of the Aryas who were living in the vehicle. They were fishing and farming on the shallow sea floor and beginning to understand what they could achieve under the water. The few survivors of the Black Cloud on the shore brought offerings of fruits and vegetables for the enormous 'fish creatures' that lived in the sea.

The *Cead's* pilot was ordered off the *Cead* when it was noted that his mate was not with him. He was brought to the Temple of Inanna, next to the Great Pyramid, where he met Lord Enlil, the Commander of the Four Regions of Kien, *'Land of the Lord.'* Deem, a distant grandson of Enlil, was puzzled. Enlil asked Deem to be patient; one of the Deep Black pilots, and his family, were about to relocate off his ship.

Enlil told Deem he was eligible to become the next pilot of the Deep Black vehicle *Rama*. The Lord *Rama* ruled the Eastern lands.

Deem was stunned. He bowed in reverence to his mighty lord. He took three steps to back away from Lord Enlil. He thought immediately of the long months in Deep Space while the *Rama* flew to catch up to their home planet, Nibiru. The aged, somewhat infirm Enlil noticed Deem's action and believed his young pilot was reluctant.

From the back of the temple room, Inanna, Goddess of Love and War, moved to stand next to Deem. When Enlil asked if they were mates, Inanna replied, "Not today, my Lord." The un-spoken words implied that they could soon be mates.

The sun began to touch the mountains west of Arad. The shadows of the Blue Mountains crawled across the valley floor; Arad turned black in the shadows. The last bit of sunlight lit the tall pole Dren and his guards erected in front of Lady Celiste's temple.

A flag fluttered in the light breeze. The women used a tightly woven sheet on which they stitched an enormous letter 'O' next to a smaller letter 'm' with a band of green cloth below the two letters. The symbol stood for 'Ninti' whose title was 'Lady Life.' The women were asking Ninti to watch over their village.

Celiste also pointed to the symbol and said 'O'magadh' which is an old expression when you do not believe what a man is telling you. "You say 'O'magadh' which means 'Oh, Really?' in our old language."

Several of the women laughed at her irreverence.

When Celiste and Lara walked back into the temple, Celiste pulled Lara aside and said, "Are you happy?"

"You mean, I believe, do I wish I had a man?"

Celiste said nothing. She knew Lara was stubborn. She was a hard worker in the cooking building.

"You know," Celiste began, "I feel a pain when I think about you."

"It is what it is," said Lara. An image of Gastan when he was angry flashed through her mind. She felt a small movement inside her belly and smiled. She touched her bulging stomach and saw her friend Celiste touch the distinct curve in her stomach.

"We have our babies," said Lara.

Celiste wrapped her arms around Lara, briefly. She released her then looked into her eyes and said, "We reap the harvest of sadness."

"A harvest caused by men," added Lara.

Lara saw tears form in Celiste's eyes; she turned away.

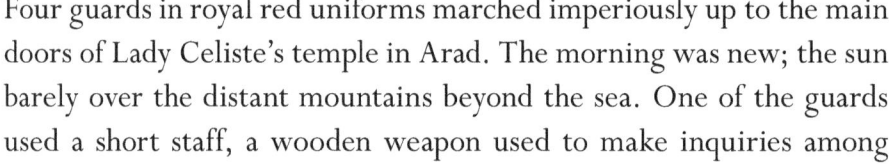

Four guards in royal red uniforms marched imperiously up to the main doors of Lady Celiste's temple in Arad. The morning was new; the sun barely over the distant mountains beyond the sea. One of the guards used a short staff, a wooden weapon used to make inquiries among prisoners when they are reluctant 'enemies.' He rapped three times on the doors to the temple.

There were neither women nor guards about this early in the day. The four guards stood in casual rest and waited. The original guard hit the door with four loud bangs from his staff. He stepped back to wait.

They were young, thin men with black hair and the pale skin of the Titans, the watchers in space. Each of them had the straight nose of the Aryas, and the deep black eyes of royalty.

One of the guards coughed. When the leader looked at him the guard nodded toward what the women called the 'Washing House.' They saw a face peering from behind the door.

The guard yelled, "You. Come here."

There was silence from the Washing House. The door slammed shut. The four guards had no time to react. They turned in unison toward a second group of four guards as they approached. Behind them walked a man of exalted rank. His red tunic reached his knees. He wore sandals with leather straps wrapped around his calves. His face was severe; his demeanor impatient. He wore the rank of Major, a silver circle with the five pointed star of Nibiru inside the circle.

His skull was bare on the left side. From the midline of his skull his long black hair had been pulled over his right ear and woven into a black rope that hung to his shoulder. He looked at the guards and said, "Nothing?"

"No, my Lord," said two of the guards in unison.

At that moment there were sounds of a heavy beam turning inside the temple doors. The sounds stopped. They heard a latch slide and the right hand door began to creak and groan as it was pushed outwards. A woman in a dark blue gown with a shawl around her shoulders leaned outward around the door. She saw the group of men in red tunics. Beyond them she spotted the shuttle. *Dara's* captain Aonim and one crewman stood near the exit ramp of the shuttle.

"My Lord," said one of the guards "requires a meeting with your mistress, Lady Celiste of Arad."

The woman turned and disappeared. The men stood for a long moment while a frown formed on the face of the Lord. He eventually said, "So open the door," and indicated the nearest guard. The guard moved quickly, pulled the door open then bowed in deference as the Lord entered.

Celiste sent her maid to fetch Dren and his squad, which had swollen to six men recently. She told her maid to say, "A royal at the temple. Your best uniform would be appropriate."

Celiste spent time with her hairbrush to pull the snarls out of her hair. She washed quickly in an effort to get the tired feeling out of her face. The entire community worked hard the previous day to remove all of the full onions and radishes from their fields. The men, meanwhile, harvested the barley. Today they were to beat and sort the barley heads.

She found her long white gown, rarely used lately. There had been no one to entertain. She wrapped the gown around her body and secured it with a cloth belt. Into her hair she mounted three yellow blossoms. Her silver emblem, the circle with six gems, she placed on the mid-line of her chest. Then she wrapped a bright red necklace around her neck and fastened it to the silver emblem.

She turned to look at herself in a burnished mirror just as her maid announced Dren and his squad were at the side door into the temple.

Celiste walked into the main meeting room then crossed to the side door. She allowed Dren to marshal his men into the large room where they formed a single line behind the small altar. Only then, when her men were ready, only then did she look up to see the elegant man in his long red tunic with its badge of rank.

She walked between her men then stopped next to Dren. Two of the other man's guards had weapons on their belts, the kind of weapon that fires a pellet of iron or copper. She pointed at one of the weapons then glared at their leader.

"You insult the house of Essa and Dea, my parents."

The man looked at his two guards and said, "Remove your Shar. Ur."

To Celiste he said, "They are effective weapons from our engineer."

"This is good," said Celiste slowly. "We accept them as tribute."

"But these are…" began one of the guards.

The man's fist came up in a blur of motion and smacked the guard on the side of his face. The guard reacted by staggering for one step, then he stopped. He removed his Shar.Ur and gave it to Dren. Dren took both weapons and placed them on a table near Celiste.

"We accept your apology, and your tribute. We are but a small village and our children will thank you for helping to protect them." At the end of her speech she bowed to the man.

"You will accept the two weapons as apology for the bad behavior of my men, I expect."

Celiste smiled and looked at the guards. "Your men may withdraw. We will do no harm to you."

The man looked at her briefly then waved at his guards and told them to wait outside. When they turned toward the large wooden doors, Dren motioned to his men to withdraw. Dren moved back to where he could intervene if needed. He felt responsible for the safety of Mistress Celiste.

"You may explain to me…" began Celiste.

"…why I am here," finished the man. He took one step toward Celiste and then stopped. "I am the one you never knew."

"Never knew?"

"I was prevented from traveling to your planet, to Lahmu, while you were growing. I so much wanted to share my life with you. Your father, Essa, was a good man."

"Did he prevent you from traveling?"

"Not your father, I assure you. It was Lord Enlil's decision. He ruled my 'indiscretion' prevented me from returning to Lahmu."

"You followed his order?"

"Yes. I am a man of Nibiru. I love my planet. I am only briefly here at Kien. And in thirty days, when the moon is again full, we will leave for a flight to catch Nibiru on her lonely circuit through the heavens, as Lord Enlil describes the 'deep black'."

"My father described you."

"Yes. I am Seth.Dar."

"My mother never said a word about you."

"She was... how to say it ...angry but quietly excited by the prospect of having a baby. Your father could not..."

"I understand," she said. *Across her mind flashed an image of Essa with his arms around her.* She walked around the large empty space of the temple. She kept her distance from Seth.Dar.

"I am your father."

"Yes. *My father Essa*, the man you betrayed, told me you seduced my mother."

Seth.Dar said nothing. He watched Celiste circle him.

Chapter 60

Celiste glanced at her friend Dren, then stared at Seth.Dar. "You betrayed my father," she argued, "yet you come here to confront me?"

"Not to confront you, surely."

"So, all this time, what do the Aryan lords want of me?"

"You have the rank of Counselor, rank 25. You are a granddaughter of Ningal. If she retires or dies you will be asked to serve on the Council of Twelve here on Kien."

"I know this."

"We leave in 30 days aboard *Rama*."

"What is it you do not tell me?"

"Your mate Deem is the new Captain of *Rama*."

Celiste turned away from her father. She walked over to Dren and shyly put a hand on his arm. "Help me stand," she whispered.

She wavered, then leaned toward Dren but corrected herself and straightened her back. *I prayed he would choose me.* She began to turn toward Seth.Dar.

"Was it his choice?" she demanded.

"I do not know."

"Where is he?"

"At the Temple of Isis."

"Doing what?"

"He is trying to avoid the attention of Inanna, my half-sister, the Goddess Inanna as they call her."

"You said he is 'trying to avoid' her attentions?"

"She is persuasive. She will succeed in seducing him."

That woman, with her wiles and charms and curves and long legs could seduce any man. He has been away for 65 days.

There was silence for a long moment. A piece of hard wood crackled in the fire pit. Celiste looked at Seth.Dar and added, "Again, I ask. What do you want of me?"

"I, nothing."

"You want me aboard *Rama*?"

"Yes, in 20 to 22 days."

"Will this 'Inanna' be aboard?"

"Probably. She has asked Lord Enlil to approve of her new mate."

"Does Deem know you are here?"

"No. I felt it my duty."

"Your duty?"

"To meet my daughter and offer her a long life."

"On your planet? Your *Nee-bur-ooo*?" she drawled.

He was silent. "Yes," she added in a quiet tone.

He paused and glanced at Dren. Dren took one step toward the older man. Seth.Dar said, "And you?" with a nod toward Dren.

"Dren has a mate. She is with their baby."

"Ah, I see. The loyal scribe."

Celiste glanced at Dren and saw his face covered with dark frown. She saw also his fist, an indication of his anger.

"You want me to abandon my village, my people, for a half-possible life with a pilot who has been out of my life for 65 days."

"You must know you have the option."

"You are my father? You offer me a good life aboard *Rama?*"

"Yes," he said quietly.

"You are not my father. My father died in an explosion that brought the Black Death to the people of our village on Lahmu. My mother died there, also, when I was six years old."

"You are Aryas."

"I know this."

"You would live out your life defending these… Beag?"

Celiste paused for a moment then said, "You Aryas. You are uncaring. You would allow us to be erased by an impartial force that cares nothing for the lives of our people…this shall be a banner and sign of your lives of anxious desperation."

Seth.Dar looked at her then at Dren. He turned away, toward the main entry doors, while Celiste said, "You disrespect me? Now, go!" [Endnote[xvii]]

Chapter 61

The morning was quiet. The sun peeked between dark gray clouds, a pre-cursor of rain. In the cooking house two women used an open pan to scrub bowls from the morning meal. Near the river one woman was washing long sheets of fine woven cloth, purchased by Dren in Salem during his last visit. The other men and women were in the fields, collecting the last of the beans, radishes, and onions. The stalks of barley were now stored in the best house in Arad with the best roof.

The men worked with two short, squat animals hitched to the Arad wagon. They were tarpon, a short semi-wild animal with a thick heavy head and yellow-brown skins. One of the tarpon had mottled brown spots on its yellow skin around both shoulders. The two animals were reluctant to pull the wagon; Dren had stated they would learn, "In two or ten days."

Dara came down in a whirlwind of dust, directly onto the plaza in front of Celiste's temple. The woman at the river frowned at the dust cloud when it swirled over her and her wet sheets. The ramp on *Dara* came down and cloth bags were thrown onto the dusty square. An apple escaped from one bag and rolled a short distance through the dust. The bags continued to fly through the air until the pile was half the height of a man.

A man in a black tunic with a black cap came down the ramp. When he turned the woman at the river saw his badge of rank, a silver disk with straight lines radiating from the center. At his waist he wore a thick leather belt that held a leather device, probably for holding a weapon. Under his tunic he wore black leggings with a silver stripe sewn on the outside seam. His feet were protected in black leather attached to leather soles.

The woman at the river thought to herself, *'Straight nose, flat forehead but he looks like a possibility.'* She left her wash on the 'altar' and began to walk in his direction. The man turned and said something to a person aboard *Dara* then began to retreat away from the shuttle while its ramp closed upon itself. The two engines on *Dara* began to whine and blast a stream of energy down from its vertical vents that swirled a storm of dust around the woman and the young officer. *Dara* lifted off and flew in the direction of Salem, to the north.

In the fields work stopped. The field crew heard and watched *Dara* as it landed, dumped its cargo and one man, then took off. They saw the man turn to the woman and say something. They saw her point out at the fields. They saw the man try to pound the dust out of his tunic just before he began to walk in their direction.

Dren came quickly to Celiste's side. He looked at the man making slow progress though the shallow river and said, "Who is he?"

Celiste thought for a moment. "A Titan must be. They of the watchers wear black."

The man climbed up the small slope from the river and began to cross the field of barley stubble. He stopped for a moment, shaded his eyes and scanned the fields and workers. Then he changed his course so he was aimed, more or less, directly at Celiste. He was nearing the radish field in which she stood when she suddenly said, "He escaped."

"Escaped, my lady?"

"Yes, Dren, escaped from the clutches of a wily goddess."

"Who is it?"

"And he should not be here. I told him to stay away from Arad."

"Is it Deem?"

"Go forward. Tell him to wash himself in the Washing House. I will not receive him until I am myself ready to deal with him."

In the main audience hall of the temple, Dren formed a single line with his six guards. They flanked a large chair that was placed on a small platform. A small altar with a jug and two bowls stood in front of the raised dais with Celiste's chair. Off to the side four logs had been placed on the fire in a 'tent' formation; they began to flare and flame and heat the walls. When Dren felt the temple chamber was prepared, he said "Lady Celiste" and she walked from the back, stepped to the platform and sat in the chair.

"Now," she said in a voice full of command.

Near the temple door the man in the black uniform had waited. He walked slowly, with what dignity he could muster, until he stood in front of the altar and looked up at Celiste. His hair was washed and slicked back. He wore it cut short in the style of the Titans, the Watchers in Space.

He saw a woman radiant with sunshine. The chair was placed to receive the mid-day sun from a slit high in the roof. Her hair was lighter; it reflected glints from the sun. Her freshly washed face was darker than last he saw her. Her lips were a straight slit; she appeared formidable and capable of defending her small community. She wore the long red coat of an Arya officer with her silver badge of rank mounted between her breasts.

"My lady…" he began.

"I hope the water was cold," she responded.

"My lady…" he tried.

"And you are shriveled to the size of a small round radish."

"My lady…" he tried again.

"And you were told not to come here."

"Yes, my lady."

"And yet you come?"

"I bring you as much as *Dara* could carry. Dates, figs and melons from the land of sand. Apples, grapes from the southern highlands, with a tuber, a vegetable they call 'Papa.' Oh, and a strange device with a shell you must peel, called Arange. It is sweet inside."

"You expect me to be sweet inside." It was not a question.

"Why do you treat me in this manner?" he said imperiously.

"My lady!" stammered Dren with anger. He had been instructed what to do if Celiste raised her left hand with one finger. He walked around the altar and kicked Deem behind the knee. Deem fell forward and banged his head against the altar.

Deem shook his head then put both hands on the altar and raised himself until he stood. His head was down. A small cut in his forehead dripped red upon the white cloth of the altar. He slowly brought his eyes up to meet her frown. Her hands were now in her lap, cradling her stomach.

Celiste saw a drop of blood run around his eyebrow, past his blue eyes and down his cheek until it ran off his chin. Her stomach churned. She motioned with her hand and Dren moved away; he returned to his place.

"My lady," began Deem slowly, "Is this why?"

She saw where he looked at Dren and said, "Dren is my most trusted advisor. He was there when the Black Death roiled up the canyon and past our cave. He was there when our guard died. He was there when Arad held piles of black poison."

"My lady," Deem tried to say.

"And you were not," she added.

Deem stood. His head dropped until he seemed to stare at the jug and the bowls on the altar.

"Some who visit us are welcome. We share from a common jug."

Dren began to walk toward the altar.

"But you are not."

Dren stopped in confusion. He had not seen Celiste act this way with other guests. Especially with a man who brought bags upon bags of produce to help their small village.

"Yes, my lady," said Deem and he raised his eyes to hers. He saw, he believed, a tear in the corner of one eye.

"Who are you? For the record. Our scribe will record your visit."

"Deem, Captain of the *Rama*," he began and then added "great-grandson of our Lord Enlil, Commander of the Four Regions."

"And I am Celiste, Mistress of Arad, my Rank is 25, granddaughter of Ningal who sits on the Council of Twelve and approves decisions made by your *high and fearless* Lord Enlil."

Deem seemed confused. He did not know the protocol.

"I am not a goddess," she added. Dren launched into a smile.

Deem saw the smile in the corners of Dren's lips and frowned. "Your advisor insults me," he warned.

"And you would do what? Drop a weapon on us? Destroy us?"

"No, my lady."

"Deem, I trusted you. In fact, I believe I loved you."

"The decision to launch the weapons, to destroy the restricted zone, was made by the Council, and agreed to by Anu, King of Nibiru."

"We are not loyal to Enlil, or to Anu, *great king* as he may be. Nor are we loyal to a pilot who intends to direct the *Rama* away from Kien."

"My role, if I choose it," he remarked.

"You wear the uniform," she countered.

"I do. I can go anywhere. My rank gives me privilege."

"Except in Arad."

He looked up at her face. She did not smile. It was clear she was not warming to his style and bravado.

"When do you leave?" she asked.

Off to her side there was an intake of breath. She glanced at Dren and saw he was clearly upset by her question.

Deem's head dropped. He looked at the two bowls on the altar and picked up one.

"I have not decided," he began.

"Then decide," remarked Celiste with grim finality.

"Ten days," he said.

He looked up at her face. She seemed grim. He began to hiccup and smiled. He knew the hiccups came on whenever he was in a difficult situation. To his mate Celiste, the smile seemed prophetic. She instantly knew he would leave in ten days.

Chapter 62

The river from the mountain gorge gurgled as it ran with intensity past the old campsite. A wagon stood near an old gnarled, half-dead tree. Two horses were hobbled near the river. Celiste sat on a box near the tree, her long robe wrapped around her legs. Her hair wrapped in a long cloth, she seemed to be quietly happy. Her eyes betrayed her calm exterior; she was anything but calm.

She watched Deem while he hobbled the horses. A soft breeze blew down the gorge and cooled both of them. They waited while Shen and a squad of six women walked up to the mountain cave. They had come to the canyon mouth with a small party to retrieve jugs and blankets and other items left behind in the rush to vacate the cave.

She watched 'her Pilot' turn from the horses and walk to the wagon. He took an old blanket and spread it on the ground. A soft breeze from the canyon ruffled his hair after he stretched out on the blanket.

"If you think, somehow, you are going to get me to lie on that blanket next to you," she began, "...you are a typical male."

"This blanket smells of onions."

"We cover the onions when we take them to Salem."

Deem looked at her. She watched the river. A crooked piece of log floated by. He watched her face. He saw her brush something away from her eye. *Was that a tear?*

"We have nothing here in Arad," she said wistfully.

"You believe…?"

"I was to be a leader of my people. Lead them to build a great city. Build a busy marketplace, at least one day each seven days. Build a place of learning for our children."

"You are disappointed in yourself?"

"Not myself," she said with conviction.

"With the Council of Twelve?"

"Yes …the Anunnaki lords who could abandon their cities in Shin'ar and leave their people to die."

"Did no one give thought to lifting some of the Beag out of those cities while the Black Cloud approached?"

"There was no time."

They sat quietly. Deem watched Celiste. She watched the river flow silently by their campsite.

"Three of our horses died here," she said in sadness. Her head dropped toward her knee. "And three of our people died in Arad."

"Your people?"

"They were caretakers. Their daughter was with child. Her mate was coerced into the Army of Enlil, down in the Land of Tilmun."

"Your people?" he repeated.

"Yes, they were my people. I am the Lady of Arad. It is my duty to rebuild our village."

"But Lord Enlil and his mate Ninlil, blessed be their names, and other lords are leaving aboard *Rama* for an extended period. It will be many years of turns around this yellow sun."

"They can leave?"

"Yes. They go for chemical treatment for their aging bodies," he commented and looked at her. She turned to look at him. Her face was blank, as if she accepted her fate.

"You said, 'our village' a moment ago?"

"Yes, I belong here."

She bent over from her chair and touched his arm. "The only question?" she began but stopped. *Do you belong here?*

Chapter 63

A period of silence followed. Celiste looked away and up the mountain gorge, as if she wondered when Shen and the six women would return. Deem sat up then slowly stood up, stretching his legs. He walked to the river and knelt down. He gathered water in both hands and splashed it across his hair. He did the same with his face.

When he stood up he looked back at Celiste. Her face was calm.

"I have asked this river to bless me."

He smiled. His dark hair and dark eyes reminded her of a word said by Eglan when describing Deem: 'mysterious.'

She almost smiled, then thought, *No, he wants to turn the past with his charm.*

Deem saw what he thought was concern in her eyes. *She has rejected me?*

He began to walk toward her before she said, "Evil winds blow from the East." Celiste knew the best winds brought the rain from the west. She remembered the evil black cloud that brought death to four members of her small village. She glanced at the canyon. Did she hear her people returning?

Deem walked to the blanket and took it to the wagon. He shook the blanket vigorously, as if he could shake away the mistakes of his past.

"But then a strong wind came from over the mountains and down the canyon and scrubbed this tree and other trees in its path and blew away the Black Poison that scarred our country."

Deem did not react. He felt uncertain of his role in her world. Celiste had placed him in charge of the strong horses. When their crew left for the cave, she stayed behind with him.

"You have worked these eight days without complaint."

"Yes, my lady."

"And your shoulders have turned the red of sunset."

"Long time at the helm of *Dara* then *Cead*," he said as explanation.

"Why did you come?"

"Here? You told me to…"

"No, back to Arad. Why did you come back?"

Deem studied the water in the river where it meandered past their tree. The water was clear with a dark brown sheen on the rocks of the bottom. An occasional leaf floated by their spot on the bank. Celiste sat quietly and folded her hands in her lap.

He picked up a stone and threw it across the stream. He was in the act of throwing a second stone when she said, "Why?"

He looked up at her and saw her eyes and light from behind her pale brown hair. "My mate lives in Arad."

She waited. He paused, then "…It seemed my duty."

"Your duty?"

"Yes, to see if my mate was still my mate, my companion from our days floating together with joy and happiness aboard *Cead*."

"Why did you doubt your mate?" she hesitated with fear.

"You sent a message not to come back to Arad."

"Ah, yes. I meant what I said."

He looked down at his knee and flicked off a small bug. He slowly lowered himself onto his knees in front of her. He put both hands on her knees and leaned down to place his forehead on her knee. Without looking he added, "I was greatly sad from your message."

She said nothing. "Why sad?"

"I believed, all this time, bringing royals here and there, helping them escape the Black Cloud, that in Arad I had a mate who was loyal and determined and waiting for my return."

He turned his head away from her. He felt, at that moment, that if he looked his eyes might begin to shed water.

"It has been four moons," she said. "You performed for others."

"Four moons?"

"That long, yes." She wanted to tell him about her meeting with her father Seth.Dar and his assertion that she could join the *Rama.*

"You and the Goddess Inanna can have the *Rama.*"

"What do you say?" He looked directly into her eyes.

"I know all about the lovely Goddess. I saw her once, she of the long legs and curled hair and flowing gowns, she and her maidens and their wiles and wine and songs and padded sleeping platforms."

"What do you know?"

"She decided to capture your soul, we heard."

Deem took a long breath and turned his head toward Celiste. He could hardly believe she would listen to stories about the 'handsome pilot' and his lady at the Temple of Isis. What she and all others did not know was that Inanna asked him once. His response had been an emphatic rejection of her entreaty. *Capture my soul? …* he mused.

What do I say? he thought.

"Once, just once," began Deem, "I knew you for a demon who captured my soul." She smiled and thought, *A demon?*

"A beautiful demon in a dream. Was it not real?" he began but added, "There was once I think... my beautiful demon loves me."

"And now?" He looked at her. "I do not know."

"You know that we will have a baby?"

"Yes. I am glad. Even to the edge of exploding with joy."

"You are happy that I have your baby?"

"Who could not be happy?"

"Why? Tell me why?" she asked.

"The baby is ours. Yours and mine. We created this baby."

Celiste turned back to look at him. She reached out to touch his arm. He felt her hand and jumped. She frowned at his reaction but said, "Can you help us to find the joy we first felt aboard *Cead?*"

"What do you ask me? Your words? They confuse me."

"In your mind, in your memories, am I still the spirit that you first joined with aboard *Cead?*" She smiled at the thought.

Deem turned to look at the stream. A small branch of tree floated by. There was a flash of light in the water. A small fish swam to the surface and grabbed a fly. He knew his words might determine their future. With slow reluctance he began "I do not..."

Celiste felt more than saw his confusion.

"If you do not know, then you do not belong to me and our baby."

Chapter 64

On the tenth day, the pilot Deem did not come to the morning meal. Dren, to no one in particular reported that the captain was dressing himself in his uniform and boots. Heads around the table drooped. The women knew a few details about Celiste's treatment of the young captain, but wondered why she would send him away.

Celiste entered the dining hall wearing her usual work clothes, a short tunic across her swollen stomach with gray cloth leggings. Her hair was bound in a red rag that held her hair tight to her head. In one hand she held several cloth bags; the bags would hold produce from the field. Her other hand held a digging stick used to chop plants.

She stopped near the end of the long table and looked across her friends and her fellow workers. Dren raised himself off his bench and indicated a spot for Celiste to sit. She waved him off.

"Today we finish the melons. They cannot last longer in the field."

There were two or three groans from among the workers. Lara stood up and waved an arm to indicate the women.

"Drenay and Eglan both say the melons will be ripe…" began Celiste before Lara held up a hand with a fist

"This is not a Council meeting to decide," said Celiste. A flash memory of her father at the Council on Lahmu crossed her mind.

"I want to say something," said Lara.

"About melons?"

"No, about my situation."

Celiste looked at Dren, then Drenay, then the rest of the gathered women. They did not look eager to head for the melon field.

"Go ahead, Lara," she said but added needlessly, "Lara may talk."

"You asked, some days ago, whether I was happy."

Celiste's face became blank and then began to frown.

"I lied. I miss having a man."

Dren stood up and raised a hand. Lara ignored him.

"Those of us who have no mates," she added then paused. *Should I say this to my friend? Our mistress?*

"...wonder if you realize what you are doing. Your man has worked nine days elbow to elbow with all of us. He says words to describe you that any of us would collapse on the ground and cry to hear said by a man."

"This is not your place," said Celiste.

Dren raised his hand and said, "Drop your hand."

"I am not improper," stated Lara. "This question relates to all of us here, those with mates and those without mates."

Celiste's face began to show a smidgen of light red in her cheeks. She looked around the women and the two guards who sat near the end of the second table and said, "This is our village."

"Which means what?"

"We can be proud in what we have done. Rebuilt seven of the houses, raised crops, birthed two babies with two on the way. And I shall not be silent about this ...none of you are slaves. You are my sisters. We will build our village into a safe place for children and families. We will ignore the animosity between the royals, those Lords who fashion themselves to be gods."

Eglan stood up. The color seemed to rise in her cheeks.

"I know," said Celiste. "I am Aryas …I am royal, as are you Eglan." She stopped for a long moment then added, "I should not admit this to you."

"Then do not," said Dren.

"But I must."

She looked across her squad of twenty-four women. "There was a time when I believed the Beag, you in front of me, were worth less than an Arya."

"But I have watched you with our two babies, how you care for them. In a way, I am jealous. All of you want to be mothers."

Lara raised her hand with a fist. When the murmuring of the women died down, she said,

"And yet you would cast away your young man, because he shared his attentions on a vain and seductive woman?"

"He had no chance, at all, a'tall," said a woman.

Laughter erupted. It was a form of release. Several women tapped the table top with their bowls, signifying agreement.

Chapter 65

A guard, who was posted near the entrance to the temple entered the cooking house and walked over to Dren. He said something quietly into Dren's ear and Dren nodded at Celiste. She took it to mean the shuttle was on the ground, her mate would be leaving.

Outside, she saw the shuttle was once again on the flat ground near the temple. A cloud of dust was slowly dissipating from a slow breeze from the west. Deem was not in sight.

Celiste waited, confused. She turned to look in the direction of the men's house and saw him stepping out from the doorway. *Time to get paint on that house,* she thought in distraction. She watched him approach. He looked regal in his black uniform with the black cap. He wore a colored ribbon around his neck that held a copper and gold medallion.

When he stopped in front of her, she blurted "that is beyond belief." She nodded toward his medallion.

"Yes, I suppose. Awarded by Enlil, our master and lord. For my four 'moons,' as you call them, service to the royal family of Anu, Enlil, Enki, Seth and Ninƕarsag."

"Five moons," she blurted.

He ignored her comment and said, "I am leaving."

"It is your choice," she said. *Is it my choice?* she asked herself. She felt a mote of dust in her eye and rubbed at it.

"It was your decision," he added. He reached up to flick a large nodule of dirt off her cheek and said, "*Dara* kicks up a cloud of dirt."

Her hand came up and grabbed his hand. To herself she said, *you are still my best friend, from years past.* Deem looked into her eyes and saw his face reflected in the water that welled up in her eyes. He rested his hand on her cheek then bent over to kiss her lightly on the other cheek.

He straightened up.

"You do not know?" she asked. *You do not know if you love me?* flashed through her mind.

He looked at her, turned away and walked toward the shuttle. The ramp lowered to admit him as he approached. He put one foot on the ramp and stopped. He stood without moving. She watched him. A crew member appeared at the door. She could not hear what they said to each other.

His cap came off his head. He grabbed it and threw it into the shuttle. She saw him reach to his neck to remove the medallion and ribbon, which he also threw into the shuttle. By this time the engines on the shuttle were beginning to turn. A cloud of dust rose from underneath the shuttle. He disappeared. When she saw him his black officer's tunic was gone; the shuttle rose out of the flying dust behind him.

He walked directly back to her and said, "I do know. If you do not yourself know, then I will serve your village of Arad for as long as I am able. To be near you…" he added but she put two of her fingers across his lips.

"We have a saying, among the Titans and shuttle crews. 'Sand builds hills.' You will build this village, and its fields. I know, my love."

My love, she said to herself. Aloud she said, "Your words are music."

The sun broke across the distant mountains. A heron flew across the sleepy village of Arad on its path toward the eastern sea. A guard, standing lonely vigil in the early morning, watched the heron and said aloud, "You will not like it. It tastes of salt."

In the cooking house one of the women stirred herself, rubbed an eye and added kindling to the embers of the cook fire. In the washing house the oldest of Celiste's women began her daily task of bringing water from the river. The guard by the temple scanned the area then walked toward the men's house to nudge his relief out of his slumber.

When he entered the men's house someone in the gray light said, "Where is the pilot?"

Someone else said, "Where he belongs. Now stop your chatter."

In the sleeping chambers of Lady Celiste, all was quiet. The encroaching light from the east showed the lady herself, stretched out on her sleeping platform next to her mate. He was asleep on his back with her blanket on his chest and one hand under his head.

His other hand, one might surmise, was under the blanket and rested on the small curve of her stomach.

She waved a flying distraction away from his face. He must have sensed her action because he suddenly said, "There is one thing. We must get rid of this blanket."

"You do not like onions?" she blurted.

He smiled with his eyes closed.

EPILOG

A cataclysm occurred. The survivors lost the history of the technological civilization that built structures on the Earth *before* the comet, or asteroid or supernova debris hit the Earth. The *Pilot's Mate* tells a story of the Anunnaki Lords who brought mathematics, law and temple construction to a chaotic world on which they wished to mine gold. *Sources are remarked, thus* (41) (43) (46).

The story of Aryas and Beag living on Mars and the evacuation is fictional. However, there were bases on Mars that were evacuated sometime before an enormous blast (nuclear or asteroid?) hit the pyramids on the Plains of Cydonia. *This novel* is historical fiction; it is an attempt to popularize the story of the Anunnaki Lords and their guidance of the new race of *Homo Sapiens*.

The pre-history of Sumeria and Egypt is in the background; the foreground tells the story of Celiste and Deem, two members of the Aryan race who face challenges during the war of 2024 B.C. This is Celiste's story. (10) (55b) (62) (44) Strongly recommended: (37)

This war, with its devastating destruction of nine cities actually happened and is recorded in the Sumerian tablets, copies of which were found in the library of King Ashurbanipal at Nineveh. This was the period when the Third Dynasty of Ur rose to pre-eminence and cultural influence and then fell into decline in the period 2124 to 2024 BC. Ur was the home-village of Abraham (AB.RAM in Sumerian; Abraham in Akkadian). *Sources, by Number are:* (23) (36) (4) (72).

Abraham and his family left Ur and went to Harran. At the age of 70 Abraham led a 'cavalry' of 100 camel mounted warriors in the War of the Kings. AB.RAM was a member of the family Ib.Ri in Sumerian; (the term later becomes 'Hebrew'). (36) (56) (23)

The land of Shin'ar (also Sumer) became an arena for contending loyalties and opposing armies in the period 2100 BC to 2000 BC. A large number of culturally strong centers (Indus Valley in NW India and the Akkad-Sumer Empire) suffered a major cataclysm. In the Indus Valley the power centers of the Hittite Kings (Mohenjo-Daro and Harappa) were attacked with nuclear weapons. (9) (18) (71). Sodom and Gomorrah and Zoar in Israel were destroyed. (56)

Historian Zacharia Sitchen proposed a blast of seven nuclear missiles (called Brilliance of ✗Enlil) hit southern Israel and the Sinai in 2024 BC and the radioactive cloud devastated the seven southern cities in Sumeria. Those seven cities were Eridu (Enki's Temple), Ur (called EN.LIL.KI, place of Enlil), Erech (Anu's City), Larsa, Lagash, Nippur (the Command Center) and Babylon. The nuclear blasts (in Israel) were for the purpose of destroying 'wicked cities' and the army of Mar.Duk. The radioactive cloud that destroyed seven cities was an unforeseen accident. In the aftermath, the people and their animals and plants were killed. It required 70 years before these cities were again declared habitable. (52) (56) (51).

✗Enlil, the Sumerian name for 'Lord of the Land' became Elohim in the Hebrew Scriptures, according to Josephus (36).

There is, however, no record yet located of *when* Mohenjo-Daro and Harappa, in the Hittite Empire were destroyed by Rama, unless a reader interprets the war described in the *Mahabharata* and *Ramayana*, epic historical poems of India.

WHY THIS NOVEL?

In the western world so little is known about the history of the world before Sumeria and the Great Flood.

A Side Note: The Galactic Clade (a progenitor civilization) referred to as the 'Anunnaki Civilization' possibly built Puma Punco and Tiahuanaco (an ore processing center) in Bolivia; Machu Picchu in Peru; Great Zimbabwe; Guang Panang in Indonesia and many other monolithic stone 'temples.'

A technological civilization existed and built the Sphinx, the Great Pyramid, and brought law, mathematics and astronomy to early cultures. Recent research suggests the Great Pyramid was a producer of microwave energy used to fuel Anunnaki ships 'on station' above Egypt. The engineer Christopher Dunn believes diluted hydrochloric acid and hydrated zinc were sent down the shafts into the Queen's chamber to produce hydrogen gas as an energy source for the resonating chamber (the King's Chamber). (20) (63)

Comets and asteroids have 'attacked' Earth. Did the Vela Supernova debris cause the end of the Ice Age? Did an attack of seven 'flaming swords' in 7640 B.C. cause the flooding of the Persian Gulf and flood of Sumeria? Did a later comet/asteroid attack (2,807 B.C.) cause the Great Flood of Noah? (41)

There is a theory that Mars was devastated, destroyed by an enormous comet or asteroid attack. The attack created the Tharsis Bulge and opened the 2,000 miles long gorge, *Valles Marineris*. There is an alternative theory that a passing planet sent a 'thunderbolt' of electrical energy that 'carved' the *Valles Marineris*. (29) *Recommended:* (64)

Velikoysky's ground-breaking work *Worlds in Collision* suggests a bright, burning star visited Earth at the time of the Exodus (1450 BC) from Egypt and turned our world over four times in six days. The sun set in the East, then the West, the East then the West. This close encounter also produced enormous thunderbolts from the star into the Earth. The star became Venus. (64) (Part II, Chapter 3). Or, is there a brown dwarf star traveling with Nibiru (Planet X) as it approaches Earth?

Could such a close pass from Mars have created the enormous gorge known as the *Valles Marineris*? In 747 BC a series of by-passes with Mars began. Mars continued to revolve in 'near-earth' orbit until 687 to 669 BC. A thunderbolt discharge created Lake Bolsema (Italy). During this century the length of the year was revised several times. After 669 BC the Earth assumed her orbit and time of rotation of 365.25 days. In 747 BC the Earth's rotation was 360 days. (64) (Part II, Chapter 8).

The evacuation of Mars, and abandonment of the 'city' of pyramids on the Cydonia plain occurred before the comet/asteroid hit Mars. (12) (24) (26) (28) Zacharia Sitchen hinted the Anunnaki lords had a 'way-station' on Mars to which gold ingots were transferred to be loaded on large 'Deep Black' vessels for shipment to Nibiru. (That will remain conjecture until Earth's astronauts actually visit the ruins of buildings on Mars).

What of more recent attacks? In 1178 AD a comet/asteroid esti-mated at two kilometers in diameter hit the moon with a force of

100,000 megatons of TNT. Current nuclear weapons are rated at 50 megatons. The crater was seen when astronauts flew around the Moon.

In 2028 an asteroid 1997 XF11 with a diameter of almost two kilometers may pass or collide with the Earth. A collision would destroy much of our planet.

In 2126 comet Swift-Tuttle will return on its 134-year cycle. If it reaches perihelion with the Sun on 26 July 2126 it will collide with the Earth. Current research predicts perihelion on 19 July 2126. (True, that warning is off in the distant future).

There are reports that a small asteroid, 30 kilometers across, broke off a much larger body. They are both inside the Taurus 'doughnut' through which the Earth passes twice each year. Is it possible the 'much larger mass' is a remnant of the planet Tiamat (or possibly Nibiru)? And when will that 'larger mass' become a threat to the Earth? (26)

Ukranian astronomers (in 2013) received credit for locating a 400-meter asteroid with a dangerous trajectory. They have projected a potential collision with earth on August 26, 2032. They also said the odds of an impact are 1 in 63,000. Did Mayan astronomers predict this event? If Spanish priests were off by one Ka'tun, the end of the last 'Mayan' age will occur on 7 September 2032. (And not 21 December 2012).

Your task is to begin to learn the ancient history of our planet. Your immediate task is to ask why the leaders of our troubled Earth are doing so little to prepare for an asteroid or comet attack.

The Need to Hold an Open Mind:
When we look to the past to 'divine' and understand mankind's history, we look through the distorting lens of the present. (13a)

The Need to Prepare:

We of Earth suffer from collective amnesia. We have forgotten the disasters that destroyed earlier cultures. We have forgotten the nuclear war of 2024 B.C. and we have ignored the causes of the two great floods in our pre-history. The pyramids that were hit with a massive blast on the Cydonia plain of Mars are a reminder that our Earth could be hit by a cataclysm of cosmic proportions. We must prepare, and not just put words to the need to prepare but hold our leaders responsible: We must act now!

(Dr. F. Martin Duncan, 2015)

READ MORE ABOUT IT...

(THIS ANNOTATED BIBLIOGRAPHY IS FOR THE USE OF HISTORIANS AND RESEARCHERS.) © 2015. It may be reprinted for educational (and non-profit) purposes. It will appear in a novel of Historical Fiction: *The Pilot's Mate* by Marty Duncan, Ed.D.

SOURCES LISTED ARE FOR THE READER'S INFORMATION

Reference (1) Anderson, Pia. "Ancient Alien Brothers, Ancient Terrestrial Remains," article in *Alien Worlds*. Tumminia, Diane, ed. Syracuse, NY: Syracuse Univ. Press, 2008. (pp. 264-274). *Alien Worlds* is a study of the sociology of contactee religions and abduction mythology; with two appendices and references. The noted article reviews *Ouranian* (alternative) history of the world.

(1a) Balter, Michael. *The Goddess & the Bull. Çatalhöyük: An Archaeological Journey to the Dawn of Civilization*. Walnut Creek, CA: Left Coast Press, 2006. The text describes the practice of archaeology, the Neolithic (New Stone Age) Revolution and reveals the growth of a farming community (7500 BC to 6250 BC) while scientists debate the causes of communal living.

(2) Barondes, R. de Rohan. *The Garden of the Gods: Mesopotamia, 5000 B.C.* Boston, MA: Christopher Publishing House, 1957. The editor includes the epic poem 'Ishtar and Izdubar' (aka Nimrod, founder of Babylon). The poem illustrates the violent tendencies of Assyria; was translated into Greek by Berossus.

(3) Bauval, Robert & Adrian Gilbert. *The Orion Mystery.* New York, NY: Three Rivers Press, 1994. Bauval and Gilbert report that most Egyptologists do not agree with 'astronomical' concepts related to the Giza pyramids. They report the pyramid shafts align to prominent stars (in 2450 BC) which implies an astronomical religion in which the King's soul flies to Orion to join Osiris.

(4) Berossus. *The Babyloniaca of Berossys* (Commentary by Stanley M. Bernstein). Malibu, CA: Undena Publications, 1978. Written in 281 BC, the Babyloniaca 1) describes the culture of Babylon, and 2) was an attempt to explain to the Chaldeans that civilization was a product of divine intervention. It was a source for Josephus in the First Century AD.

(5) *Berossus and Manetho;* (Historians) edited by Gerald P. Verbrugghe & John M. Wickersham. Ann Arbor, MI: University of Michigan Press, 2000. The editors present translated fragments, no complete works. Berossus glorified Babylonia and the importance of the worship of Mar.Duk (Enki's son). Manetho's work is "embellished, altered and excerpted" (p.116). These historians present 'King-lists' for Sumeria/Assyria and for Egypt.

(6) Blumrich, Josef F. *The Spaceships of Ezekiel.* New York, NY: Bantam Books, 1974. NASA engineer Blumrich designed a re-entry vehicle from words of Ezekiel. *Spaceships* contains (perhaps) an illustration of the 'chariot' seen by Ezekiel.

(7) Breasted, James Henry. *A History of Egypt: From the Earliest Time to the Persian Conquest.* New York: Charles Scribner's Sons, 1905. The two kingdoms became one state under Menes around 3400

B.C. Art and mechanics reached a peak of excellence during the III, IV, V and VI Dynasties (2980-2475 B.C.) In this period the 'gods' ✕EN.LIL and ✕NIN.HAR.SAG controlled the people and civic projects of their state.

(8) Budge, E.A. Wallis. *The Book of the Dead.* New York, NY: Penguin Books, Inc. 1989 (1st edition, 1899; revised edition 1923). Budge introduces the chapters of the Theban Recension of the ancient (pre-dynastic) prayers. The pious Egyptian lived with the teachings before his eyes and believed in the possibility of immortality.

(8a) Budge, E.A. Wallis. *The Kebra Nagast: The Queen of Sheba and Her Only Son Menyelek.* South Carolina: Amazon & Create Space, 2011. *Kebra Nagast* is a 14th Century account written in Ge'ez of the origins of the Solomonic line of the Emperors of Ethiopia. The text is a 'pastiche of blended legends,' oral traditions derived from Jewish and Islamic commentaries.

(9) Buitenen, J.A.B. van. *The Mahabharata.* Chicago: The University of Chicago Press, 1973. This is an epic of 24,000 couplets (Book I) and 100,000 total for the 18 books. The epic tells of the marriages and mystery surrounding the succession to the throne of Bharata the kingdom in middle India. It is a genealogical mystery recited in public then expanded by the poets over many generations.

(9a) *Bhagvad Gita.* Trans. by Gavin Flood & Charles Martin. New York, NY: W.W. Norton & Co. 2012. Recorded from an ancient oral tradition, this poem describes the ethical dilemma faced by Arjuna when he challenges his 'duty' as warrior to fight his own cousins in a battle for succession to the throne of Bharata. (700 stanzas from the longer *Mahabharata*).

(10) Charles, R.H. translator. *The Book of Enoch*. London: Hollen Street Press Ltd. 1917. 17th Printing, 1980. Enoch was taken into space and received training (from Uriel) on the operations of the natural universe. Enoch describes the behavior of the 'Watchers' (*I.gi.gi* in Sumerian) such as Azazel who taught men to make swords, & knives or Jegon who brought the 'Watchers down to earth and led them astray through the daughters of men. [The righteous] "cast them into the abyss." (*Book of Enoch*, LIV.5)

(11) Childress, David Hatcher. *Lost Cities & Ancient Mysteries of Africa & Arabia*. Kempton, IL: Adventures Unlimited Press, 1989, 1997, 2002. Childress is a 'maverick archaeologist' who traveled in a quest to find lost cities, to understand their history, and to visit and enjoy the current peoples where he traveled. His books include:

> Lost Cities of China, Central Asia & India
> Lost Cities & Ancient Mysteries of Africa & Arabia
> Lost Cities of Ancient Lemuria & the Pacific
> Lost Cities & Ancient Mysteries of South America
> Lost Cities of North & Central America
> Lost Cities Atlantis, Ancient Europe & Mediterranean

(12) _____. *Technology of the Gods: The Incredible Sciences of the Ancients*. Kempton, IL: Adventures Unlimited Press, 2000. Childress reviews ancient megaliths, metallurgy, electricity, aerial warfare, atomic warfare and the "earth as a giant power plant." He also reviews 'stories' of flying chariots and nuclear weapons.

(13) Churchward, James. *The Lost Continent of MU.* London, UK: Neville Spearman, 1959. Once labeled as Science Fiction, Churchward is known for interpreting Naacal tablets from India and Mexico. He proposed a continent (Mu) disappeared from the Pacific Ocean and left behind scant traces of its culture.

(13a) Clow, Barbara Hand. *Catastrophobia: The Truth behind Earth Changes in the Coming Age of Light.* Bear & Company, Rochester, Vermont: 2001. Spiritual leader Clow posits "there is a titanic struggle going on over human access to the ancient wisdom records," (Clow, 273) and suggests the human race needs to open itself to a New Age of spirituality. She notes the Sphinx, the Osireion and Valley Temple are from the *Zep Tepi* (First Time – many centuries before the Cataclysm in 9500 B.C.). She notes that evidence suggests the long, slow shift of crust occurred before Earth was 'attacked' by debris from the Vela supernova that led to the Deluge.

(13b) _____. *The Pleidian Agenda.* Rochester, Vermont: Bear & Company, 1995.

(14) Coppens, Phillip. *The Ancient Alien Question.* Pompton Plains, NJ: New Page Books, 2012. Coppens reviews many anomalies: Stones of Carnac (France), the Saraiyana weapon in India; Crystal skulls; the Metal Library; the Piri Reis map. He quotes Louis Pasteur: "Life as we know it here on Earth is always *derived* from life that existed before." (Pasteur, 1857) Coppens argues that science is [un]willing "to explore and accept any evidence in favor of the Ancient Alien question."

(15) _____. *The Lost Civilization Enigma.* Pompton Plains, NJ: New Page Books, 2013. It might be better titled: The Lost Archeologists

Enigma. Coppens reports on the 'older' archeologists who argue that cultures develop in isolation; they resist changing the paradigm. Coppens reviews Gobekli Tepe (in Turkey) and Glozel (near Vichy, France) and other cultures where evidence shows the people had technology and farming before 10,000 B.C.

(16) Crawford, Harriet. *Sumer and the Sumerians.* Cambridge, UK: Cambridge University Press, 1991 The re-discovery of the Near East, History, chronology & social organization; patterns of settlement; town planning; manufacturing; writing and the arts.

(17)   Cremo, Michael A & Richard L. Thompson. *The Hidden History of the Human Race.* Los Angeles: Bhaktivedanta Book Publishing, Inc. 1996. The authors report evidence of unexpected & exceptional artifacts that show proof of ancient humans manipulating tools in far distant ages. The evidence, they report, was ignored or written out of the record because the evidence did not fit with current archaeological ideas.

(18) Dharma, Krishna Dharma. *Ramayana.* Badger, CA: Torchlight Publishing, 1998. *Ramayana* is an ancient epic of adventure and the love of Rama for his beautiful wife Sita and his efforts to save her from the demon Ravana. Some consider it myth; others think it is historical reporting of air battles.

(19) Donnelly, Ignatius. *Atlantis: The Antediluvian World.* Blauvelt, NY: Rudolf Steiner Publications, 1971. (reprint of 1882 edition) Donnelly begins with Plato's History of Atlantis and describes the

pre-history of the world and the evidence of Atlantean outposts around the world.

(20) Dunn, Christopher. *The Giza Power Plant: Technologies of Ancient Egypt.* Santa Fe, New Mexico: Bear & Co., 1998. Dunn proposes the Great Pyramid at Giza was built to use resonance and harmonics to amplify sound waves and create micro-wave energy to support (in a previous civilization) technology (pp. 135-146). The 'Queen's' chamber was used to create hydrogen (p. 191) to provide power to the resonance chamber.

(21) Edwards, Dr. I.E.S. *The Pyramids of Egypt.* Baltimore, MD: Penguin Books, 1970 (1947 issue revised). Dr. Edwards reviews the mastabas, step pyramids, Gizeh pyramids and later, less well-built pyramids.

(21A) Feuerstain, Georg, Subhash Kak & David Frawley. *In Search of the Cradle of Civilization.* Wheaton, IL: Quest Books, 1995. Indic civilization reached maturity 2700 B.C. to 1900 B.C. The authors review the *Rig Veda,* the world's oldest scriptures and point to "no evidence" of an Aryan invasion into India.

(22) Flem-Ath, Rand & Rose. *Atlantis Beneath the Ice: The Fate of the Lost Continent.* Rochester, Vermont: Bear & Company, 2012. (Originally pub under title: *When the Sky Fell,* 1995). The authors expanded their previous work and the theory of Prof. Charles Hapgood that periodically the earth's crust moves catastrophically. Survivors of the displacement (est. 9600 B.C.) began cultivating plants in the

highlands. The world's first advanced civilization Atlantis, they propose, is under Antarctica ice.

(22A) Flem-Ath, Rand & Colin Wilson. *The Atlantis Blueprint.* New York, NY: Delacourt Press, 2001. The text follows Hapgood's work on the shifting crust (1958) with Flem-Ath's review of ancient maps and the conclusion that Atlantis was indeed under the Antarctic ice shelf. This conclusion is contradicted by recent (2015) documentaries on the ruins of an ancient city on the shore of southwestern Spain.

(23) Ginzberg, Louis. *Legends of the Bible.* Philadelphia, PA: Jewish Publication Society of America, 1978 (a compilation; original published in seven volumes). Ginzberg collates and combines the story of Biblical history; inc. Creation of Adamu (first Adam) and the history of Abraham.

(24) Grossinger, Richard. *Planetary Mysteries: Megaliths, Glaciers, the Face on Mars and Aboriginal Dreamtime.* Berkeley, CA: North Atlantic Books, 1986. The author describes implications of the face and pyramids on Mars.

(25) Hancock, Graham. *Underworld: The Mysterious Origin of Civilization.* New York, NY: Crown Publishers, 2002. Three post- glacial floods inundated low-lying coastal plains across the Earth and 'erased' cultures such as Yonaguni (Japan), Dwarka (India) and the Persian Gulf (dry with lakes until 7,000 B.C.). Eridu, first city of Sumeria was founded circa 7,000 B.C. but might have been a re-building of an earlier city in the Persian Gulf. (No evidence to show earlier cities in the Persian Gulf plain).

(25A) _____. *The Sign and the Seal.* New York: Touchstone, 1992. This text is 'Indiana Jones' in his six-year search for the Arc of the Covenant. Hancock concludes the Arc was removed from Jerusalem when a siege by King Manasseh (687 B.C.) threatened the Holy City. The Arc was removed to an island in the Nile, Egypt, then Ethiopia.

(25b)._____.*The Magicians of the Gods: The Forgotten Wisdom of Earth's Lost Civilizations.* New York: Thomas Dunne Books/St. Martin's Press, 2015. We face danger from a massive chunk of comet in the Taurus 'donut' thru which Earth passes twice each year. Astronomers estimate our Earth will begin to intersect with the danger zone in 2030. Hancock reports multiple air bursts and comets struck the Laurentian Ice Shield (10,800 BC) melting the ice and flooding Earth. In short: Earth was devastated and an ancient technological civilization wiped from our memories.

(26) _____. *The Mars Mystery.* New York, NY: Crown Publishers, Inc.1998. Hancock makes the argument that our society expects to receive contacts from an alien species by radio; therefore, we reject the idea of alien artifacts on Mars. In Part IV he reminds us of the threat we face from comet/asteroid attacks.

(27) _____. *Fingerprints of the Gods: The Evidence of Earth's Lost Civilization.* New York, NY: Crown Publishers, Inc. 1995. Hancock proposes a prehistoric technological civilization existed before the Great Deluge. He points at carved figures of Toxodon (a semi-aquatic hippo) helps to date Tiahuanaco to 15,000 B.C. Hancock reviews Incan, Mayan, Aztec, Olmec and Egyptian cultures before he leads the reader to this conclusion: the earth- crust displacement moved Antarctica south by 30 degrees and launched the melt-down at the end of the last Ice Age.

(28) Hapgood, Charles H. *Earth's Shifting Crust*. New York NY: Pantheon Books, Inc. 1958. Evidence shows melting of North American glaciers and growth of Antarctic ice cap at 10,000 B.C. Oil, fossil records and chemicals in sediment rock show climates have changed; earth's crust shifted by 30 degrees south. "...we may expect the next displacement to be in the direction of 96° East [Longitude] from the South Pole." (Hapgood, 385).

(28a) _____ *Maps of the Ancient Sea Kings*. Hapgood proposed the crust shifted a mid-Atlantic land mass to the South Pole in *Earth's Shifting Crust*. In *Sea Kings* Hapgood proposes the Piri Re'is map (1513) and the Oronteus Finaeus map (1532) show river draining the land when there was no ice. These maps are compilations of older maps drawn by 'local' seafarers. (Hapgood, 89).

(28b) Hart, George. *Eyewitness Ancient Egypt*. New York: DK Publishing, Inc. 2004. Photographs/artifacts that describe how Egyptians lived.

(29) Hoagland, Richard. *The Monuments of Mars: A City on the Edge of Forever*. Berkeley, CA: North Atlantic Books, 1987. The author analyzes the Viking photo of the face and 'city' and the false horizon built on Mars. Astronomers suggest the sun came up behind the face 500,000 years ago.

(29A) Hodder, Ian. *The Present Past: An Introduction to Anthropology for Archaeologists*. Croydon, England: Pen and Sword Archaeology, 2012 (reprint of 1982 edition). The text is a 'classical text' that details the archaeological insights which may be gained through historical understanding of today's societies.

(30) Hodges, Henry. *Technology in the Ancient World.* New York, NY: Alfred A. Knopf, Inc. 1970. The earliest use of technology in Sumeria and Egypt are described: the birth of agriculture and the plow, the ziggurat, uniform measurement, bronze, chariots, ironworking, ships, looms, etc. from 5,000 B.C. to end of Roman 'domination' (5th century A.D.)

(31) **Valley of the Tigris & Euphrates Rivers**

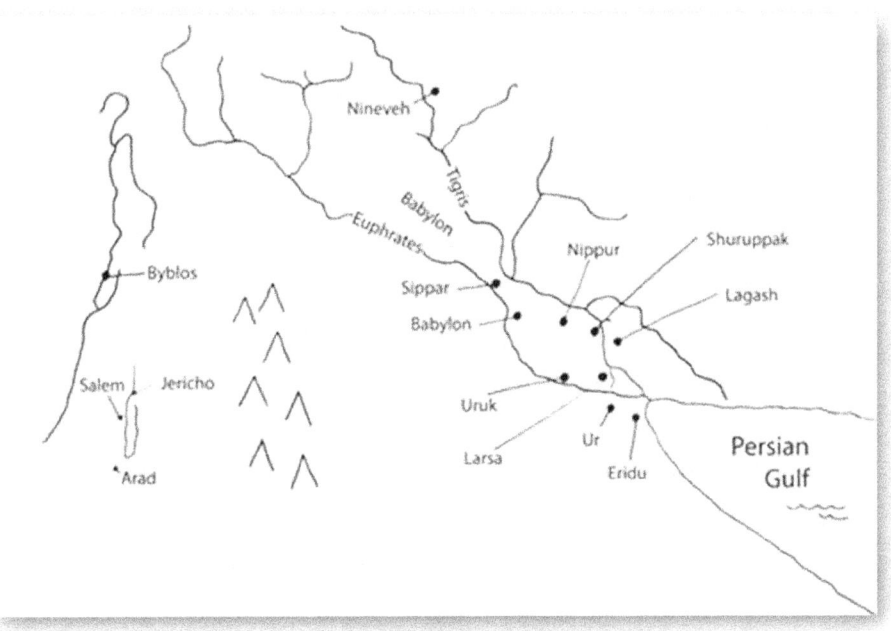

(Ur, 'En.Lil.Ki' Place of Enlil) (Eridu 'Enki's Temple')
Map by: Colby Marble, & Creative Ad Solutions, 2015

(32) Janusek, John Wayne. *Ancient Tiwanaku: Case Studies in Early Societies.* New York: Cambridge University Press, 2008. In this study of Tiwanaku culture, the political, economic and religious tenets of an ancient 'cultural' area are reported. The ports (on Lake Titicaca) and farming villages were semi-autonomous. Tiwanaku

was cosmopolitan, a place of diverse ideological views and of religious rituals focused on the sun and water, in 500 A.D. to 1000
A.D. The regional basin was inhabited by fisher/foragers, raised
field farmers and herders (of camelids).

(33) Jones, Tom, ed. *The Sumerian Problem.* New York, NY: John Wiley &
Sons, 1969. This is an academic review of archaeological mono-
graphs on this problem: Were the Sumerians the first to settle in
Eridu and the Lower Valley? The site excavations revealed Eridu
was the first city and Nippur was the most important religious center. The Sumerians are credited with transforming pictographic
text into ideographic then cuneiform syllables (ie. KI.EN.GI is
Shumer or *Sumer;* KI.EN is *Earth*).

(34) **Sumerian Time Lines (Ages of Sumer)** **notation below
    4250 B.C.   First arrival of Sumerians (in primitive society)
    3100 B.C.   barbaric Sumerian Heroic Age (not primitive, not
    civilized)
    2900 B.C.   Proto-Literate stage
    2700 B.C.   Early Literate Period (cuneiform tablets)
    2300 B.C.   Sargon of Accad (King of Sumer and Accadia)
    1750 B.C.   Reign of Hammurabi
    ** Time Line proposed by S.N. Kramer, "New Light on the
Early History of the Ancient Near East," *American Journal of
Archeology,* LII (1948), 156-164.

(35) Joseph, Frank. *Atlantis in Wisconsin: New Revelations about Lost Sunken City.*
St. Paul, MN: Galde Press, 1995. Researchers propose one-half billion
pounds of copper were taken from mines in Upper Peninsula, Michigan
and Isle Royale. Ingots were sent down river to Cahokia (Illinois) then

(perhaps) to Atlantis. Round stone pyramids are submerged in various lakes; suggesting the 'Atlantean' culture was world-wide.

(36) Josephus, Titus Flavius. (trans by William Whiston, A.M.) *The Life & Works of Flavius Josephus.* New York: Holt, Rinehart & Winston, (no printing date). Book I: *Antiquities of the Jews* inc. Adam & his descendants; Great Flood; Moses & Exodus.

(37) Kenyon, J. Douglas (Editor of *Atlantis Rising* magazine). *Forbidden History: Prehistoric Technologies, Extraterrestrial Intervention, and the Suppressed Origins of Civilization.* Rochester, Vermont: Bear & Co. 2005. Alternative historians present reasonable evidence for an advanced civilization that built large monuments prior to the Great Flood and the Earth Crust Displacement. Establishment historians refuse to accept probable evidence. The authors 'urge' acceptance of alternative interpretations and future actions to save mankind from annihilation.

(38) Kolosimo, Peter. *Spaceships in Pre-History.* (Listed with *Timeless Earth,* below at #43.

(39) Kramer, Samuel Noah and Diane Wolkstein. *Inanna, Queen of Heaven and Earth.* New York: Harper & Row, Publishers, 1983. The authors present the family tree of XAn/Anu, XEnlil, XEnki/ EA. The book contains Epic poems of Inanna and seven hymns to Inanna as compiled by Wolkstein. A concise history of Sumer is presented by Kramer.

(40) Kramer, Samuel N. *Enki and Ninḫarsag: A Sumerian "Paradise" Myth.* Monograph printed by American Schools of Oriental Research, New Haven, Connecticut, 1945. It may have been a 'myth' but it

reads like a long poem extolling the ability of Enki to get his daughter, granddaughter and great-granddaughter pregnant.

(41) Knight, Christopher & Robert Lomas. *Uriel's Machine: Uncovering the Secrets of Stonehenge, Noah's Flood, and the Dawn of Civilization.* Gloucester, MA: Fair Winds Press, 1999. Knight and Lomas, working with many archeologists, reveal the secret of Stonehenge: [*Uriel's Machine*] was built to locate the Spring Equinox at 51 degrees north latitude; and the 'computer' warned the vanished builders (the Grooved Ware people) of the arrival of a devastating comet in 3150 B.C.
Of Note from this text: Ancient oral traditions tell of a civilization that existed before the Great Flood. The Book of Enoch (discovered perhaps in Ethiopia) seems to be a source of Freemason oral traditions. This text reviews a report by Edith and Alexander Tollmann of the Carbon 14 spike that occurred in 7640 BC when seven cometary fragments struck the earth (pp. 55-58).

(42) Kolata, Alan L. *The Tiwanaku-Portrait of an Andean Civilization.* Cambridge, MA: Blackwell Publishers, 1993. Kolata reviews the myths and evidence of the cultural emergence of Tiwanaku and its step pyramid ('Akapana'); their impact upon the later Aymara culture and the Bolivian Altiplano.

(38) Kolosimo, Peter. *Spaceships in Pre-History.* (Trans. Lovett F Edwards) Secaucus, NJ: Lyle Stuart, Inc., 1975. Wherein the author reviews hundreds of symbols, painted images, pottery, statuary that hint spaceships were 'on' the earth in ancient times. Kolosimo mentions 'earth-crust' displacement, reported by Martinus Martini (in *History of China*, p. 362). He also mentions 'radioactive' paste that could allow stone to be molded into desired shapes.

(43) Kolosimo, Peter. *Timeless Earth*. New Hyde Park, New York University Books, 1973. (translation © Granstone Press). Kolosimo reports the conjectures of many noted historians and archaeologists that there was an advanced, intelligent technological civilization on Earth in 'pre-history' before the Egyptians and Sumerians. He suggests the continent of Mu was submerged in the Pacific, and proposes a 'great civilization' existed before a world-wide cataclysm. His ideas are presented in a more readable format in von Daniken's *Chariots of the Gods*.

(44) Lambert, W.G. & A.R. Millard. *AtraḤasīs: The Babylonian Story of the Flood*. Great Britain: Oxford University Press, 1969. AtraḤasīs presents the Sumerian story of the creation of humans and of the Great Flood as recorded by scribe Ku-Aya in the reign of Ammi-saduqa (1635 B.C.) in Sippar. This Epic notes that Lord XEnlil lived in Ekur, his shrine in Ur and he 'ordered' the flood in response to the 'noise' of humans (interpreted by some as 'evil sexual behavior').

(45) Layard, Austen Henry, Esq., DCL. *Nineveh and Its Remains*. New York, NY: Skyhorse Publishing, 2013. (Original publishing: John Murray, London, 1849) These are Layard's journals of travel and excavation in Syria and Turkey. Layard is entertaining and descriptive. A true Indiana Jones deals with obstacles in the desert.

(45a) Layard, Sir Austen Henry. *Discoveries Among the Ruins of Nineveh and Babylon*. Forgotten Books, 2012. (Original Publishing: A.S. Barnes & Co, New York, 1856). Ten years after his first expedition, Layard returns to excavate in Nineveh, Sennacheril, Kouyunjik, Nimroud and Babylon. At Babylon he finds no notable artifacts due to Xerxes who required the people to destroy Babylon. "Marduk appears" as the principal deity of Babylon (Layard, 422).

(46) Lewis, L.M. *Footprints on the Sands of Time.* New York, NY: New American Library, 1975. Lewis makes the case for a 'Master Race' with advanced technology and hydrogen bombs (today known as the Anunnaki) who manipulated justice & economic prosperity of Mesopotamia & Egypt.

(46A) Mellaart, James. *The Neolithic of the Near East.* London, UK: Thames & Hudson, Ltd. 1975. Mellaart was the first excavator at Çatal Hüyük, in Anatolia province, Turkey. This is the earliest known (8,000 B.C.) site where farmers domesticated goats and sheep and grew wheat and barley.

(47) Michell, John. *The New View over Atlantis.* New York, NY: Thames & Hudson (revised edition) 1983. Michell reviews earlier writer's descriptions of 'ley' lines and their electro-magnetic properties. He suggests stones and 'flying carpets' may have been levitated by magnetic currents that were guided by ley lines.

(48) Morris, Desmond. *The Naked Ape: A Zoologist's Study of the Human Animal.* New York: McGraw Hill Book Company, 1967. Morris describes the origins of the hunter-ape who pair-bonds with a female. He notes the naked ape developed cultural tasks that sometimes 'clash' with biological imperatives. (p.39).

(48a) Muller, Richard A.; Marc Davis & Piet Hut. "Extinction of Species by Periodic Comet Showers." *Nature* April 19, 1984. Proposes a comet shower extinguished the dinosaur species.

(48a) Muller, Richard A.; *Nemesis – The Death Star: The Story of a Scientific Revolution.* New York, NY: Weidenfeld & Nicolson,

1988. Muller proposed a killer star —Nemesis- orbits the sun and bombards the Earth (every 26 million years) with a cataclysmic shower of comets.

(49) Parrot, André. *The Flood and Noah's Ark.* London, UK: SCM Press, 1955. Parrot briefly describes the Javistic, the Priestly and the Assyrian versions of the Flood story and notes these versions are based on much older versions.

(50) Petrie, Sir W.M. Flinders, with update by Zahi Hawass. *The Pyramids and Temples of Gizeh.* London, UK: Histories and Mysteries of Man, Ltd. 1990. Original 1st edition, 1883. Petrie reports the measurements and alignments of the three pyramids. Hawass (Director General of Giza) describes efforts to preserve/repair the Great Pyramid.

(51) Posnansky, Prof. Arthur. *Tihuanacu: The Cradle of American Man.* New York: JJ Augustin, 1945. Ancient and well-developed cultures evolved on the high plateaus (Tibet, Mexico, and the Andes). "The islands of the Pacific are the most elevated peaks of a submerged continent," and land masses continue to rise and fall. Tihuanacu was in ancient times a much lower basin that has risen, trapping sea water.

(52) Pye, Michael & Kirsten Dalley, eds. *Exposed, Uncovered, and Declassified: Lost Civilizations and Secrets of the Past.* Pompton Plains, NJ: New Page Books, 2012. Notable essays include "Oppenheimer's Iron Thunderbolt: Evidence of Ancient Nuclear Weapons;" and "From the Pyramids to the Pentagon: The U.S. Government and Ancient Mysteries."

(52a) Pye, Michael & Kirsten Dalley. *Lost Cities & Forgotten Civilizations*. New York, NY: Rosen Publishing Group, 2013. The authors cover a variety of 'pre-history' subjects including 'Evidence of Nuclear Weapons,' and 'Race Interrupted: Ancient Aliens and the Evolution of Humanity.'

(53) Rice, Michael. *Egypt's Legacy: The Archetypes of Western Civilization 3000-30 BC*. New York: Routledge, 1997 (Paperback 2003). Rice proposes, in Jungian style, that archetypes such as the nation-state and an isolated god are powerful drives that 'create' Egyptian society. Egyptians asserted their way of life was god- driven, that in ancient memory Egypt was ruled by gods then by semi-divine kings. The Atlantis myth acts to explain the idea of Nile civilization brought to Earth by extraterrestrial visitors.

(54) _____. *Egypt's Making: The Origins of Ancient Egypt 5000-2000 BC*. Rice adds a new introduction to the 2nd Edition in which he notes a) no evidence to show Khufu built the Great Pyramid; b) the pyramids of Giza and Sphinx are much older than earlier estimates. Rice reviews the histories of the kings of Egypt and their management of the state.

(54a) Rich, Nathaniel. "The New Origin of the Species." NY, NY: The New York Times Magazine, March 2, 2014. Early stages of lab work to decipher the genomes of vanished species indicates that in five to ten years scientists may be able to 're-create' the Mammoth, the Passenger Pigeon or any vanished species.

(55) Rudgley, Richard. *Lost Civilizations of the Stone Age*. New York, NY: The Free Press (subd. of Simon & Schuster) 1999. Stone Age

cultures were violently destroyed; the earlier cultures have been "disguised and shunned" by today's writers of history. The developed cultures are imposing 'development' on the less developed people and damaging their ecosystems. Rudgley reviews tools, surgery, ceramics, mining in Eastern Europe.

(55a) Schoch, Robert M. *Forgotten Civilization: The Role of Solar Outbursts in Our Past and Future.* Rochester, Vermont: Inner Traditions, 2012. Schoch makes the case for a major solar outburst and plasma event that extinguished much of life on Earth at the end of the last Ice Age (10,800 BC).

(55b) Silverberg, Robert. *Lost Cities and Vanished Civilizations.* Philadelphia, PA: Chilton Book Co. 1962. The author describes six civilizations that rose to prominence then disappeared: Pompeii, Troy, Knossos of Crete, Babylon, Chichén Itzá and Angkor. The gods of these cities were believed to be myths. The deciphered tablets of Ashurbanipal at Nineveh say otherwise.

(56) Sitchin, Zecharia. *The Wars of Gods and Men.* New York, NY: HarperCollins, 1985. Archaeologist Sitchin reviews recently translated Sumerian and Akkadian tablets to reveal the history of the Lords of Earth and their descent into wars that involve men.

(57) _____. *There were Giants upon the Earth: Gods, Demigods, and Human Ancestry: The Evidence of Alien DNA.* Rochester, Vermont: Bear & Company, 2010. Sitchen reviews the history and rebellion of the Anunnaki that led to the creation of human man. He proposes the two most unusual tombs at Ur of the Chaldees held an Anunnaki princess and her demigod spouse.

(58) _____. *The Stairway to Heaven.* New York, NY: St. Martin's Press, 1980. Sitchin ties the Egyptian 'Book of the Dead' (and the Epic of Gilgamesh) to the landing site (space port) found at Baalbeck in Lebanon, and reviews old stories told by visitors to the site.

(59) _____. *The 12th Planet.* New York, NY: Harper & Avon Paperbacks, © 1976. As of 2007, the book is in its 45th printing; translated to 21 languages. Sitchen amalgamates the work of hundreds of archeologists and translators to give the reader the story of the Anunnaki Lords before the Deluge that almost wiped out humans. The arrival of the 12th planet (Nibiru) every 3600 years and its impact in 9703 B.C. is reviewed. Footnote: A Reports suggest Sitchen erred; the rotation may be 360 years.

(60) _____. *The Lost Book of Enki: Memoirs and Prophecies of an Extraterrestrial God.* Rochester, Vermont, 2002. Sitchen writes a comprehensive history of Ea/Enki the engineer and his work to find gold for the atmosphere of Nibiru; and the wars that result from animosity between Enki and Enlil towards each other.

(61) Smith, George. *The Chaldean Account of Genesis.* New York: Scribner, Armstrong & Co. 1876 (Reprint by BiblioLife, LLC, no date) Smith describes the recovery of tablet fragments of pre- history copied by scribes at Nineveh (circa 670 B.C.) of the Genesis and Flood stories. He reviewed 'religious' epics which may have been, in reality, poetic style histories, reported by Berossus, who reports Oannes (Lord Enki) arriving out of the sea. He lists the Lords and their 'sacred' cities in Chapter Four.

(62) Speiser, Ephraim A. *Mesopotamian Origins: The Basic Population of the Near East.* Philadelphia, PA: University of Pennsylvania Press, 1930. Researchers are confronted at Sumer with an elaborate culture that bursts upon the scene fully literate. Speiser infers a 'linguistic pale-ontology' for guidance of the original settlers; place names indicate Elamite origins in southern Sumeria.

(63) Tompkins, Peter. *Secrets of the Great Pyramid.* New York, NY: Harper & Row, Publishers, 1971. Tompkins noted Sultan al Mamun found ½ inch of salt crystals on the walls of the 'Queen's' chamber. Many researchers have speculated on who was the master architect who built the Great Pyramid (tradition says Enoch).

(64) Velikovsky, Immanuel. *Worlds in Collision.* New York, NY: The Macmillan Co. 1950. The close approach (and re-approach) of an incandescent comet is remembered in world-wide historic accounts of floods and thunderbolts wreaking havoc at the time of the Exodus –1450 BC. Egyptian priests (according to Herodotus) report the sun set twice in the east during this cataclysm. The Israelites (in Sinai) wandered for 25 years under the cloud created by the tail of the comet. The comet Venus returned 52 years later (in Mexican sources). Mars 'by-passed' 700 years later that lasted a century and 'pulled' Earth to its current 365.25day orbit.

(65) Velikovsky, Immanuel. "The Weakness of the Venus Greenhouse Theory," publ. in *Kronos: A Journal of Interdisciplinary Synthesis,* in the issue titled: "Scientists Confront Scientists who Confront Velikovsky." October, 1978. The editors make the position that celebrity scientists were too quick (and wrong) to deny the theories of Velikovsky. In the

Forward the editors show calculations to show how an incandescent planet (of the mass and surface area of Venus) would cool in 3500 years to 750 degrees Kelvin.

(66) Von Daniken, Erich. *Chariots of the Gods.* New York, NY: Putnam & Sons, 1970 (© 1968) *Chariots* is the international best-seller that proposed the 'Lords' in pre-history were in fact aliens who landed in chariots that spewed fire and smoke.

(67) _____. *Twilight of the Gods: The Mayan Calendar and the Return of the Extraterrestials;* foreword by Giorgio Tsoukalos. Pompton Plains, NJ: The Career Press, 2010. A study of Puma Punku (aka 'Winay Marca' or *Eternal City*) and Tiwanaku with pictures that provide evidence the stone was cut and polished using alien technology. Von Daniken also comments on the 'Return Myth' of the gods, found world-wide and theories about the spread of intelligence in our Galaxy.

(68) _____. *The Eyes of the Sphinx.* New York, NY: Berkley Books, 1996. The author suggests Egyptian priests mummified millions of animals in homage to the ancient Lords (Anunnaki) who created genetic mutations. The Labyrinth remains lost. The stones of the Great Pyramid were 'mixed' on site from an ancient formula. The Great Pyramid (of Enoch) contains hidden chambers and tunnels and perhaps the Tablets of Enoch.

(69) _____. *History is Wrong.* Franklin Lakes, NY: New Page Books, 2009. Von Daniken reviews the cryptographic mystery of the Voynich manuscript, the golden plates found with Father Crespi in Ecuador and the Book of Enoch, who may have been instructed by Alien Technicians.

(70) _____. *Odyssey of the Gods: The History of Extraterrestrial Contact in Ancient Greece* Franklin Lakes, NY: New Page Books, 2012. There are ancient revered sites in Greece and Crete that hold the remains of sacred temples built long before the classic age of Greece. Von Daniken suggests the network of 'sacred sites' were 'way-stations' for fuel used in flying machines (possibly balloons).

(71) Wheeler, Sir Mortimer. *Civilization of the Indus Valley and Beyond.* London: Thames and Hudson, 1966. Thirty skeletons in Mohenjo-Daro indicate a sudden death occurred and the city was abandoned. The two major cities Mohenjo-Daro and Harappa show town-planning with well-designed water and sewer works. The buildings show a new culture in its early years. Wheeler does not speculate on what caused the sudden down-fall.

(72) Woolley, Sir Leonard. *Excavations at Ur: A record of Twelve Years' Work.* New York: Thomas Y. Crowell, (no pub date) (circa 1855). Excavations reveal the 'al Ubaid' people lived on the site before the Flood. The Bible story of Noah's Ark was a Mesopotamian story told by survivors of the Flood. Ur lived for 4,000 yrs and was excavated by Woolley who reports their finds: statuettes, pottery, mausoleums, entire streets and temples.

SOURCE BOOKS: GENERAL INFORMATION & VIDEOS

(73) *'Legendary Times'* Magazine: 'Exploring the Unsolved Mysteries.' Magazine of the Archaeology, Astronautic SETI Research Association; Box 6400, Oceanside, CA 92052; (at) legendary-times.com

(74) Engel, Frederic André. *The Ancient World Preserved: Relics and Records of Prehistory in the Andes.* New York: Crown Publishers, 1976. Engel reviews the history of the cordillera & the high plains & the Incan empire.

(74a) Fagan, Brian M. Editor. *Discovery! Unearthing the New Treasures of Archaeology.* New York: Thames & Hudson, 2007. This text provides 320 illustrations of recent excavations, pottery, burials and artwork.

(75) National Geographic Society. *Builders of the Ancient World.* Washington, D.C. Special Publications Division, 1986. A brilliant review of ancient buildings, forts, and temples.

(76) Sherratt, Andrew, Ed. *The Cambridge Encyclopedia of Archaeology.* New York, NY: Crown Publishers, Inc., 1980. Cover Note: "An integrated global survey of Archaeology [on] "the origins and development of civilization."

VIDEO SOURCES:
YouTube Videos with Primary Contributor Noted

Hancock, Graham, (Author) with Robert Bauval, Archaeologist
Egypt Exposed: True Origins (Robert Bauval) 0:59:56
Evidence from Our Ancient Past 1:44:38 (ancient maps)
Mysterious Origins of Man 1996 (3 videos)
Quest for the Lost Civilisation (movie) 2:31:13

Secrets of the Pyramids & Sphinx 0:43:00
Underworld: Flooded Kingdoms 47:45 (Dwarka, Kristna's city)
Martell, Jason, Researcher *w* Dr. Tom Van Flandern Astronomer
Planet X Research Lecture 1:26:11
    (Central Coast Science UFO Conference 2008)

Shoch, Robert, Geologist
Forgotten Civilization (radio discussion) *(Book details at 55a Above)*
Mystery of the Sphinx; with John Anthony West, Egyptologist
    Charlton Heston, Narrator, 1 hr 34 min.
Re-Dating Puma Punku & Tiwanaku 12:07

Sitchen, Zecharia, Linguist
Anunnaki, Nephilim, Aliens, Enki & Abzu Mines 4:23:55
Sumerians and the Anunnaki 1:51:48
The Twelfth Planet (by Sitchen) Audiobook 2:18:08

Tellinger, Michael (Archaeologist)
Ancient Anunnaki Cities of Africa 1:06:23
Anunnaki and Ancient Hidden Technology 2:02:37

Vallogia, Michael (Archaeologist) Dobbrey, Vassil (French Institute)
Ancient Egypt: Pyramid of Djedefre (the 4th Pyramid) 1:30:34

Unknown Editors:
Phobos: Ultimate Ancient Alien Out post Beyond Earth 7:14
The Best Nibiru Documentary 2015 58:25

"Ancient Aliens," produced for History Channel, available on DVDs
Episodes with relation to this novel _only_ are noted:
Year One:
Ep.1 'Evidence:' -Vimana, Ezekiel's Chariot, the Giza 'power plant.'
Ep.2 'Visitors:' -targeted mutation of human genes by extraterrestrials.
Ep.3 'Mission:' -gold miners & star people who mated with hominids.
Ep.4 'Encounters:' -Sodom & Gomorrah; Noah; Columbus' encounter

Year Two:
Ep.2 'Gods & Aliens:' -Unexplained brain development;
Ep.3 'Underwater Worlds:' -Atlantis; Yonaguni; Dwarka (India).
Ep.6 'Alien Tech:' -Sonic weapons; Advanced Energy Weapons
Ep.8 'Structures:' -Gobekli Tepe (Turkey); Cuzco; Carnac; Coral Castle.

Year Three
Ep.3 'Sacred Places:' -Temple Mount; Ajanta; Mecca; Baalbek.
Ep.8 'Lost Worlds:' -Copan, Honduras; Garden of Eden (Persian Gulf?)
Ep.16 'Creation of Man:' -In ancient history a 'Special Event' adds the Fox-P2 gene to Hominids.

Season 8 (2014)
Ep. 8 'Alien Encounters:' -In ancient myths gods are portrayed intervening in human affairs.

Season 9 (2014)
Ep. 3 'Aliens Among Us' -by extraterrestrial design our technology developed.
Ep. 8 'The Great Flood' -alien beings are the reason we survived?

Season 10 (2015-2016)

Ep. 1 'Aliens B.C.' -enormous man-made caves, structures, underwater discoveries.

Ancient Aliens: Special Edition: Examining a theory that aliens helped ancient humans construct megalithic structures.

Ancient Aliens: The Monoliths: massive stone structures; balls in Costa Rica; obelisk on Phobos; obelisks that receive or send energy. (Host: Giorgio Tsoukalos, Publisher of Legendary Times Mag.).

AUTHOR BIO

Marty Duncan, EdD, is a lifelong educator, having spent thirty years as a school administrator in Minnesota schools. He's the author of historical novels, including *Gold…Then Iron and Vengeance*, *A Civil War Romance*, and *New Americans*, a trilogy born out of his research of Minnesota regiments during the Civil War.

Duncan's newest novel, *The Pilot's Mate*, compiles forty years of extensive scholarly study of Earth's forgotten history, the fascinating time period between 10,000 and 1,500 BCE. *The Pilot's Mate* sheds light on a credible alternate historical perspective, taken directly from translations of ancient Sumerian, Akkadian, Hebrew, and Hittite writings.

The author comments, "This novel is written with my appreciation for the hundreds of archeologists, historians, and translators of Sumerian, Akkadian, Chaldean, Hebrew, and Hittite cuneiform tablets. Please remember this novel is fiction. The novel is a salute to all those translators."

ENDNOTES (WITH CHAPTER NOTED)

[i] **Chapter 20:** The people of Ibri on Mars learn that their Arcology called *Phoebe* cannot take them to their home planet. Lord ✕Enlil grants the colonists permission to emigrate to Earth provided two squads will serve in the Army of Abram or in the growing fields of Arad.

Note: One picture of 'Phoebe' shows what could be an exhaust vent for a rocket engine. Phobos II, a Russian mission was somehow destroyed while imaging Phobos, one of the small moons of Mars.

A recent release from the 'Russian Space Agency' (ie. 2010) shows a light streak coming from Phobos toward their mission. Was it a missile? Or possibly a laser weapon?

[ii] **Chapter 22:** The people vote to agree to Lord ✕Enlil's conditions. When the Council votes to confirm Gastan's right to join with Celiste, two Counselors vote no, her father abstains, and Gastina does not vote.

Note: In the ancient cuneiform tablets unearthed in Sumeria, in Eridu and Nippur and Ur, the scribes describe the rules for succession among the Anunnaki. Enki ('EA' in Akkadian) arrived to mine gold from sea-water in the delta called E.Din in Sumerian texts. His half-brother Enlil was the legal successor of ✕Anu, king of Nibiru ('Crossing' in Sumerian). Enlil's father was Anu and his mother was Anu's half-sister. Anu's first born son was Enki, by Anu's official spouse, his sister. But birth from a full-sister did not qualify Enki to be the legal successor. Thus was born the on-going rift between the brothers Enlil and Enki. The Anunnaki, as a race, cherished purity in their bloodlines; this belief controlled the rules of succession.

Enlil's first born son with NinMah (Enlil's half-sister) was Ninurta. Enki's first son with NinMah (his half-sister) was Mar.Duk, known as Ra in the land of the Great Pyramid. Mar.Duk believed his father Enki was unjustly denied the succession to the kingship of Nibiru. This was the root cause of Mar.Duk's on-going efforts to control Eridu and E.Din during the period after the Deluge.

Chapter 24: *Dara* flies the colonists up to *Cead* where Captain Shar reminds them to use the 'hand-holds' he calls poles when they are in weight-less condition.

The first of the twelve Anunnaki (those whose father was Anu) was an engineer named Ea. His name meant, 'He who makes the water move.' His purpose was to reclaim gold from seawater. He landed at the delta of the four rivers at the head of the Persian Gulf. Here he built what would become the first city of the delta, Eridu, his blessed city.

'Four rivers:' the four rivers were the Pishon, from Arabia, the Gihon from the mountains in the northeast, and the Tigris and Euphrates rivers that flowed southeast past Nippur and Eridu to the Persian Gulf.

Ea built canals to force seawater past his concentrators. He quickly discovered there were only trace elements of gold in the seawater. He sent a message to Anu and the Twelve arrived and began the search for sources of gold. Nibiru, the home planet, needed to disperse atomized gold into its atmosphere to increase the reflectivity of its upper atmosphere.

Ea became known as ✝Enki, the Lord of the Waters.

Chapter 29: Celiste learns that a nuclear weapon has destroyed her village of Ibri on Mars.

"By fractal analysis there is reason to believe the Cydonia structures were not made by natural forces." (Clow, 192).

Note: *History in the Sumerian tablets records that when the goddess Inanna's pure love Dumuzi died in an accident, Inanna launched a series of fierce attacks against the perpetrator Lord Mar.Duk/Ra. The battles lasted for years and resulted in imprisonment of Mar.Duk/Ra in the Great Pyramid.*

^v **Chapter 30:** The shuttle *Dara* brings the colonists to the southern Highlands of South America where they will become acclimatized to Earth's heavier gravity.

Note: *Lady ⚹Sud.Lan was mistress of Shur.Rup.Pak, the medical facilities in the Land of Shin'ar (Sumeria). At the time of the Deluge (ie. 10,800 B.C.) the King of Shur.Rup.Pak was Utnapsihtim, aka Noah.*

The book written by Enoch before he stored his tablets inside the Great Pyramid relates how he was flown into the heavens. "And I came to a river of fire in which the fire flows like water and discharges itself into the great sea towards the west." (Book of Enoch XVII.5)

When animosity threatened to lead to war between the Lords of Kien, the 'civilized' world was divided into four quarters: the desert river with the Great Pyramid called E.kur; the land between the Two Rivers above the Gulf; the Land of Rama in the Far East and Tilmun, the Land of Missiles, the prohibited area of the Sinai Peninsula.

^{vi} **Chapter 31:** A ceremony sanctified the pyramid Saspéir.

Note: *Tiahuanaco was already an ancient city when its warrior-kings began a program to conquer their regional neighbors. Victorious warriors wore the severed heads of their enemies attached to their coats/tunics when on parade or in ceremonies.*

Tiahuanaco and the Altiplano of Lake Titicaca were destroyed by the Great Flood. In the following years survivors arrived from Atlantis and continued to develop crop strains (wheat, barley, maize, radishes) in the highlands of Bolivia.

An Arab historian Al-Magrizi noted Enoch "read in the stars that the Flood was about to come. So he had the pyramids built and had hidden inside them treasures, learned writings, and all those things he feared might get lost or disappear, so that they would be protected and well pre-served." (from the Khitet, written by Al-Magrizi)

Enoch, builder of the Great Pyramid, also known as Hermes (in Greek) or Idris among the Arabs, was the son of Jared, son of Mahal'aleel, the son of Ca-i'nan, the son of Enosh, the son of Seth, the son of Adam.

Some recent undersea research seems to suggest a similar pyramid con-tinues to operate inside the Bermuda Triangle.

'White Wall' is the large mound in Ireland known as New Grange. Sitchen suggests Lord Enlil brought 200 I.gi.gi ('Watchers') to chastise them for 'knowing' the Daughters of Earth.

x **Chapter 41:** *Salem, also called 'Shalem,' was the Radiant Place; also called Ur-Shulim, which meant 'City of Shulim' to the Sumerian scribes, was the 'Supreme Place of the Four Regions.' It was also the Mission Control Center northwest of the Dead Sea. It is called Jerusalem today.*

xi **Chapter 45** *Among the Anunnaki the matter of accession to the throne was a serious matter. Mar.Duk, son of Lord Enki, was third in line behind Lord Enlil, Lord Enki and Ninurta (Enlil's son). He grew up believing his father had been denied his heritage; Enki was the first born of Anu, but Enlil was the first-born of Anu with Anu's half-sister Antu.*

As a consequence, Mar.Duk continued to maneuver to achieve control of all of Kien (aka. Earth) although Lord Enlil was Commander of the Lands. It is quite possible that Mar.Duk was responsible for the accidental death of Dumuzi, the Aryan beloved of Inanna. He was ordered to be shut-up in the Great Pyramid; to die slowly was his punishment. The sisters of

Mar.Duk pleaded with Enlil for his release from the pyramid. They were successful.

^{xvi} **Chapter 56** *Lady Ninti: her name in Egypt was Hat.Hor, or Hathor, mistress of Ekur, the Great Pyramid. Her title was also Ninḫarsag, mistress of the Sinai Spaceport, in the Restricted Zone.*

Salem, the Radiant Place, also called Ur-Shulim or 'City of Shulim' meant "Supreme Place of Four Regions." Salem became the Control Center for the shuttles and ships after the nuclear catastrophe.

Lord Mar.Duk, in Babylon, refused to abandon his claim to Command of the Four Lands. The Council of Twelve, including Enlil and his father Anu, voted to obliterate the Spaceport on the Sinai Peninsula. [Sitchen suggests] there were seven nuclear missiles available. Mount Most Supreme, the Spaceport was destroyed, as were Sodom, Gomorrah and two capital cities in Indus Valley (Mohenjo Daro and Harappa), the capital city of the New Hittite Empire in the Indus Valley.

In the aftermath, the deadly black cloud came out of the Sinai and killed every living thing in seven cities in Mesopotamia. It required 70 years before these cities were again declared habitable: Ur, Eridu, Nippur, Erech (Anu's city), Lagash, Larsa and Babylon.

^{xvii} **Chapter 60** *Nin.Ti held the title of 'Lady Life.' To the Egyptians she was Hat.hor, mistress of Ekur, the Great Pyramid. Her title was also Nin.ḫarsag, mistress of the Sinai Spaceport, the Restricted Zone. Her granddaughter Inanna was trained in medicine but achieved fame as a seducer of men.*

www.ingramcontent.com/pod-product-compliance
Lightning Source LLC
Chambersburg PA
CBHW060357260626
47160CB00006B/2345